30119 0

KU-410-665

HELEN

Helen Mort was born in Sheffield in 1985 and grew up in nearby Chesterfield. Five-time winner of the Foyle Young Poets Award, she received an Eric Gregory Award in 2007 and won the Manchester Young Writer Prize in 2008. Her first collection, *Division Street* (2013), was shortlisted for the T.S. Eliot Prize and Costa Poetry Award, and won the Fenton Aldeburgh First Collection Prize. *No Map Could Show Them* (2016), her second collection, about women and mountaineering, was a Poetry Book Society Recommendation. Helen has been the Wordsworth Trust Poet-in-Residence and the Derbyshire Poet Laureate and was named one of the RSL's 40 under 40 Fellows in 2018. She is a Lecturer in Creative Writing at Manchester Metropolitan University and lives in Sheffield.

Black Car Burning is her first novel.

ALSO BY HELEN MORT

Poetry

Division Street
No Map Could Show Them

HELEN MORT

Black Car Burning

VINTAGE

LONDON BOROUGH OF SUTTON LIBRARY SERVICE	
30119 028 712 80 2	
Askews & Holts	12-Aug-2020
AF	

Helen Mort has asserted her right to be identified as the author of this Work in accordance with the Copyright, Designs and Patents Act 1988

First published in Vintage in 2020
First published in hardback by Chatto & Windus in 2019

penguin.co.uk/vintage

A CIP catalogue record for this book is available from the British Library

ISBN 9781784706630

Extract from 'World Shut Your Mouth' © Julian Cope.
Reproduced by kind permission of Julian Cope

Extracts taken from: Bridges LJ in *Hicks v. Wright* [1991] UKHL 9 (5 March 1992); Griffiths LJ in *White and Others (Respondents) v. Chief Constable of South Yorkshire and Others (Apellants)* [1993] 3 WLR 1509 House of Lords; The Report of the Hillsborough Independent Panel, September 2012.

Printed and bound in Great Britain by Clays Ltd, Elcograf S.p.A.

Penguin Random House is committed to a sustainable future for our business, our readers and our planet. This book is made from Forest Stewardship Council® certified paper.

MIX
Paper from
responsible sources
FSC® C018179
www.fsc.org

For Jess

'There are days when, driving home from some gloomy hole in the hillside near Bolton, you wish the whole world was like this: white bungalows on a hill, floating against a blue cloud full of rain. A one-track road looping across the moor. Old pop music on the radio. Sore fingertips. Nothing ever again but crags you have never seen before, made of a wonderful new kind of rock.'

M. John Harrison, *Climbers*

Hillsborough

Today the sky is full of thunder. Great gobs of cloud above the Penistone Road. The girls don't have an umbrella and they're shrieking, laughing as the rain starts to strike. Three of them, outside the sandwich shop, hair in identical braids. The two blondes have their heads bowed together, leaving the third out. One cups something in her hands. They giggle, call their friend over and tip it down the back of her neck, but she doesn't flinch. When they're bored, they walk on and the brunette stays a pace or two behind, eyes fixed on her trainers. The clouds are grey knuckles above them. I watch them drag their feet towards the park, and I watch the man, too. I notice how carefully he parks his van outside Cee Dees, stares at the glass as if his reflection is a face on a 'Missing' poster. He's hesitating beneath the boards. *Tuna Mayo. Corned Beef. Cheese and Pickle.* He lifts his hand up. Builders are leaning against the counter in their hi-vis. The man walks out without buying anything, opens and closes the boot of his car. Inside, there are two coiled, fluorescent half-ropes, just in case. Climbers' ropes. I know him. I never forget a face. I could have done the first inquest myself if I had a voice. I can speak, though, if you know how to listen. I speak in blown litter by the tram stop, a bird trapped in the flue of a house. I clear my throat and it sounds like traffic on Middlewood Road. I speak like the spin of a tumble dryer in the Valley Cleaners laundrette, faster, faster, so you have to bend to hear. I watch the man drive away. I keep watching him. It begins to pour.

Him

He was never sure where Hillsborough began. Mid-morning, sun on the windscreen like a knife, thin and bright from the storm clouds. He'd call it pot-luck weather, rainbow weather if you were jammy. At the Shalesmoor Roundabout, he almost pulled out in front of a lorry and the driver slammed his palm down on the horn.

Open your fucking eyes.

He tried to keep fixed on the road, ignoring every landmark. He knew this route by heart, roads the shape of his own veins. He passed the turn-off to the climbing wall, the river stretching away to the east of Penistone Road, glassy and quick, clogged with shopping trolleys. Somewhere out right, he sensed the bones of the old dry ski slope on the hill, abandoned now. Then he passed the flash expanse of the car showrooms. The New Barrack Tavern with its bold yellow window frames. Swann-Morton Limited, the huge leisure centre with its bright struts. He indicated left, following signs for Stocksbridge.

It was on him before he knew it. Catch Bar Lane, the stadium. The more he tried not to look up, the more he knew it was there.

The car juddered: he was in the wrong gear and almost stalled. Leppings Lane, a sign like any other.

He got half a mile down the road before it hit him, and the memory itself was like a tunnel. The ground tilting away, the air scarce. Everybody jostling to move, raising themselves to breathe, somebody lifting a young lad – maybe eleven, maybe younger – up and away. Then the memory was around him, a holding pen, a pen with meshed fencing, and a woman was lurching towards him, gradually turning purple in the face, a man was scrambling his way up the fencing, clawing at holds. He put the radio on, like always: Hallam FM. It was not so difficult to sing along. As he drove slowly down Middlewood Road, and as the flats petered out and he started to notice the height of the trees, the sparse landmarks of Oughtibridge, he imagined the tunnel closed off, a darkness sinking over it. He imagined himself leaving it behind, then he glanced in the rear-view mirror to check he had.

* * *

In Wharncliffe he parked past the garage, the place where the track was badly kept and rocky. He killed the ignition and sat there for a moment with his hands steepled on the wheel. In the afternoon quiet, he felt as if he was still moving. Like when you step off a funfair ride and everything keeps going. The tightness in his chest was back. He got out and slammed the door, didn't bother to lock it. He crossed to the track without looking and set off into Wharncliffe Woods.

You could go in circles here. Once, coming down from the crag at sunset on his own, he'd missed a turn-off and followed a path he thought he recognised until it was almost dark. He'd seen nobody, convinced himself there was no way out of the woods. In the end, he fetched up at a pool where a man was throwing a stick to a muddy Labrador. In the half-light, he wasn't sure if they were real. Then the bloke whistled and his pet loped back towards the copse. They both stared right past him, man and dog, as if he was the ghost. He thought of them again now as he neared the tunnel. Locals used to say there were dragons in the woods, a beast slayed by a knight in Sheffield armour. Now, it was all the same myth: the dragons, the Deepcar railway station. Even the climbers. Once, he found a young lad sleeping rough in the clearing, his bivvy bag damp and filthy and covered with dark spots, scraps beside him that might have been the bones of rabbits. The boy's face had reminded him of another face. It had happened before, like that: a lad on the bus, glancing round to look at him, and suddenly the years collapsing, the day caved in. *I can't reach you. I can't get to you. You'll have to climb down.*

He followed the steepening path. It was eerily quiet, apart from the distant sound of the Stocksbridge Bypass. When he came out of the trees, the crag stretched away like a long wrist, something you could almost hold. He noticed the hum of pylons, tried to count them. There was something sombre about their vigil. It was hard to walk along the top of Wharncliffe once you left the path, but harder to pick your way along below the crag, giant blocks of stone making you stumble. He stood on the top and tried to breathe. When he did, the pressure on his chest lifted, but as soon as he exhaled, it was back. He felt sick. Not nauseous, but as if something was filling him. He stared hard at the bypass, the sewage works, the distant, scrappy flats. How could you love Sheffield, standing like this? But he did. Always had. The wide, fast road. The sky like something almost rubbed out. Years ago, when he

9

was courting Angela and the scent of her perfume and the heat of her hand in his made him shy still, he'd stood here with her. *What do you see in it?* she'd asked and he'd shrugged.

Today he had brought nothing. He clambered down, slipping, righting himself, until he was at the bottom, beneath the square walls. Wharncliffe always felt like a closed room. When you were on top, the woods seemed open. Down here, everything hemmed you in. Short routes. Sharp corners, wide, imposing cracks. This was all he needed. He zipped his jacket up, then wondered why he had. He was in his approach shoes and the route was just a few metres to his right. He had chosen it because of the landing. The stone prows, the overcrowded boulders and hewn-off bits of rock, how the ground shelved towards the woods. He did not think of anyone. He tried to picture Angela, but he couldn't. When he shut his eyes at the foot of the route, he saw a sea cliff in Wales instead. *A Dream of White Horses* maybe. Nobody on it, just the wheel of a gull in the air. He began to climb then, imagining it was the sea below him now. His foot slipped on the first ledge and he felt his heart lurch, despite himself.

Hand, then foot. He was almost at the top before he knew it. Stopping, he faced the rock. There was nothing spectacular to see anywhere. The hum of the pylons seemed to grow around him and he thought about what it would be like to have climbed one of those instead, the crackle and thrill of them, the hugeness of the struts up close. He remembered the boy on the fencing. The boy who would have been a man by now. *Let go.*

In the end, he couldn't go through with it. He held tight. He clung to the rock until it was dusk and his fingers were chill from being clenched. He hung on. When it was completely dark, he climbed down very slowly and wept like a child.

At home, on the sofa until dawn, he stared at the small light of his phone. Google. A bar where you could search for anything, find what you liked. His mind was blank.

Hillsborough is a village, townland and civil parish in
  County Down, Northern Ireland.
The Hillsborough disaster was a human crush.
Hillsborough (grid reference SK332896) is a suburb in
  north-west Sheffield, South Yorkshire, England.
The story of Hillsborough is the story of 96 individuals.
Hillsborough is blooming once again after winning the Large
  Village category in the 2015 Translink Ulster in Bloom
  competition.
The real tragedy of Hillsborough is the families of the 96.
The truth about Hillsborough is still out there.
Hillsborough is the cheapest day out for Yorkshire football
  fans.

Pitsmoor Road

Here's a girl. Here's a woman, alone. She's got blonde hair and a police uniform, sitting on the wet grass, just shy of Burngreave, between the trendy bars near Kelham Island and the start of Pitsmoor. It's always me she comes back to, always my fat green shoulder. I don't know why. But I like to guess what she's thinking. She's looking at the tops of tower blocks and offices to the west, remembering a drawing she once saw that could be my portrait. She's thinking if she could draw the city, she'd put more spaces in. She'd draw it the way it looks in her mind when she tries to plan a route. The supermarkets and roundabouts the size of marbles, the Porter like a pencil line and other things looming massive: the neat square of Devonshire Green, her dad's house, the old rec with the broken tyre swing and chipped wood floor, places she can't go to any more. She'd take a marker and do everything with thick, black lines around it. She'd sketch the way she used to as a child, when she was young enough to get pocket money but old enough to practise kissing on the back of her hand. I draw a breath and suck the sun back in. Eventually, she stands up, but she won't leave just yet, not until the moon comes out.

Alexa

In a house to Alexa's right, a light came on in an upstairs window and a woman peered through the curtains, trying not to be seen. There was always someone watching her in Page Hall, someone turning to their partner or their kids in the room behind them and saying, *What are they going to do about it, then?*

She clipped her walkie-talkie onto her belt, started to speak before she reached them.

'You need to move along, please.'

They looked at her and some of them moved back out of the glare of the street lights. Others started talking again, a rising murmur. She was supposed to know some words in Roma – all of the community support officers were. They'd sat through classes after hours with that brisk woman from the local authority, the one with pinstriped legs. She could repeat the words then, but as soon as she was here – out on the street with the sodium lights and the scuffed front doors and the barbed wire around the back walls – it all leaked out of her head. *To help strengthen our relationship with the Roma community in Page Hall, the dedicated police team have learned the basics of their language, so that issues can be dealt with more quickly and to allow our officers to better engage with residents.* She could see her boss, Bill Apsley, with his spokesman face on, getting the words right, putting everything in the correct order.

'You need to go now, OK?'

Someone was playing music too loud from a bedroom window. Dancehall or reggae. She'd have to deal with that later. She could hear lads laughing on the main road, outside the takeaway. Someone shouting for *Damo. Oi, Damo! Get here!* The Roma men were moving along now, without really looking at her. They'd be back once she was gone and the woman from Number 16 would be at her window again, tutting behind glass.

Alexa didn't know how you could explain to someone that they couldn't stand outside, together. Not in any language. That other people – people she couldn't point to – thought they were in the way. That a few of them was OK, but too many of them was bad. *Yes, that's too many. Yes, that's still too many.* That was what people were always complaining about. *There's twenty of them in one house. The area's changed. There's loads of them, hanging round the streets. We can't take any more.* But they always could take more. They had to.

She walked back, heading towards Firth Park Road. Night made everything strange. The piled-up sofas and stained mattresses in the gardens looked like new landforms. A house on the left had a bedsheet draped across the window instead of a curtain, but she could see through it into the living room, where at least ten people were crowded together, trying to watch TV or drink or just sit the evening out until dawn. She looked away and carried on, walking past the halal chip shop on Page Hall Road and Mega Fashion with its shutters down and the grocer's. She passed the Pakistani Advice Centre, too, the place where the Page Hall

Residents Association met. Every time she looked at it she thought about the conversations they must have about the police in there. All that shouting at the walls. *They don't do nowt. They move them on and then they're back five minutes later. And where's the police then?*

When she went to The Fat Cat or the Kelham Island Tavern down by the river with Dave and Sue on Fridays after work, it was all *I didn't join the police to do this* after the third pint. Sue shaking her head sadly, talking about what areas like Parson Cross and Burngreave and Pitsmoor used to be like. Dave cracking the same jokes he'd been telling on the beat all week. All of them angry about Page Hall and the police needing a Section 30 or just needing more power. So that gathering after 9 p.m. could be a crime. All that anger and the empty pint glasses never big enough to hold it. Alexa couldn't say *I didn't join the police to do this*, because she didn't know why she'd joined. She could answer if she was pressed. She could say it was something to do with coming from round here and wanting to give something. The kinds of things people say. But really, it wasn't anything she could put into words. It ran deeper than that.

A car sped past towards Barnsley Road, the driver over-revving the engine. Alexa took no notice. She was here to move people along. To listen to takeaway owners and shopkeepers complaining about the groups that gathered outside every night. To hear locals saying *I'm not racist. They've got to respect how we do things here.* Warning her trouble was brewing. That someone would take things into their own hands. And she'd explain what a PCSO could do, what efforts the police were making in Page Hall, and she'd stop listening to herself halfway through each sentence.

There were other voices too. There were the eager teachers at the Academy who spoke proudly about the school's thirty-eight

17

languages, the four Roma speaking staff they'd employed. There was the elderly Jamaican woman Alexa often met beside the shops who shook her head at the papers, tutting *this is 2015. And still you don't know the words 'love thy neighbour'?* There were families of all nationalities chattering across back gardens, sharing food over the hedges. There were members of the Roma community who were met with smiles and back-slaps in the cafés. When rumours of a documentary TV crew started, Page Hall was alive with jokes and shared anger and conspiratorial, delicious suspicion kicked like a football in the alleys between the two-up two-downs. *Who do they think we are?* These streets brimmed with warmth and companionship. But it was the fear that cut through to Alexa, the fear that the police fretted about.

She called in to the chippy, the one she often ended up in. The owner always reminded her of someone, and she liked him for that. The backs of his hands had swallows tattooed across them, bluish now. He was the kind of person you thought you might have spoken to in a pub once at last orders, surprising yourself how easy the conversation was. His slicked-back hair was trying to remember the shape of a quiff. He had a circle of gold in one ear and a smoker's cough. When he smiled, his teeth were the same colour as the fish batter.

'All right, love.'

It was too hot. The smell of fat and vinegar socked her in the face.

'All right. Been busy?'

'Steady,' he said.

The walls were covered in old Pukka Pies posters. One showed a blonde woman and a well-built man reclining under the sheets, sharing a pie. The picture next to it was of a businessman, driving his open-top sports car with a Pukka Pie occupying the front seat, a fork sticking out of the middle of it.

'Any trouble this week?'

He stopped shovelling chips into a cone and laughed.

'Get this, right. Thursday, I had two of them gyppo teenagers trying to sell me a baby. Didn't speak hardly any English. Took me ages to work out what they were saying. I thought one of them had something tucked under his jacket … Tiny kid. Just born.'

'A baby?' If she stared at him hard enough, kept her gaze level, perhaps she'd know if he was lying.

'They wanted 250 quid for it.' He shook his head. 'I've already told your lot about it.'

'Would you know them if you saw them again?'

'They've not been back. I gave them a fucking earful. God knows where they went after here.'

'That's shocking.'

Alexa hated the way she could only ever think of the obvious thing to say. *That's terrible. That's shocking. How awful for you.* But what else was there? Sometimes, she wished she could think sideways like her girlfriend. Caron would know how to respond.

'It's disgusting.' He was piling the chips up too high in the cone, sinking the shovel too deep. 'I were speechless.'

'I can't even think about it.'

'I'm not being funny, love, but it's your job to think about it, in't it?'

'Tell me about it.'

'I mean, I know you're doing your best. I know you're out on the streets trying to move them along, but something's got to blow. Sooner or later.'

'So you say.'

'I could tell you some right stories. It's not them I mind, not most of them. But if they're going to all move to Page Hall, they've got to learn to live by the rules. Our rules.'

Alexa knew there was no point answering.

'I don't mind them when they're not coming round trying to sell me babies ... I'm going to the papers with that by the way. Most definitely.'

'They'll lap it up.'

'Salt? Vinegar?'

* * *

On the way home from every shift, she couldn't shake the habit of looking in through people's windows. When they were lit up, it was almost like an invitation. Crossing the city from east to west, you'd see the living rooms and kitchens change, just as the houses got bigger and the streets got quieter. Once, near Owlerton, she saw a couple naked in an upstairs window, not doing anything, just standing together and looking out with mugs of tea. Back towards home, it was all ginnels and Nepalese prayer flags in the windows and tasteful plants. Chests used as tables. Large pine chairs. Streets where all the double-parked cars left at 7 a.m. and came back at 7 p.m. Where people argued about parking slots and didn't realise how much space they'd got.

Sometimes, she'd take the long route back, just to cycle past Dad's house. It was the last one on the road. Often, he still had the light on when she went by. She was thinking about the baby, bundled up in a cardigan or in newspaper, like the hot parcels of fish and chips passed over the counter in the chip shop. The weight of the child as the mother gave it away. Dad's house was dark tonight. It made her feel better, somehow, knowing he wasn't behind any of the windows.

When she got home, she took her boots off in the hall and tiptoed upstairs. Caron was like an Egyptian mummy under the duvet, thin sheets pulled up over her face. She had her back to Alexa and her breathing didn't falter when Alexa slipped in beside her and kissed the back of her neck, just under the hairline. She thought about pressing her body against Caron's to try to wake her up. Instead, she lay on her back in the dark.

Last week, outside a house in Page Hall with the front door smashed in, she'd found an elderly Slovakian woman pacing the narrow stretch, back and forth, the same small square of light outside the house. When Alexa stopped to ask her if she was OK, she grabbed Alexa by the wrist, placed her other hand on top of her arm and started to talk. It was a stream of words, the same phrase repeated over and over. Alexa nodded as if she understood. She wrote the words down in her notebook later, spelling them wrong.

It took her some time to look it up at home, face lit by the glow from her laptop, piecing the words together. When she did, she started.

Do you believe in ghosts?

She thought about Dad, the times when his silence seemed to grow over him like a second skin. The way he used to look past her. The things she could never see. As she closed her eyes in bed, she thought she was staring into a crowd. Red and greenish bodies behind her eyelids, very small. There were loads of them and they all seemed to teem together. A flock. No, denser than that. Packed like snooker balls in a triangle. Like a football stadium.

But something denser than that, something that made it hard to breathe. Like how she imagined the Leppings Lane entrance, the stand, when people talked about Hillsborough. Because she had to imagine it, every time anyone said the word. She couldn't just hear the name or have an abstract image.

People in your face and over your face and everywhere around you. People blocking the light and people on the ground. People under your feet. She tried to look at the bodies until they became dots, shapes in a kaleidoscope. It never worked. Not really. Eventually, they turned into the crowds of Roma men outside the shops in Page Hall, men pushing and jostling and laughing with each other, and she could send them away just like she did every shift, back to their houses and out of her head. When the alarm clock went off, Alexa felt like she hadn't even been asleep.

Norfolk Park

It's early, not yet light. I'm stretched out like a sleeper – black pavements slick with rain. You leave the car engine running, but you get out of the driver's seat. The door is left slightly ajar. You stand by the railings and take me in. The cholera monument is behind you, tall and slender, adorned with moss. In front, there are trains pulling out reluctantly, the distant sound of the announcer on the tannoy. *Chinley. Stockport. Manchester Piccadilly. Manchester Oxford Road.* You light the joint and light it again when the breeze snuffs it out. Inhale. *Widnes. Liverpool South Parkway and Liverpool Lime Street.* Exhale. The headlamps of the cars as they sweep past The Showroom. The high university buildings and the higher flats, the steeples and towers like needles, injecting the sky with dawn. Signs to Chesterfield, Barnsley, Rotherham. The shape of the moors in the distance, a dark cloth thrown over a tabletop. The stars above them. The satellites. The galaxy. The smell of something heavy, cloying as it fills the air. A single crane, still above the ex-workshops and foundries. The grass amphitheatre behind the station, a boy who is crouching, bending to write his name on the wall, beautifully, in three colours.

Leigh

Leigh squinted out of the pub window, through dregs of light. The clouds that had been scudding all evening were gone and now everything was drained. The wind couldn't be arsed to blow and even the gritstone edges standing guard above Hathersage seemed less vivid than usual, teabag-coloured. Up there by the crag, the Popular End car park would be emptying now; vans taking school groups back to Sheffield, couples in patched-up down jackets wandering over to The Norfolk Arms, or down in to the village. A single kestrel overhead, perhaps, drawing circles in the air only it could see.

She wished she was high up, in the half-light, underneath all the routes she knew by heart. Inverted V, Thunder Road, Ellis's Eliminate – names said with respect and regret like the names of ex-lovers. She wanted to feel the rock around her fist, taking her skin off. A gritstone handshake. As if she could get inside the landscape for a second.

'She's called Caron by the way.' Pete broke her reverie. 'The lass you couldn't take your eyes off earlier, the one looking at bouldering mats.'

'Fuck off!'

'She climbs E5. Well, she were climbing E5 last year.'

It was quiz night in The Robin Hood and groups of women with fuchsia lipstick and spidery eyelashes were huddled round the best tables, but Pete didn't want to do the quiz because it would be *all friggin' Lady Gaga and Take That*, so they propped up the bar instead, Pete with his pint of Dizzy Blonde and Leigh with a half-full pint glass of red wine, because they'd run out of wine glasses. The microphone was broken, too, so a man with a triangle beard and a megaphone was leaning against the pool table, intoning questions.

'Well, Pete, if I can't have you …' Leigh grinned at him.

'Exactly!'

'Body like that … You're only twenty years past your prime.'

Pete had been in the climbing shop long before Leigh started there. At first, she thought he was shifty, like an uncle at a wedding. When the manager introduced him, he didn't lift his head. She clocked him. Wiry, athletic, with a shock of silver hair he ran his hand through when he was exasperated. Leigh was used to seeing men like him at the crags on Tuesday nights, fifty-somethings who'd been great climbers once, who'd lost some of their strength, but none of their skill and determination. Steady. Hard to age accurately. But there was something awry about Pete, too, something she didn't quite trust. His glasses were on a string around his neck, tied with a piece of climbing tat and one side of his face seemed more closely shaven than the other. At first, she moved round him the way she'd step past strangers on a train, careful not to touch. But working side by side behind the counter every day, she became curiously dependent on his photographic memory for which guidebook was stored where, vaguely entertained by his habit of humming Simple Minds tunes under his breath. Within a month, they'd started climbing together. Within two months, they were drinking buddies, holed up in the overpriced, tartan-carpeted pubs around Hathersage and Grindleford, bitching about the management, idly speculating about routes they'd climb one day, on limestone and gritstone, ushering each other to bus stops and taxis at the end of the night. Leigh preferred him to the lads in their early thirties who climbed topless at The Works on Saturdays, their single earrings and their white-boy dreadlocks, the women in black crop tops, the clear chime of their voices. Before they set off up a route, they'd check to see who was watching. Pete was utterly unselfconscious.

'I'm just saying. You were staring.'

She fiddled with a beer mat. 'I don't know what you're on about.'

That was bullshit. Leigh remembered her. She was short, only up to Leigh's shoulders. Mahogany hair, dyed and cropped below her ears. Unplucked eyebrows, the glint of a nose stud. Her weird, slow movements as she stooped to handle each mat in turn, freezing with her palms pressed into them. Like someone doing tai chi. Or taking the piss out of someone doing tai chi. In fact, she was the kind of person who looked like she was taking the piss all the time: she had a permanent half-smile, humming to herself as she moved round the climbing shop.

'Didn't buy owt anyway.' Pete was talking too loudly now. 'Her and the rest. If tomorrow's that slow I'm bringing the dog to work.'

'I thought I might have seen her bouldering a few times, that's all.'

'You should see her shoulders though, her back. Like a concertina. Nothing to her most of the time, but when she's tensed ...'

'So?'

'Just saying. You could climb like her if you tried.'

'I've not got the bottle.'

Pete looked at her for a moment.

'No,' he smirked. 'Probably not.'

'*In what year was "Spinning Around" a hit for Kylie Minogue and what position did it reach in the charts?*' The megaphone rattled the whole room.

Pete propped his arms on the table, leaned close to Leigh as if he was going to tell her a secret. 'I heard Caron's after a route on Apparent North. Something big.'

'Like what?'

'Black Car Burning.' He said it slowly.

Leigh had heard of it before, a short, tough climb out at the very edge of Stanage, the part where the rocks begin to peter out into broken teeth, ground tumbling towards the lower moors. She'd always wondered why that clutch of boulders was called Apparent North, whether it meant nobody was really sure where north began in that edged, hemmed landscape. Black Car Burning was a hard route, arduous and steep, poor handholds under a great gritstone roof. It was an E7, so far beyond anything she could ever dream of climbing she'd never even glanced at it. But it wasn't one of the classics either, not a test-piece climb like Careless Torque, a boulder problem on a prow of rock; or Archangel, a smooth, forbidding aerate with no holds on it, a sharp fin rising from the Plantation.

'Why does she want it?'

Pete shrugged. 'Why not?'

They were words Leigh wanted to say out loud. *Black Car Burning*, savouring the locked sound of it. She thought about the logic of route names. Valkyrie, named for a woman who could choose who would die in battle and who would survive. Chameleon, named for its shifting character, the awkward moves it forced climbers into. Black Car Burning was a name that seemed to smoulder, something acrid and tense about it. It made her think of sudden death, a car wrapped round a tree, or three men standing back with cans of petrol while the windows and doors went up in flames.

'Have many women climbed it?'

Pete swirled the last of his pint round in the glass. 'My missus did,' he said softly.

Leigh stared at him. He hardly ever mentioned his wife. As if saying her name might irritate her ghost. Just then, a businessman in a suit with an off-putting sheen nudged their table on the way to join his friend at the bar, almost knocking Leigh's wine over. The man smiled weakly, held his hands up, looked Pete and Leigh up and down, taking in their bashed knuckles, dirty jackets, the pair of rucksacks on the floor. Pete turned back and winked at Leigh.

'See if he'll get the wine in. Don't mind if I leave you to it soon, do you?'

'No, 'course not.'

Pete was always the last to arrive and the first to leave. She never asked questions, even though she knew he was only going home to his empty terrace, back to the long night and the last measure of Johnnie Walker. She's never set foot inside his house, but she understood what it felt like, needing to get back to nothing.

Pete levered himself off the bar stool with an exaggerated groan.

'Never know, you could be in there.' He nodded at the two businessmen.

'Christ, Pete.'

'Get yourself a nice fella ...'

He hoisted his rucksack up on to his shoulders, nearly swiping the empty pint glass off the bar. Cackling and punching her on the shoulder, he was off out into the car park and the calm night, his stride quickening. Pete always walked as if he'd just seen someone he recognised, or someone he wanted to avoid. Head down. Shoulders forward. It was the walk of the professional loner.

Megaphone man approached the bar, seemed to holler right in her ear.

'What is the real name of the singer Lady Gaga?'

Leigh drained the rest of her wine in one.

* * *

Back at the house, Tom was waiting for her outside, shivering slightly in a summer jacket. He'd got the last bus over from Sheffield to surprise her. He clearly hadn't expected her to be out. Perhaps his girlfriend was away for the weekend, or drinking Prosecco with her manicured friends. She'd learned not to ask. In the light from the porch, his cheekbones seemed sharper, his black hair shone. She couldn't help taking him in, angular and still. He was kissing Leigh before she'd even got the door open. Inside, he held her face in both hands, then moved them down to her waist, tugged at her belt. She pushed him away gently. He followed her upstairs.

What she wanted wasn't sex. Not really. Or not the most part of it, the shoulder-gripping and swearing. Not that endless swimming, treading water under Tom's body, looking up at him open-mouthed. They were on the bedroom floor now for no good reason, on the landlord's oatmeal rug. She was holding her knickers to one side. What she wanted was the moment just before he entered her. The relief of knowing it was going to happen. Just that and no more. Like this all had a beginning.

She could see his shadow on the wall, the outline of his back. She thought about Black Car Burning then, a crouched, intent body of rock. A smoke-coloured surge. That morning, driving into the village, there'd been a cloud inversion over the whole valley, pure white. She'd taken the bends slowly for once. It felt like she was driving into the sea.

'Stop,' she said. 'There.'

Shining Clough

If you try to find me, you'll get lost. You'll walk under the crack-ling pylons and follow the signs for 'Open Country' by the gate, congratulating yourself on your keen eye. By the copse, you'll pick a good line through the undergrowth, skirting the rhododendron bushes. It's twilight, and a barn owl flies out of one of the trees behind you, glides on muffled wings. It seems darker under the trees. The path is dividing, lessening. Soon, you'll slow through heather and bracken, anxiously checking your bare legs for ticks. You'll lean into the hillside, fix your sights on me, think of the solidity of rock. It was summer down by the reservoirs, down in the lap of the Woodhead Pass, but by the time you reach me, I'll be cloaked in mist and silence. Scottish weather. You'll stand under a corner climb, uncertain where the route goes, how to start. There will be no one to nod a greeting to, just a pair of climbers from Hayfield on the far buttress; a man who seems poised forever on the same hard move. You'll place your hands against me tentatively, lean against me as I lean back at you, taking your weight, feeling all the bones inside your body. On the way back down, you'll lose the path again and stumble on a mink trap, its snarl a furled lip. Dragging your feet along the track, you'll meet a gamekeeper who slows in his Land Rover, wants to know if you've touched anything, if you've interfered with his traps. You'll look down at your hands as if they don't belong to you.

Him

Asphyxia. He did not think he could spell it. He did not belong in the library with its tidy women behind desks, its serial numbers and grey trollies. But he felt like he was a proper researcher in here, not like in the house with its street noises and crap central heating. He had chosen the computer furthest from the reception, the one tucked away in a booth on its own. They probably thought he was looking at porn. He pushed his reading glasses higher up his nose. He didn't wear them when he was supposed to and they made him feel clumsy. The screen kept going black. Energy preservation, no doubt. The efficient girl with braids on the front desk had asked him if he needed any help with the PCs and he felt ancient. She was attractive in an unobtrusive, tidy kind of way. Twenty years ago he could have asked for her number.

In cases of death from traumatic asphyxia caused by crushing, the victim would lose consciousness within a matter of seconds from the crushing of the chest which cuts off the ability to breathe and would die within 5 minutes.

He opened his black notebook, the one he'd bought from Smiths on Fargate this morning, running his hand over the leather cover. It was the first notebook he'd had since the force. He never even wrote shopping lists these days. He'd got a flashy pen, too, one of those rollerball ones. He clicked it to distract himself.

Traumatic asphyxia. He wrote it down. It looked wrong, so he crossed it out and tore the page out.

He started again.

Hicks v. Wright (Chief Constable of South Yorkshire Police).

He stopped. He added the word RESEARCH in capitals, drew square brackets around it. You should always start with a title, that's what they said in school, in English Literature. His English teacher was the only good teacher he ever had. He couldn't think of her name, but he could see her face blink into life when she talked about *Macbeth*, holding up her hands and pretending they had blood on them. *Out, damned spot.* He stared at his writing for a minute, relishing the neatness of the 'v' – 'v' for versus – remembering how meticulous his notebook always used to be at work. He drew a line under it. The thick black mark reminded him of something. Another page. Other words. Underlining the parts that didn't fit.

He wrote *asphyxia*, neater this time. He dropped the pen. He could see another A4 sheet. His own handwriting. Crossed out and annotated. The careful word-processing. *This is a personal and graphic account. He may wish to reconsider the statement ...* He must have sworn out loud. The braided girl at the desk looked over at him sharply, and he bent down to the floor to fetch his pen. His hands were shaking. He could do with a drink, but it was only quarter past ten. Start again. If he couldn't write, he could read.

Unless the law were to distinguish between death within seconds of injury and unconsciousness within seconds of injury followed by death

within minutes … these findings, as Hidden. J himself said 'with regret'
made it impossible for him to award any damages.

Death within seconds and death within minutes. He wondered how he could read the words *death* and *unconsciousness* so many times and almost feel nothing. And yet a scarf could set him off, a clutch of flowers in cellophane, a view of a stadium on the news. It was as if the words on a screen didn't mean the things they were supposed to. They were bubble-wrapped.

It is perfectly clear that fear by itself, of whatever degree, is a normal
human emotion for which no damages can be awarded.

He found that phrase unusual. *Damages can be awarded.* Damage was something that happened to you, not something you got. But in the eyes of the law, damage was money. Damage was something to be proved. He wrote down *fear is a normal human emotion.* He closed that window, opened the next case. This one was about psychiatric injuries and how you define them. He looked back and noticed there was a man asleep in the wooden chair behind him, next to the 'Life & Leisure' shelf, and he'd started to snore. He had a white beard flecked with ginger and a small bottle of vodka sticking out of his anorak pocket. Beside him, one of those square shopping bags on wheels. The girl behind the desk went on with her paperwork.

Watching the man's chest rise and judder back down made him shiver. Some nights, he fell asleep in The Byron, after last orders. They never said as much when he came to, but he knew he did it. It was Absolution that did him in. He was all right on Moonshine, but the stronger beers made him drowsy. He hoped he never slept long, hoped his mouth never lolled open like this man's.

He scanned the screen. *The law expects reasonable fortitude and robustness of its citizens and will not impose liability for the exceptional frailty of certain individuals.*

He wrote *exceptional frailty* and finished it with a question mark.

This is not to be confused with the 'eggshell skull' situation, where as a result of breach of duty the damage inflicted proves to be more serious than expected.

The man in the chair almost choked on his own snore. He was spread-eagled right next to a display of books on Mindfulness, the white covers printed with pictures of brunettes doing yoga poses or standing next to waterfalls.

The law cannot compensate for all emotional suffering even if it is acute and truly debilitating.

Above this, there was a numbered list, a set of criteria for establishing whether psychiatric injuries have been sustained. He decided not to look at it. He wanted to make his own list instead. He wrote DAMAGE TO THE MIND in large letters and scribbled the numbers 1 to 5 underneath. Then he started to fill them in:

1. Seeing things you never asked to see.
2. Not being able to forget.
3. Loss of livelihood.
4. Loss of mental faculties.

He realised he did not have a fifth idea. He went back to number 3 and wrote *i.e. job, sense of pride etc*. Then he looked at the real list. It was nothing like his – it mentioned plaintiffs and victims and immediate aftermath. When he read these court cases, he couldn't picture anything. Not even the face of the lawyer who said the words. But he liked that, liked to be able to switch his imagination off for once. Skimming the screen again, he wrote down *eggshell skull*. He wondered if he had an eggshell skull. It felt like it was more than that. He felt as if he was made of cement.

After that, he shut the computer down and shouldered his bag and walked through the maze of shelves for a while, clutching his new notebook and thinking about the word *asphyxia* and how it almost crushed you just to say it. He thought about climbing accidents in the news, how an avalanche presses down on the hill, how the snow presses down on the climber's chest. Then he just tried to picture the snow without thinking about things underneath it. A white sheet. The first page in the notebook he'd bought when he first picked it up in the shop this morning, imagining all the things he could do with it.

Wharncliffe

I know you, old man. I know your Lowe Alpine rucksack with the corners frayed, your walk more cautious than it was ten years ago. I know your damaged skin and your leathery palms, the silver afterthought of your hair, your surprisingly wide shoulders and your surprisingly narrow waist, legs skinnier than they should be. Strangers might put you in your early fifties, but I remember how long you've been coming here. I know you the way I know the curve of the bridge that nobody walks across, buried under green leaves. You're a black dot among the clustered trees, then you're a slip between the angular, black rocks. I smell of the bypass and the garage up-wind, the slight musk of wet leaves and wild garlic, but you smell of coffee and new sweat. An hour ago, you were a premonition – the way dogs can sense a car approaching before it turns into the road. I see you until I barely notice you, part of me, like the hunched, miserly overhangs and lost paths, the woodland tunnels, the open land where I'm trodden lightly by sheep, grazed and gently tended. Every night this week I've been washed clean, the ferns sagging with water, the rocks a private bowl for mist and dampness, soaked then dried too fast by the wind. When I feel a man grip down on me and start to climb, unroped, I'm patient and calm. The birds that scatter from the wires and pylons and clatter skywards are not a sign of fear.

Leigh

That girl, Caron. She was back, gliding round the climbing shop, last customer of the day. Pete had been jangling his keys for a good five minutes now, clearing his throat theatrically. He wanted to get gone, off to his old five-a-side reunion. It was Derby night, the pubs off Bramall Lane would already be sweating out United fans. But Caron was standing in front of each display shoe in turn, stroking the uppers or picking them up and holding them. She reached to get one from the highest shelf, then stared at it as if she'd picked a rare apple.

Leigh shot him a pitying look. 'I could lock up if you want to get off?'

He was turning a screwgate round and round in his hands.

'Traffic on Eccy Road ... don't want to get stuck in all that.'

'Go on then, piss off.'

'Do you remember the code? For the alarm.'

'Yes. Get out of here.'

He scooped up his bag from the corner behind the counter. 'Don't forget to do the lights.'

'Piss off before I change my mind.'

'I'm already gone!'

'Oh, Pete?'

'What?'

He was half in and out of the doorway.

'Don't do anything I wouldn't do.'

His two raised fingers were the last thing to disappear. He'd be in town in twenty minutes, wiping the sweat from his brow, flanked by men at the bar who wouldn't look directly at each other, then he'd carry his pint back to the table and sit with other men who didn't know what to say. They'd meet twice a year out of a sense of duty. None of them ever shared any news. *What's new with you, lad? Oh, you know – keeping on.* There'd been deaths, grandchildren and separations, lawyers and minor heart operations, but none of it was spoken of. If they saw each other in the supermarket or in town on Saturday in the intervening months, they'd nod and wave cheerfully.

Caron was facing away from the counter and Leigh could see the slim tattoo on the nape of her neck, red hair cut close. She moved as if she knew people were always watching her. Leigh slipped out from behind the till.

'Sorry to be a pain, but we need to shut up shop.'

Caron just carried on, pressing the tip of a shoe against the wall to test its grip. It was only this close that Leigh could see the silver of her small, in-ear headphones. She wondered what she was blasting through them. Electronica, probably. Or something transcendental. Whale song. Leigh always liked to imagine that those tapes were really made by a load of blokes in a basement somewhere in Barnsley, honking and wailing into a borrowed microphone, someone splashing a bath out back for effect.

Leigh wanted to touch her, but she didn't know how. She just reached out her hand, hesitated, let it fall lightly on Caron's shoulder.

'Sorry,' Leigh backed away. 'Didn't mean to startle you.'

'No, I was miles away.'

With one headphone trailing down her top, Leigh could hear the bassline of an Arctic Monkeys' track. She was obscurely relieved.

'We're closing now.'

'I was trying to get some more shoes, left mine at the wall yesterday.' Caron handed the shoe to her, the movement only slightly too lavish. 'Some arsehole will have made off with them by now.'

'Never know. One of your mates might have them.'

'Exactly.' Her laugh was like a sneeze.

'We must climb with the same utter bastards.'

'Haven't I seen you out with Steve?'

'Depends which Steve you mean. I know an embarrassment of Steves.'

'Four foot something. Goatee.'

'Big Steve. Guilty as charged. He used to work here. Left to train dogs in Stoney Middleton. That's why he's only got half an ear. He – ' She tailed off, ashamed of her own sudden earnestness.

Caron looked at her sideways. 'I'm sure we have lots of people in common.'

There was a short silence that felt long. Caron held out her hand. 'Nice meeting you, Leigh.'

Caron's handshake was firm. Leigh didn't know when to let go. 'How do you know my name?'

She was already walking away. 'I said we had people in common.'

It was turning dark. A reminder that the days of climbing after work were on their way out, and the evenings spent in the cottage, nursing a whisky and an imaginary cat were on their way in. Practising how she'd answer the phone if Tom called.

'We drink in The Sheaf on Tuesdays. If you ever want to compare Steves.'

Caron was out, without waiting for an answer. Leigh beat the shoe absently against the palm of her hand a couple of times. Then she put it back on the shelf, scooped her bag from behind the counter and, before setting the alarm, switched the light off and stood in the shop in the dark for a moment, liking how the place looked.

* * *

Leigh went back to the house with no storage cupboards, her naked house with everything on display. Five minutes from shop door to front door. Back to the *Peak Advertiser* wedged in the letterbox and the sound of the old woman next door running a loud bath. She was restless, so she made herself climax, jeans still on, and then fell asleep on top of the covers with her flies undone, and dreamt badly. A woman like Caron, soloing on Stanage. Or someone she thought was Caron, seen from a grey distance, her car in a lay-by with the engine ticking over. Then the focus shifting, the dream tightening, a close-up without permission. Not Caron's face at all. The hair too light, the lines around the eyes and forehead revealing someone older. How carefully she reached the top and turned round, incredulous at how she'd got there.

Leigh woke, shook the dream away and sank back into a fitful sleep.

'I want you to watch me,' dream-Caron said, her face wobbly as if she was underwater.

Leigh felt her whole body stir – in the dream, Caron was naked and close. She straddled Leigh, made her keep her hands locked behind her while she touched herself, slow, holding her stare. Then neither of them was naked any more and she was out on Froggatt in summer, under an impossibly pink sky, and Caron was above the first break of Three Pebble Slab, stepping gently. Leigh was below, watching the whole performance. And it *was* a performance: every time Caron placed her palm against the rock or moved her feet up, it was exaggerated. Slow motion. Big. Leigh watched until her neck ached. And as Caron went for the last moves, she cried out – a single, shrill cry – and Leigh saw that it wasn't rock she was climbing after all but the smooth, untouchable face of a mirror. Her hands slipped off. The glass let her go. And as she fell, Leigh realised that when she said *Watch me* she had meant *Guard me, spot me, hold your hands out to catch me*. She meant *Break my fall*.

Leigh woke up, sweating, on the wrong side of the bed. She stared up at her painting of Stanage, its beige and grey lines. The millstones watched her with cool, unblinking eyes.

Stanage

I'm strewn with beads, cast-offs from a giant, stone bracelet, dropped and forgotten in the heather. In the right light, I'm decorative and the tourists like to pose beside me – sometimes couples perch on the stones, one either side, grinning for the camera. Sometimes teenagers come out from Sheffield and Manchester and leave crumpled cans of Strongbow in the empty centres, scrawl on them with spray paint and make them into smiley faces. I stay silent in the face of this indignity, because I know what I was, how my body was turned. I remember being hefted and lifted when the valley was a hub. I cannot forget my usefulness. When the work ran out, they left me here, stones angled on the hillside, sheltered by bracken. Over the centuries, foxes nosed me, sheep shat on me, dogs cocked their legs, and I kept motionless while the patient weather did its work, flattening parts and sharpening others. I hardly recognise myself. If a climber were to fall and roll down the bank, I might catch and hold, startle back to life, as if I've only been sleeping all this time, waiting for someone to touch me with their weight.

Alexa

'We need to talk about Page Hall,' said Inspector Apsley.

It was an emergency meeting. Or an everyday meeting, Alexa couldn't remember. She was watching the orange and gold tree outside, bending backwards and forwards in the wind, trying to break itself. Inside the room, Inspector Apsley had his hands steepled on the Formica table. He was a brisk man with gelled black hair, combed over in a kind of quiff. Alexa saw him in Fagan's one night, dressed in a red checked shirt and skinny braces. He looked as if he'd walked straight out of 1950s America. It was hard to imagine the man at the table ever taking off his uniform and holding a pint of Abbeydale's Deception.

'What is there to say?'

Dave's tone was brusque. He was sitting next to her, leaning back on his chair like a kid at school. The legs groaned under his weight. His shirt rode up a little, showing his paunch. She had an urge to pull him back, so he was sitting properly.

Inspector Apsley cleared his throat. 'We've been called out every night for the past three weeks. Reports of anti-social behaviour. We get called out because of the groups. The Roma. But if they aren't doing anything apart from talking, there's not much we can do. There's growing tensions, especially from the shopkeepers and representatives from the Pakistani community. They all want us to do something.'

There was nothing but the tree behind the window. Alexa had always wanted to live on a street with lots of trees, to watch the year change through them. To see everything through the leaves. At home, Caron had taken to sleeping with the curtains open. She said it was more natural to wake up with the light. Then again, she didn't do night shifts.

'The problem is the number of people that have arrived in Page Hall in the past few years. We don't know how many it is exactly ... but the council reckons there are about 1,500 Eastern European Roma children in the city as a whole. That's just kids, so maybe 600 to 900 families in total. And most of them are in Page Hall.'

Sue was shaking her head. Someone was talking about washing being stolen from washing lines. Greg, the other PCSO, was repeating an anecdote he'd already told Alexa, a night last week when a group of lads had been kicking a football against an elderly couple's window on Popple Street and they'd wanted him arrested, because it wasn't just about the football – they'd had enough.

'I've known them years. I think they felt like I'd let them down ...'

'Yes,' said Inspector Apsley. 'What we're facing here is an issue of trust.'

An issue of trust. Wasn't it always? Alexa wondered how many times a day she heard that word. She imagined Caron's mouth saying it and the word became beautiful. *Don't you trust me, Alexa?*

Then she saw Inspector Apsley repeating it and it sounded harsh again, cracked at the edges.

'We are approaching breaking point in Page Hall. As I say, it all comes down to winning trust.'

'Oh aye,' said Dave, 'and we've got a shitload of that, haven't we?' He said it a bit too loud. Inspector Apsley's face sharpened.

'David, if you want to continue your one-man mission to turn every meeting into a discussion of Operation Resolve, maybe you'd better do it elsewhere. My priority is Page Hall.'

'Did I say owt about that?'

'Operation Resolve is a completely separate inquiry.' His voice was leaden. 'The results of the inquests will not affect our other work.'

There was a heavy, hot kind of silence. People shifted in their chairs. Operation Resolve had been talked about for months, muttered in the corridors. The latest criminal inquiry into the Hillsborough disaster, headed by an investigation team. Dave was obsessed with it.

'To repeat: what we need in Page Hall is a clear and visible presence.'

Alexa stared at the huge tree. She tried to make up some kind of private analogy. Like the trunk was South Yorkshire Police and the leaves were all kinds of things, the leaves were Page Hall and Burngreave and Parson Cross, but the leaves were also Hillsborough and the Miners' Strike and Orgreave and investigations and shouted orders and cover-ups. And you couldn't have the tree without the leaves.

Dave didn't say anything for the rest of the meeting. His balding head gleamed with sweat. Leaning back with his paunch almost touching the table, he reminded Alexa of a greying Friar

Tuck. He sat still and listened to Inspector Apsley's solutions. *That's what we do here. We frame problems and we look for solutions.* He listened to the anti-social behaviour figures for East Sheffield. He listened to the Inspector's decision to apply for a Section 30. He listened to him saying they'd all have to work hard and show they were present in Page Hall. Alexa watched his leg judder under the table.

Afterwards, she caught him hurrying down the corridor.

'Dave!'

They walked in time. He was leaning very close to her. She could smell that he hadn't showered. He'd been out last night in The Kelham Island Tavern until late. Maybe he hadn't slept. He didn't look at her.

'Think your dad would have stood for this if he'd stayed a copper?'

She said nothing. Her face reddened. Eventually his walk slowed down, he was breathless from hurrying.

'Sorry, Al. I didn't mean ...'

'It's all right.'

'I just meant, people have no idea. How much we're meant to do. And with what?'

Most people got louder the angrier they got. Dave got quieter. He sounded almost hoarse now. Alexa followed him out into the car park. He pressed the key in his pocket and the lights flashed on his dirty silver Fiesta. He got into the driver's seat. Alexa opened the passenger side door.

'Watch your knees, love, my snap's in the glove compartment.'

He reached down to get his tin of sandwiches out and offered her one.

'Cheese, peanut butter and cucumber. Bloody lovely.'

She shook her head.

'Are you eating? Is he feeding you properly at home?'

Alexa faked a laugh. Dave still assumed she had a boyfriend, never wondered why he didn't join them in The Fat Cat on Fridays. Sometimes, people aren't as interested as they think. Once they've sketched a picture of you, they're content. She had never bothered to put her colleagues right. It wasn't to do with shame, just apathy. Dave's mood had lifted now, halfway through his first sarnie. A small piece of cucumber dangled from his lip. He'd parked in front of a high brick wall and they both sat, staring directly into the red and brown patterns of it. The car smelled of feet. Dave must have his trainers in the back. Alexa knew he was frustrated that she couldn't get angry about it all like he could. Page Hall. Hillsborough. Staff cuts. Blame. If she was a better person, she'd be able to make him laugh right now. But Alexa wasn't good with humour. Not the kind where you could say something funny on cue, or take someone's words and turn them round so that they suddenly realised the whole thing was ridiculous. Banter. She wasn't any good at that.

Caron was good at it. And confrontation, too. She did it in a way that made you feel like she wasn't furious about things, just passionate. Caron always let you know she was right. Alexa couldn't remember the last argument they'd had. This morning, she'd already gone out when Alexa got up. There was no note, just no bread left and a pile of dirty clothes snaked at the top of the stairs. What was that phrase? Ships in the night. They weren't ships. They were rowing boats. Small. Rained on. Alexa looked at herself in the passenger side mirror. Her roots needed doing. She had her hair scraped back in a high, severe pony tail and it only emphasised it. Her whole face felt pulled taut. She was paler than usual. Her chin was growing a spot. At least she didn't look like Dave with his three-day stubble and pothole eyes.

'Why did you mention my dad, back there?'

'I don't know. Sorry. Wanted a reaction, I guess.'

She nodded.

'He was a top bloke. Always good to me.'

'Yeah? Then how come you don't keep in touch?'

Dave had just bitten off a big chunk of peanut-butter-and-cheese sandwich. His eyes seemed to bulge. He was chewing frantically.

'How come you don't, Alexa? In't that the question?'

His mouth was all claggy. It ruined the drama. But she got out of the car and slammed the door anyway.

* * *

Eva was in the doorway of her house on Wade Street, chain-smoking, like always. Her black hair was tied back and gelled down at the front. She nodded to Alexa when she saw her on her beat.

'Time for a brew?'

Alexa checked over her shoulder, as if there was someone there. Dave or Inspector Apsley, watching her. She was at work. She shouldn't be spending time with the locals. But Eva was gone already, into her cream-tiled kitchen, leaving the door open for Alexa to come in. Alexa knew every corner of that room. They'd been called out to Eva's countless times the previous year, before she finally sent her husband packing. Eva said he'd gone back to their hometown in Slovakia. Her eyes flicked from side to side whenever she talked about him. This visit was pastoral. She was

56

only checking up on things. But she still ducked through the doorway, furtive. Hard to be inconspicuous in Page Hall.

'Sugar, love?'

Alexa sank into the plastic chair. She liked the way Eva said *love*. How her accent hardened briefly into Yorkshire. She nodded.

'Two?'

'Three. It's a three-sugar day.'

Eva raised her painted eyebrows, ladling the granules in and fishing out the bag. She put the mug on the table, resting it on unopened envelopes. Alexa tried not to look too closely at them. The block capitals that said URGENT, CONFIDENTIAL, TO BE OPENED BY THE ADDRESSEE ONLY. Official logos. Eva's surname spelled wrong on the front of half of them.

'Three sugars, hey? Why so bad?'

'It's nothing. Long day.'

Eva pursed her lips.

'Trouble with your boss?'

'It's nothing important. How've you been keeping, anyway?'

'Good, good. I spoke to my mother yesterday, on Skype. My dad's not so well.'

'I'm sorry.'

Alexa remembered all the times she'd said those words to Eva, she and Sue, sitting in the strip-lit kitchen, holding her hands, taking notes. Writing the unspeakable. *Did the argument take place before he tried to push you down the stairs? Do you remember what happened next, Eva?*

Eva shrugged. 'Nothing to be done. I need to find the money to fly back, when the time happens.'

'How much does it cost?'

'Depends. But too much. For me.'

Alexa looked at Eva's hands, bare, with the gold band she wore so stubbornly for months removed now. They were small hands, quick hands, hands you could fold into your own. There was something delicate about her thin face, too.

'Did you have any luck with the agency?'

Eva shook her head. 'They keep saying they'll call me. But you know how it is.'

Music started from next door. A jumping bassline, so deep it seemed to get into your chest and shake it.

'Bloody kids,' said Eva. 'It's like this always.'

'I'll have a word. Pay them a visit after this.'

Eva laughed. 'They'll start again when you go.'

Alexa took a swig of her tea. The sweetness was almost unbearable.

'Did you hear about the baby?' she said.

'The Roma boys in the chip shop? Yes. I don't like to think of it. Not much.'

'What do you mean?'

'I don't like to think of what happens after. You know? If the baby …'

She paused. The music from next door cut out abruptly. Alexa put a hand on her knee and squeezed. She remembered Eva's belly, the neat swell of it. She remembered the aftermath, the weeks of recovery. The silence.

'You know what they do back home for this? When a child dies?'

Alexa shook her head.

'It's bad luck if you die unmarried. Very bad luck. So the funeral … it's more like a marriage.'

'What do you mean?'

'The Wedding of the Dead, it's called. It happens in lots of places. Tradition, you know? In Romania, in China ... I think in China they call it a ghost marriage, actually. If someone dies and they aren't married, there is this ceremony – if it is a child, for instance, they are married to another dead child at their funeral.'

'Like a party?'

'No, not really. The couple – the ones being buried – they wear clothes for a wedding. But the guests dress for a funeral.'

'No way.'

'Yes. Sometimes they are married to a living person. It depends on the tradition.'

'And you really think it's bad luck, to die without being married?'

Alexa was thinking of the games she used to play when she was small. Lining her teddy bears up on the carpet and marrying them, the other soft toys and plastic figures in a dumb congregation just behind. She used to pick dandelions from the garden and place them in front of the teddy called Blossom, the one she had decided was a girl. When her dad found her, sitting cross-legged in front of her audience, he laughed. *Are you going to get married one day, just like Mummy and Daddy?*

Eva turned to her sharply. 'Who says I think anything? It's tradition.'

'Sorry. I didn't mean ...'

'Birth, marriage and death. The three important stages of life, no? They say it's bad luck if you break the cycle, if you die before someone marries you. So that's why. They must do it after you die.'

'Do you believe it?'

Eva shrugged. 'I don't know. I don't care. I'm already unlucky.'

'Maybe you can make your own luck.' Alexa winced as soon as she'd said it.

'There are lots of things like this back home. Mostly my parents believe, people like that. It's bad luck, too, if you don't spend time with someone before they die, make your peace with each other. I know my mother thinks so.'

Eva looked down at the table, at her folded hands. Alexa wanted to comfort her, reassure her, tell her she'd find a way home. But all she could think about was her own dad. The old, jinxed house where they used to live. His face at the window, angled towards the garden, as if he was watching something happen there or beyond there, out on the tower-block horizon. Something happening again and again, right in front of him.

She hardly noticed when Eva started to speak again. 'I think they believe this. In Page Hall, yes? The Roma, I mean. Many of the things they do, they do them because they believe. Nobody understands this. It's their way of life.'

'Like gathering in the street.'

'Yes. Like so. It isn't threatening, it's just … you know. How they do.'

Alexa sighed. 'Some people don't see it like that.'

'People see the things they want to see.'

Alexa rinsed her mug and put it on the draining board. When she got back on to the streets, she walked slowly, hesitantly. She did not look like an officer. A man was leaning at the bus stop by the main road, a hat and a hood pulled over his face, fiddling with a mobile phone. When he looked up, she saw he was older than she'd thought, almost her dad's age. He turned to his right, as if he was about to say something but there was no one there.

He lifted his hand as if to steady someone's elbow. As if there was a woman next to him. Alexa could imagine the shape of her. Ghost bride. She wrapped her uniform round her and moved on.

Page Hall

Days like this I lie low, keep as still as I can and listen to the things people say under their breath. The city's bristling; nobody knows what to do with their hands. It's too hot; it shouldn't be so hot, not at this time of year. Lads square up to me, then slump back like someone's stuck a pin in them, bang their fists against the walls. Sometimes, grown men call me names they heard their fathers call their mothers, names repeated in the playground after school. Kids tell me I'm boring, riding their bikes at full tilt, pedalling towards the edge of the sky or throwing a cricket ball so hard they almost take down the sun. Women call for home, call the others back, have their tea ready at five. Then there are quiet conversations. Some I don't like. Men outside the pubs talking too low to be overheard. A group of blokes who come from out of town in a discreet van, walking the streets with hands stuffed in their pockets, eyeing the houses, listening to the languages in the gardens, the lovely hubbub. By evening, they've gone. Soon I'll be steady, everyone inside their houses with the radio turned low. There'll be kids play-fighting in the yard outside. A man helping a grandmother cross the street. Two Somali teenagers coming back from the shops, throwing a word back and forth between them in the warm air. *Babe. Hon.* The Bangladeshi newsagent taking the sign in from outside his shop, straightening the magazines, putting everything right.

Him

He was awake. Listening for the soft hiss of tyres outside and hearing nothing, he worked out it must be about 3 a.m. No birds yet and a single light on in the street – the man from Number 62 whose front room was crammed with cardboard boxes and who stayed up through the night at his dining table, hunched over books and papers like an accountant. He checked the digital clock: 3.25 precisely. He had come home from The Byron sweetly exhausted, his mouth dry from whisky chasers, and fell asleep early, on the side of the bed that used to be Angela's once, allowing himself to think about her. He tried to remember his dreams. He never slept properly when he'd been drinking. Angela's hard shoulders. His hand at the nape of her neck. Her brother's wedding in St Helen's, the guests in formation, doing the conga. A football match they went to together when they were first courting.

He turned to the notebook on his bedside table and opened it. He wanted to write down all the things that flickered back to him in the night, as if they might mean something when he read them the next morning. A dream diary, was that what they called it? The first half of the book was spidery now. Pages of notes from court cases and reports, copied out neatly. Then other passages, written quickly, the letters flat and hurried and joined up, but never written fast enough to keep up with his thoughts when they came.

It wasn't a surge. It was like a vice, getting tighter and tighter.

He'd started that and got no further. He felt silly, writing things down. As if he was going to have to submit the lot for review. Even when he wrote alone in the tight kitchen or in the storeroom at work, he kept startling, imagining someone reading it over his shoulder. It made him think about the way he used to be in bed with Angela, how he'd always whisper, even when there was nobody to overhear.

The match he'd been thinking about when he nodded off was at Anfield and he'd refused to wear red, even though they were in The Kop, even though she'd teased him all the way there. *Not my team*, he'd said, all mock-pride. But really, he'd loved being there with her. Held in the bowl of the stadium, held in the noise. It was so cold you could see your breath when you spoke, hanging in the air like an afterthought. Everyone was wrapped up in thick winter coats. Angela was wearing one that looked like a railway signalman's jacket. They were both deliciously young.

Angela told him about coming here with her dad as a kid and climbing on his shoulders so she could see better, climbing him as if he was a tree. And he asked her – half-joking – if that was where it came from, her love of heights, that urge to climb mountains. And she turned the headlamps of her stare on him and said *Maybe*, and he was an animal under her gaze, slipping his hand into her hand and holding it in the oversized pocket of his coat. Tweed. He even had a flat cap in those days as well. A Yorkshire cliché. And then she was telling him about climbing trees in Sefton Park as a kid, about wanting to sleep in the branches in summer, hidden above the city. And he laughed when she said that the only time she'd even felt like that since was bivouacking on a mountain, waking up on the hill and forgetting where you were for a minute. He almost kissed her then, even with the noise around them, even though the men would have whistled and jeered, but it was kick-off and there was a song forming in the air. He squeezed her knuckles and knew he didn't need to say anything.

The players were electric. They moved so fast he could hardly keep his eyes on them. Blood-red colours and grass stains. A header that seemed to last forever, the ball sailing through the air, almost suspended there. At half-time the air smelled faintly of gravy. In the end, Liverpool beat Everton 3–1. Kenny Dalglish scored twice, ran in triumphant circles as the other players massed around him. Ian Rush finished things off with a third goal in the seventy-fifth minute and the stadium erupted then, people kissing each other, looking like they were going to nut each other. Angela squeezed his hand hard and jigged up and down, trying to get a better view over the heads of the others.

Years later, when he joined the force, she laughed the first time she saw him in uniform. She stroked his chest and slapped him on the arse too hard and told him he looked like he was booked for a hen do. She never had to wear a uniform in her life. Only her Liverpool kit and she never kept up with the new ones each season. Angela was lithe and sinewy. She wore her hair loose over her shoulders and she never put on make-up, not even if they were going out to a do. She always moved very deliberately, on the rock when she was guiding someone up a route, or in the house, stooping slightly to fill the kettle. She made everything she did seem important. Like the precision with which she packed for expeditions, setting all her kit out on the floor in neat rows: pairs of gloves, crampons, axes. The first time, he begged her not to go and he didn't care how weak he must have sounded. But it was her job. More than her job – her vocation. She was a natural climber, fluid and confident.

Slowly, over the years after they married, their house filled with photographs, bright with ice: the Karakoram, the Alps, the Rockies. He still had them in a shoebox – his favourite was an unnaturally blue photo of Angela climbing in Canada. In the picture, she was leaning in to the slope, he could almost feel the points of her axes biting into it. Back turned away from him, intent and purposeful, small on the great face. After each trip, he'd ask her what it was like and she'd be lost for words; the photographs held more of the mountains than she could. He understood that. Even though he could never climb like her, he loved the speechlessness of it, the way some climbs refused commentary. That was something they'd always shared. He felt closest to her when they were on a rope together, him belaying her usually: holding her ropes, making sure they were tight enough, trying to guess her movements, ready to brace if she fell. They spoke best through the easy language of climbing. *Watch me. Climb when ready.* When their daughter was born, he paced up and down in the hospital, wishing there was a code for that, too, or something that tethered him to her. When they cut the child's umbilical cord, purplish and thicker than he expected, he thought of rope, thought of Simon Yates, the Sheffield climber who cut the lifeline that linked him to his partner, Joe Simpson, when Simpson fell down a crevasse. Angela was always sanguine about it: Yates had no choice. If they'd stayed connected, they'd both have died. She was always more logical than him, better equipped to let go of things. He was sentimental sometimes, romantic, in the grip of high ideals. No good for a copper really.

3.28 a.m. He got out of bed and unhooked his dressing gown from the door. He was so practised he didn't even need to turn the light on. The wooden floorboards protested under his weight and he creaked downstairs, shrugging the gown over his shoulders. He sat in the darkness on his small sofa and flicked on the TV, lighting the room palely. It was a twenty-four-hour shopping channel. American. A woman with a neon-green crop top and cycling shorts was demonstrating the different uses of an abs trainer. He watched with the sound off as she did crunches with her knees tilted to either side. Behind her was a topless man with a defined six-pack, arms folded across his chest to accentuate the muscles. Now he was using the crunch trainer to do tricep dips. The man's bristling shoulders and large hands looked fit to crush it. His teeth were like dice. There was an untouched can of Oranjeboom next to the sofa, along with some empties, and Pete opened it now, enjoying the deflated sound of the ring pull. The first sip was lukewarm. A new advert for jogging bottoms was playing on repeat. He took another swig and found it hard to swallow.

How many did you have to drink that day? How many people did you see drunk? Did your son like to have a drink before the match? The families shaking in the waiting room. The interviewing officers who didn't let their faces show a thing.

When he got home that night in April, close to midnight and found her shaking in the lounge, she was holding her Liverpool top like a cleaning rag, balled into her fist and they'd clung to each other and thanked God she wasn't there, thanked a god they didn't believe in that she'd taken a mountaineering client out that day and didn't even know about it until she got home and switched on the telly. And she rang her mum and dad and her cousins and talked through the night, her accent getting harder, the way it always did when she talked to other Scousers. He went to check on the baby, movements like a ghost. He was numb. He felt like nothing could touch him. Angela would have to do the crying for the both of them.

Afterwards, when she'd hung up and he was still in the kitchen in his work clothes, staring at the back door, eyes fixed on the bit of paint he'd missed when he did the house up last summer, convinced he'd made a bad job of it, she came and stood behind him with her arms looped around his waist and murmured that she kept trying to work out what she'd been doing at 3.06 p.m. She thought they'd probably been on The Rasp at Higgar. She was certain that was it. Maybe she'd have been at the top by then, belaying. It had been a good day, perfect for the time of year. She'd led it well, the client was happy and they'd both got home safe.

It's like climbing, she said. *Something like this. Out the blue. You never know when it's going to be your time.* He'd tried to get those words out of his head ever since.

Kelham Island

Everything left messy as if someone might pick up tools round here again. The door of The Gardeners pub is permanently ajar. In the new apartments, students from Hong Kong and Mumbai and Tokyo sleep with their windows open, letting the sound of traffic from Shalesmoor filter in. Their neighbours are graphic designers, bakery owners from Neepsend, property developers whose nightmares are architectural, who shut their eyes and fall asleep and dream of being lost inside marble corridors, buildings that could be temples, shrines to unknown gods. All the roofs round here are slightly crooked. Car alarms sound through the night. There's the sign for the old saw manufacturers, the crocodile grin of it, the smashed glass and the rubble of brickwork. There's the mark on the side of The Fat Cat ale house where the flood water reached years ago, seeping through carpets, touching the sills. There's peace, shut inside gastropubs and cafés and boarded up inside ex-foundries, the cavernous heart of the climbing wall where nobody hangs from a rope at this hour, nobody shouts *Take me!*, nobody drops through the air like dread, like fear in the pit of a stomach.

Alexa

They'd had reports of a middle-aged woman drunk and walking the length of Willoughby Street, knocking on doors. She'd spent the afternoon in the only pub open in Page Hall, before getting ejected for smoking in the toilets. When Alexa found her, she was leaning against a propped-up mattress outside one of the houses, arms spread wide. Alexa recognised her immediately. She'd picked her up before in someone's garden after the residents had phoned in about an intruder. The woman was asleep, wrapped in a sheet from the washing line. Alexa had almost regretted disturbing her, she looked so peaceful.

'Marjorie,' she said. 'Shall we get you home?'

The woman opened one eye, then the other and laughed at her.

'I'm resting. Give us a minute.'

A kid rode past them on a scooter, veering close, almost hitting Marjorie.

'Little Paki bastard!' she shouted after him. She turned to Alexa with her hands up. 'I'm sorry. I'm not racist. It just come out.'

'OK.' Alexa took hold of her arm. 'Shall we walk?'

'Get off me! I can walk myself.'

She followed Alexa, a step behind, then drew level with her.

'I'm not racist at all. I don't understand all that. There was two of them in The Ball earlier, two blokes, blaming them Roma for the pub going under. Talking about refugees. I said to them, "Wouldn't you do the same? If it was your country that was like that? Wouldn't you move?"'

Alexa nodded. She should be asking Marjorie questions, trying to find out why she'd been knocking on the doors on Willoughby Street, but it didn't seem to matter. It was the logic of drink.

'People don't like it, though, do they? When summat's different. That's why all these bastards …' – she spun round in a circle with her arms wide, taking in the whole street – ' … that's why they've got no time for me. Because I'm different.'

Alexa didn't know what she thought about that word. People like Marjorie used it as if it was a badge. But Alexa had never felt that way. She felt marked, like she was always on the wrong side of the line, even though she was quiet, softly spoken, even though there was nothing in her appearance to mark her out and the clothes she wore didn't court attention like Caron's. She was different at school when she wanted to keep her head down, when the teacher went out of the classroom and everyone else whooped and hollered and she was scared. She was different at university when she tried to talk to her friends about love. Different in the force when she tried to sink her lukewarm white wine in the pub and the others downed their pints and talked about their marriages. It made her awkward. Detached.

Marjorie was sobbing. Very softly. Her shoulders were shaking.

'Come on now,' she said. 'Let's get you back home.'

'Where's that, yeah? Is it here?' Marjorie gestured at the long street, the packed-in cars, the abandoned bikes. She pointed to the last house on the road. 'Here?'

It was a good question. Alexa thought about all the times someone had asked her where she was from and she'd said Sheffield without thinking, without really knowing what that meant. At university, all the girls she met on the first day were from towns in Surrey and Suffolk. They had confident voices and clear skin. Some of them even said *London*, the word like a punch in the air, though she wasn't sure what it really meant to come from London either. To those girls, Sheffield was exciting. Sheffield was cheap real ale and The Leadmill and seeing bands with ironic names like Burn After Listening before anyone else and putting Henderson's Relish on your chips to prove that you liked it. Sheffield was complaining that your thighs were getting bigger because of all the hills, and shivering in winter, and sitting out in the beer garden of The Lescar in summer, smoking weed. When they asked Alexa where her home was and she said *Here*, some of them looked at her quizzically, as if to say *Why wouldn't you get away?* And sometimes at night she'd sit in her new box room in Ranmoor and think about how close she was to the street where she grew up, and how strange it was to be here, with a crap kitchen and an upstairs neighbour who played reggae before 8 a.m., just for the sake of independence, whatever that meant. And she wasn't sure which version of the city was hers, the ordinary, boring Saturdays, the markets and back gardens and late buses and the view from the green hill beyond Forge Dam she'd seen so many times she could trace the skyline, or the new Sheffield, the one that came alive at night with pills and Plug and girls in Doc Martens and crop tops who knew the words to 'Common People' better than she did. The Sheffield that was in your face or the Sheffield that was under your fingernails.

Her first term, she couldn't say the names of all the tram stops properly. *Malin Bridge*. Alexa said it with a flat 'a', instead of pronouncing it like Mailing. And the others laughed at her and said *You're supposed to be the local*, and Alexa felt ashamed, like she was only pretending to be from Sheffield. And it was funny, how there were always places in your own town that you'd never go to, just like there were places in your own body you'd never see, bones you wouldn't know the names of. Sheffield felt like that sometimes when she was a student – like a muscle that started hurting after a long walk or a long bike ride, one you never knew was there until you used it, unexpectedly.

'I was born in Page Hall,' said Marjorie. 'Did you know that?'

Alexa nodded, steering her back on to the pavement. 'You said.'

'Do you think it means owt?'

Alexa shrugged.

'Because I don't.'

They passed a lad in a hoodie and smart trousers, and he acknowledged Marjorie with a movement of his head.

'He was born here, too. Ranjit. But if you told that to some of them wankers, would they believe you?'

'If you told that to who?'

'The wankers.' She threw her hands in the air. 'They're everywhere.'

Sometimes, you could walk down the street and believe that. That everyone around you was just going about their business single-mindedly, seeing you as an inconvenience. Other days, someone would open a door or smile and call you *love* on the bus and make it all right.

Marjorie had stopped crying now. With Alexa still holding on to her arm, she sunk to the pavement, cross-legged.

'Come on Marjorie, we need to get you home.'

'I am home.' She was grinning at Alexa now, a wide-toothed smile. 'I've decided. This'll do.'

A car racing down to the T-junction beeped at her, the bass line from the stereo lingering, following it like an afterthought. Marjorie raised one hand in a friendly wave.

'This is my stop, love.'

The sun was faintly out. It was not yet dark. Alexa leaned against the wall in the brief silence of the street. She couldn't argue.

* * *

Alexa woke alone, she was on Caron's side of the bed and she'd hardly slept. Before she drifted off, she'd been trying to remember something, and she'd been groping towards it in the night. Awake with her fist clenched and Caron's pyjama shorts looped round her ankle, she felt like she had a hold.

She was a kid – she couldn't remember how old – and the Tube train was very hot, the kind of heat that gets into your eyes and your throat. Her and her dad and her uncle who wasn't her uncle, Rob. The men were wearing scarves in Rob's team colours, trying to loosen them as the carriage got warmer. They'd been to the theatre in Leicester Square, but it was match day and the Tube was heaving. Everyone was trying to get out of everyone else's way, but nobody could, not really. There were armpits and bellies everywhere. No one could make themselves smaller. They stood in silence, holding on to the rails and loops, and Alexa's dad squeezed her shoulder and asked her if she was OK. She was waist-height and the train was a forest of legs. She shifted, balancing on one leg, in case that made her more tiny. Rob was swearing and puffing, and her dad said *Not in front of Alexa* and she wondered why, because he was always saying those words in the house, on the phone or even to himself and saying them louder than that, too.

The train got to a station and stopped too quickly. Everyone jerked forwards. The doors opened and the sound was like someone being winded, and they all waited for people to spill out, but they didn't, instead more people got on; men from the football, who were shoving each other to get through the doors and who smelled of beer and warmth and new sweat. Everyone was touching now; Alexa could feel their legs pressing against her. Her dad pulled her a little closer to him and put one hand on the crown of her head, ruffling her hair, and she wanted to smoothe it back the way it was, but she couldn't really move her arms that far.

At the next station, the doors opened and there were more people, rows of them on the platform. Someone shouted that the train was full, but Alexa could feel herself being pushed backwards, her body tightening, braced against whoever was behind. A big man was shoving his way forwards and everyone was getting shunted back into the space that wasn't there. Rob was turning purple. *Mate, you have to get off the train. There's a kid down here.* The voices were too loud, jostling for their own positions in the air. *Get off the fucking train, mate.*

And all the time Alexa's dad held her hand and she stared at it and saw the knuckles turning white. She wanted to say that he was hurting her, but she couldn't; she had no breath and anyway it was nice being held by him for the first time since Mum and the accident. She stared right ahead of her. She didn't look up. Rob's voice was getting higher and louder. She wondered if a voice could break like a glass, like the pubs they'd walked past earlier where a man dropped his pint as he talked and it opened up on the pavement in front of him, in pieces.

The man would not get off the train. The doors didn't shut. Rob strained towards him like a dog on a leash, though he couldn't get close. Her dad's grip on her hand was a vice. She could feel herself going wobbly, her knees first, then everything else. She closed her eyes and tried to pretend she was back in her room, at night, one of those nights that didn't exist any more, when Mum would come back from the climbing wall smelling of chalk, and read her the story about the three little pigs, while Dad clattered plates downstairs, getting tea ready for her. She was not imagining it hard enough. The train kept getting back in. People were on top of her, she could tell even with her eyes shut.

Uncle Rob's voice and the man's voice twisted round each other until they became one. Now someone else was shouting at Rob, a man with a Cockney accent, saying *Calm down, mate. There's no need to fucking swear.* Rob saying *I'm not fucking swearing, mate.* Mate. Everyone repeating it, using it like a full stop. Alexa's dad didn't say anything at all. Eventually, the fat man inched his way just far enough into the carriage and the doors collapsed shut and the train carried on, slower than ever, and there was silence all the way, apart from people sighing and breathing and clearing their throats.

They had to push themselves out at King's Cross, wriggling through the crowd. The platform seemed huge and cool. Rob had his hand on Dad's shoulder.

'You all right, pal?'

'I'll live.'

He hadn't let go of Alexa's hand. She wondered how long it would take him to remember he was still holding on to her.

Millhouses

There's a man asleep in the park bandstand again. From a distance, he looks dead. Half the night the trains shuttle back and forth to Chesterfield, carrying drunks and office workers who stay up too late. The wide road that separates the park from the woods is an invitation to escape, to keep going, to drive without looking back through Totley, neat semis turning into stone cottages, the long approach to a country house, where cattle grids make the car rattle and sheep stand in the road, their eyes lit a supernatural green by the headlamps. Sometimes a deer skitters back into the shadows or two rabbits stop to sniff the air, bodies quivering. How contained, how small they are. How their fear propels them, but gently. Above, a bird of prey roosts on a branch, beak curved like a brass hook, and the bats are barely known, invisible, making sounds no one can hear. Above the valley, the moon is a blood moon, tinged pink like the residue left inside an egg, a wound in the clouds, an incredulous mouth, the sky around it seeping.

Leigh

Leigh had left it a whole week. Now she wasn't sure if Caron was here at all. The Sheaf's taproom was very white, but the smoking ban hadn't been kind to it – sweat and beer farts. Under one table, there was a dog the size of a small horse. Occasionally, it would shuffle out and unfold itself, large raindrops of saliva dropping to the floor. It surveyed the room with wood-coloured eyes and seemed disappointed or worried or just plain scared by what it found. The owner stared off into the distance, like the dog was nothing to do with him.

Leigh had Jim Beam vision. Before she headed out, she'd finished the bottle that Pete had brought round to her place one lonely, rained-off night. Now everything seemed pleasantly far away. A workman in paint-stained boots taking up most of the bar, who hadn't been home since clocking off. Someone in the corner who used to be a famous climber, holding court, a skinny lad with a beard more interesting than his face, hanging on every word. She could get her phone out and pretend to text someone. She had a new message.

Hey. Where are you? xxxxx

She ignored Tom's text. Her map of Sheffield was a diagram of all the places she'd once argued with him. That corner by Arundel Gate, outside the Genting Club, where he'd asked her, half-joking, if she was the kind of person who could be lived with. The park near the hospital with no street lights where they walked, drunk, bickering about a film neither of them cared about. The station bar. Fargate. The Moor. Seams of disagreement connecting up her city like a Tube map. The Sheaf wasn't on it at all. Too far from Tom's trendy, shoebox flat. The Sheaf peered down at semis and unkempt gardens, suburban cats fucking and fighting behind the dustbins.

Her pocket was vibrating again.

I've got an hour, maybe 2. Come round. X

People said jealousy was green, like sickness. But for Leigh it was better than that. Sometimes, jealousy was a spur. It woke her up at 5 a.m. It stopped her from lying in bed those days when the curtains couldn't be thick enough, when she wanted to switch the sun off. It made her body shake with anger. And anger was a kind of movement. If you knew how to control it, anger could help you do anything. It could help you sink your fingers into every crimp on a climb so hard they had to hold. It could help you reach higher and hold on.

She downed her pint and swung herself off the bar stool, swaying towards the toilets. And there they were, in her peripheral vision, huddled round a table too small for them. Caron caught her eye, but the others – two blokes nursing glasses of water – didn't notice, and she was glad as she slid down next to them. When she spoke, there was something unnaturally and briefly still about Caron. As if what she was saying pivoted around her, left her in the eye of it, calm for once.

'I know what you're going to say, Leyton.'

Leyton didn't look like he'd ever known what he was going to say. He was wearing a grey cap and Leigh could see the silvery stubble of his hair underneath.

'But it's all about being strong for your weight. Your size.'

The whisky was behind Leigh's cheekbones and eyelids, making her whole face heavy.

'You're right fucking strong.' The gap-toothed guy who wasn't Leyton stuffed his folded beermat into a pocket. Leigh noticed how his down jacket was botched with tape. He had a wiry face and a wirier beard, newspaper-print black. There was something languid about him, but his eyes were too big and too green for his face.

'Not as strong as I will be.' She punched Leyton on the arm, exaggerated. 'Sorry Leigh, I'm shit at introductions. Guys, this is my friend Leigh. Leigh, this is Leyton and Matt. Matt's just got back from Kalymnos. Leyton's just got back from the jobcentre.'

She couldn't quite work out how Caron knew the two men; if they were climbing acquaintances or something else. Leyton seemed awkward around Caron at times, touching her arm stiffly when he went to get a round in. It didn't matter. As the night rolled round the pub, they both started to look the same to Leigh. Her phone kept buzzing. She had another whisky. Only Caron was utterly herself, still at the heart of The Sheaf.

* * *

When Leigh woke she was in the quarry, by the debris of a fire. She stared past Caron to the reddish flank of London Wall, almost blank but for those big zigzags and cracks dividing it. She thought if she looked at the wall long enough, everything that happened last night might happen again on it, like TV. Someone deciding to drive, Matt maybe. The moors like the sea at night on either side of the car. Caron taking her hand in the dark on the way from the lay-by, folding it into her own pocket, making her feel like a kid. The lighters in the blackness, the ends of Leyton's roll-ups glowing. Someone pretending they could point out the constellations. *The Bear. Orion's Belt. The Great Twat in the Sky.* And Leigh not wondering where the next drink was coming from, just huddling down in the darkness with Caron. Caron resting her chin on her shoulder, so she could feel the engine of her breath. Then the parts she imagined afterwards. A tongue, warmer than anyone else's. And the heat inside her body. The heat that seemed to stay on Leigh, on her fingers and lips when she closed her eyes, then opened them and let the night sky in.

Without waking anyone, Leigh inched herself away. She was still wearing all her clothes, but she'd taken her trail shoes off, as if she was getting into bed, so she yanked them on and stood up, shaky. Took a few steps backwards, still looking up at London Wall. Leyton and Matt were off to the left, sleeping like Yin and Yang. Leyton had his cap over his face.

She dragged her hangover to Surprise View, then changed her mind and doubled back towards Higgar Tor. The ground was dry, but she felt like she was wading through mud, all the way, the bracken dragging at her legs. It was early, but already there was a woman picking her way up to the rocks with a tiny child clinging to each of her arms, like a human seesaw. Both of the kids were in crimson duffel coats and lumpy bobble hats.

'When can we have an ice cream?'

'It's too early for an ice cream, Jack!'

Leigh couldn't look at them, because they made her think of teenage Sunday walks with her mad cousins. So many, she couldn't remember their names. She had nothing in common with her family, but walks meant you didn't have to talk to people, or not in the way you did normally anyway. You could say things without looking at them and it was easier. She didn't know the names of the places back then – Higgar East, Carl Wark – but somehow, it was better not knowing. Once, they startled a tiny grouse chick from the grass and it ran alongside them for half a mile, before it threaded back into the undergrowth. Her cousins were all doctors and solicitors now, living in Birmingham and Manchester, married to people they'd met online or at work, waking up in flats that overlooked a long stretch of canal, a gentrified warehouse-turned-artisan-bakery.

'But I want a Mister Whippy!'

As Leigh passed them, she tried to soften her face into a smile. She nodded at the mother. One of the small boys hid.

At the top of Higgar Tor, she carried on – round the weird elbow of Burbage North, the car park at the crook of it. Down towards the comforting loudness of the stream, where she crossed and kicked her shoes off underneath Triangle Buttress and started upwards, following the shiny holds and signatures of chalk. Bare feet were useless, but she knew the routes so well she could just hang on her arms. She realised she was climbing almost silently, holding her breath. It was as if she still didn't want to wake up Caron. Caron, miles away.

A bird swooped down from over the top. Leigh was thinking about High Tor above Matlock, how it was used as a suicide spot. How, if you were unlucky, someone might drive their car off the edge or jump while you were climbing. She never went there late, as if something about the morning might keep the place safe. Then Pete told her about the bloke who was belaying there when his mate, reaching the top of a climb, knocked down a huge block of rock. Took the bloke's head off. Clean. She stopped climbing there after that. She wanted to laugh at herself for remembering it now. *Morbid fucker*, Pete would say. *You don't have to dwell on it.* She stopped thinking and she started to climb.

Harpur Hill

You've been standing in my shadow for ten long minutes, fiddling with your harness, strapping on your new Velcro shoes. You can hear the lads racing on their quad bikes, down there at my feet in the mud and spoil heaps. They're closer to me than you are. Closer to my core: the disused railway line; the caustic, turquoise pool; the industrial estate where those lost, metallic voices drift up to you from the tannoy. They're closer to the council houses near Buxton, the dark green of the Pennine Moors, the place where I start, hunkering down in the valley like a neglected grandparent. You're a stranger here, chalking up, pressing your fingers into the white powder you keep in a bag at your waist, then touching my quarried face, glancing up at the bolts they stapled into me. My skin is crumbling, punched metallic. I'm wondering what you and the old man belaying you have in common. Neither of you talks much. He's old enough to be your father, but you don't look alike. You fall at the third bolt and have to retrace the moves. When you get to the top, short of breath, he says *You could be good if you tried.*

Leigh

The abandoned jeep was smack in the middle of Burbage Brook lay-by, sagging into the mud. It was Thursday, Leigh's day off, but she'd lost track of the weeks lately. The frame was mostly black from the flames and the windows gaped where the heat had exploded them. Inside, it was full of rubbish bags: cans of Carling poking out, some kind of rusted wire wrapped around the steering wheel and bags. Something intestinal about it. It bothered Leigh in a way it didn't bother Caron. She was tense, as if they were going to get caught looking.

'Kids,' Caron laughed.

Leigh was imagining the night before it happened. Too many of them crammed in the back seat. The bends at Fox House taken so fast the jeep nearly tipped over. Laughter. Then the lot of them hunched over tinnies, passing a single joint back and forth. One not knowing how to light it when it went out. Burbage South utterly black above them, just the moon there, like a gatecrasher. Caron was ahead of her already, starting up the path. She glanced back.

'Leigh. Come on. It's not a museum.'

Leigh ran to catch up. They set off up the fawny track, bracken on either side. Leigh didn't look over her shoulder.

* * *

Apparent North. It had to be. She'd known it the moment they got off the bus, even though Caron hadn't said anything to her the whole journey, just smiled at her and squeezed her arm as the Sheffield suburbs got too big for themselves and then shrank again, back into the moorland and tracks they must have come from. They were here to scope out a route. Realising, she felt more like an accomplice than whatever she'd thought she was on the bus.

Apparent North was small and cut-off. Like Caron. It was also dangerous in the rain.

There were two short lads bouldering, one high on a rib, the other using his mat as a makeshift sofa, squinting up at his mate. He was shouting advice, but there was something detached in his voice, as if he didn't care if he made it or not.

'You got it, Jonno. Nice.'

They passed them, heading for a buttress that looked like a warped battleship. A titanic piece of rock with a jutting overhang. Caron chucked down her bag and grinned.

'Black Car Burning.'

'I know.'

Bouldering-mat boy had followed them and was looking up at the route, too.

'You going for it?' he asked. His voice was as big as his stare.

'Not today.'

Leigh could see him eyeing Caron, from her small feet to the large blue bobble hat she seemed to have tried to stuff her whole body into, like a sleeping bag in its sack. Today, she was 90 per cent hat. Bouldering-mat boy's look was abrasive.

'Are you the girl from that film? *True Grit 3*?'

Caron snorted. She was underneath Black Car Burning, on her tiptoes, miming out moves. Even the first break was high. It was the kind of route that seemed to glare down at you, wherever you stood. That was the way Leigh often thought of Tom's face. No matter where she went, she had this image of him, head downturned, craning towards her. She'd think he could see her whatever she was doing. It was better than thinking of him not thinking of her, him in the car with his girlfriend, or lecturing to a room of girls who thought he knew everything.

'You must be confusing me with someone good.'

Bouldering-mat was animated now, lit by his own ambition.

'Have you ever climbed Downhill Racer?'

Caron nodded. Leigh let the names wash over her like music.

'Committed?'

Caron cracked a smile. 'Not yet. Might be committed soon. If I'm not careful.'

He didn't get the joke. He was off again, tripping over his words.

'How about Malham? I want to climb there. Consenting Adults? Obsession?'

'Not if I can help it.'

'Psycho at Caley?'

'I'm more Psycho in Sheffield.'

'I'm at Sheffield, too. At the uni. I came for the climbing. It's Freshers' Week, but me and Jonno have been up here every day. We're new to grit, just doing some easy stuff. E2s.'

Easy stuff. Leigh could feel her body stiffening. She was used to this from the shop. People who had to position themselves, gauge how much better than you they might be. She'd had that stamped out of her at school. If she ever had it. The playground round the back of the leisure centre where she'd first thought of climbing, up and over the meshed fence, slipping in and hiding with all the people in tracksuits and people with wet hair from swimming. The playground where you learned to underestimate yourself in company.

'What's your name?' asked Bouldering-mat.

'Caron,' said Caron. Leigh said nothing.

'I'm Greg. Greg Sutcliffe.' He lurched his hand out.

Caron didn't take it. Leigh could tell she was impatient to be in her own world, fed up of even her own company, needing to lose herself in the guessed sequences of Black Car Burning, the thought of everything she might yet do.

There was a thump as Jonno sailed through the air and landed on one of his bouldering mats. Greg didn't even glance over.

* * *

Later, when the rain began to mesh over the valley, they walked along to Robin Hood's Cave and sheltered under the lip of it. The cave smelled faintly of piss. Someone must have slept in it recently. There were acrid logs and a couple of empty cans.

Caron was fingering the graffiti on a far wall, letters bigger than her hand.

'My name's in here somewhere. See if you can find it.'

Leigh had always wanted to bring Tom to a place like this. She'd thought they'd forget the city, drinking whisky and watching the lights go out over Hathersage, one by one like faulty, flat-pack stars. Maybe the cave and the night would give him the feeling he could be anywhere, give him the nerve not to go back home. Now, with the piss smell and litter, she realised it was just another outpost of Sheffield. A fistful of town, brought and left here. They couldn't even have fucked in the cave, it was too narrow and angular and dusty. It let too much light in.

'I can't see it.'

'It's not there. I was just messing.'

They hadn't touched since the bus. Caron came and sat next to her, so they were both staring out through the nest of rock. It felt like a concession. Leigh turned.

'You really want it, don't you?'

'The route? Of course. It's short. Bold. I like stuff like that.'

'It's desperate,' muttered Leigh.

'One day. And I want you to belay me.'

'Me?'

'Yes.'

'Why?'

Leigh knew how pathetic it sounded as soon as she said it. Like a plea for affirmation. An invitation. Sometimes, the best climbing partners were people you didn't really know – people who didn't care enough about you to hold their breath as you inched up the rock, who didn't feel the tension in the rope that linked the two of you, didn't keep a nervous silence. That's why she never tried anything difficult with Pete nowadays. They both cared too much.

'Why not? You planning to kill me?'

Caron was never serious. She was too good for that, Leigh thought.

'I'm not an idiot.' Caron took out a cereal bar from her pocket and started to eat. 'I don't want to deck it.'

'What's the deal with Black Car Burning, then?' Leigh was thinking out loud, but it was too late to take it back. Caron stopped smiling. There was a silence and she said:

'Long story. It's to do with Alexa.'

'Alexa?'

'She's one of my partners.'

'Climbing partners?'

Caron laughed. Leigh felt a slow tightening, a winding sensation in her stomach. That was how she'd felt when she saw Tom's girlfriend for the first time, from the back, in a camel coat, fumbling with the keys to their flat. Like something was being wound up, like a turning lock gate.

Afterwards, when they were scrambling back down from the cave, Leigh thought about the only time Tom had shown her anything that mattered to him. It was the Major Oak in Sherwood Forest, the tree where they said Robin Hood's men had crouched inside the hollow trunk to hide. Tom's parents used to take him there when he was a kid. They'd scuffed their feet along the trails and dragged each other behind trees to kiss. People who are good at cheating have this way of making you feel like they'd never show these things to anyone else, even when you know they do. Leigh remembered the smell of the bark after rain. She'd hated the fence around the Major Oak, the way you couldn't really get that close to it. Tom sat down on the surfaced path, so he could look up into the canopy of the branches. Leigh wondered if there'd been a warning in all of it. Like you shouldn't trust people who prefer forests to clear views.

They were nearing the Plantation, the softness of the woods, the ground turning to mulch underfoot.

'So Leyton's your ex now?'

'No. Me and Leyton still have sex, but we aren't that close really. It's not a regular thing these days. I guess I prefer to look further afield.' Something in the way she said it made Leigh laugh, nervously. There was a long pause before she spoke again.

'And Matt?'

'The boys in the house are just mates. With each other, I mean. Things are pretty fluid. Leyton and Alexa used to sleep together loads, but at the moment they're like best friends who don't fuck.'

'Friends without benefits.' It was a lame joke and she knew it.

'That would be a pretty narrow view.'

'And how does it work if you want to start seeing someone new?'

They both looked sideways and their eyes met for a second.

'You have to talk it through first.' Caron's voice seemed sharp, irritated. She'd picked up the pace, but she paused slightly and shot Leigh a backwards glance. Leigh felt her eyes move over her. It was gentle, almost imperceptible. 'Theoretically,' Caron said.

There was a woman hiking up from the car park with a backpack bigger than her. A springy lurcher with fur the colour of puddles raced ahead, zig-zagging up the hill and veering off the path. She kept shouting its name, but it was all nose-to-heather, following a better call. Suddenly, for no reason, it dug its paws into the ground, halted, then started sprinting back towards her.

Leigh felt the urge to take Caron's arm as they descended, the way she used to link arms with her friends at school.

'I met Alexa at uni. She didn't even know she was bi – '

'Too much information,' said Leigh.

'Sorry. I'm a chronic oversharer. You'll have to tell me to stop.'

Leigh jumped a rock, focusing on the leaves on the other side of it, avoiding the bog. The lurcher came hurtling past them up the track and Leigh had to jump to one side. She resented the dog. Its single purpose. Its easy lope up to the top of Stanage, not caring why it needed to keep climbing.

'You know, Leigh, most people are full of shit. Like, you tell someone you're poly and they go ... "Oh, so you cheat on each other?"'

Leigh's mind was with the lurcher, which had to be on top of the edge now, cannonballing over towards Apparent North and Black Car Burning, the overhang waiting just as they'd left it.

Caron stopped and got the guidebook out of her pocket, its list of diagrams and names. Leigh wanted to say something then, but the moment was gone.

'Where to next?' grinned Caron. But she set off before Leigh had a chance to answer.

Robin Hood's Cave

I'm a bad secret-keeper. I hold the sleepers with their small fires burning out, their crumpled sleeping bags and blow-up mats, their whispered, intimate conversations, and in the morning I let them go. When the park wardens patrol with torches, I have nowhere to hide them. I'm open to the air, open to the sun when it rises too early. I watch the climbers huddle in the evenings with cans of beans and hip flasks as if they're the first to ever shelter here. I let them write their private messages across the walls. Then I let the night in and they tremble; nothing they have is theirs alone.

Alexa

When Alexa and Caron were in the house at the same time these days, Caron was usually on her laptop, or in the bathroom playing PJ Harvey at full volume, running all the taps at once. She seemed distracted, one hand on the pocket where she kept her phone. It reminded Alexa of the look she wore years ago at Burning Man festival, that second summer after they graduated when Caron was waiting for work. They'd met some girls at Sheffield Peace in the Park who reckoned they'd never forgotten Burning Man: the mind-altering meditation practice, the Mexican food, the desert like an empty promise in the background. Caron bombarded Alexa with pictures until she agreed. Leyton was travelling round South America and Matt was working on a construction project in Bristol, so it would be just the two of them.

They flew to Reno, arrived at Black Rock City as the sun was going down, the sky a Tequila Sunrise orange. The festival shone in the distance, rose-gold. Alexa thought of their Christmas tree back in Nether Edge, how Matt always liked to wind lights around every single branch until he almost choked the tree, not draping but wrapping. At the gates, the traffic was backed-up. Eventually, they were greeted by tanned, lean women and men in cut-off shorts who told them how to get to their area. Everything inside the festival seemed circular, as if people were orbiting something central and mysterious. Caron was wide-eyed from the moment they dumped their bags. They bought vodka cocktails and expensive coffee made from beans that had been through the guts of a civet cat. They took in a lecture on astrophysics and an interview with a woman who illustrated graphic novels. Caron kept looking slightly past Alexa, over her shoulder, like a guest at a formal party, aware that there was someone else they should be talking to. When the vodka made Caron sleepy, they went back to the RV and fucked tenderly on the floor, surrounded by their half-unpacked bags. Afterwards, Caron dozed on her rucksack and Alexa got a bike and tried to head out to the central playa. She had never been to a real festival before, not even Glastonbury. There were half-naked bodies and flavoured hash cakes – salted caramel and popcorn crush. She cycled past fire-jugglers and men in fedoras and jumpsuits, slowed down beside a plywood booth offering 'Non-Monogamy Advice'. Inside, on deckchairs, a man with cropped black hair and another with dreads were talking intently. They were both topless, but one of them had dark skin and the other had a white vest from tan lines. *You have to feel jealousy to master it*, the guy with short hair was saying. *You have to become one with your envy*. The other took a sip of cloudy lemonade. They saw Alexa staring and beckoned her over.

Back at the RV, it was dark and Caron was cross-legged by a small campfire, laughing with an American couple, sharing a joint. They were called Keston and Suz and they touched each other on the arm compulsively when they spoke. Suz had Pre-Raphaelite hair and came from Georgia. Her voice was like an almond latte. Keston had workman's hands and a neat wrist tattoo. They were discussing sustainable clothing and the difficulties of finding vegan shoes. Suz thought Caron's accent was *super-cute*. They embraced Alexa several times and passed her the spliff. Suz told Alexa she had the nicest cheekbones. *I mean, the nicest.* Keston had a harmonica in his bag and his cord jacket made him look like something from the cover of *The Freewheelin' Bob Dylan*. Caron was wearing a multi-coloured sweater that Alexa had never seen before and which turned out to be Keston's, too. Suz worked in new media and took MDMA at the weekends. Her eyes were very large, dilated from the weed. While Caron and Keston heated a tin of chickpeas with some sauce, Suz described meeting Keston at a conference in Silicon Valley. *Every time he spoke, it was like someone switching a light on in a corridor, you know?* Suz and Keston lived in LA. They had been together for five years and in an open relationship for three.

'Things are so much further along over here,' said Caron. 'I mean, Sheffield's OK, but people our age … I don't know.'

'How old are you guys?' asked Keston.

'We just left uni.'

'Boy!' squealed Suz. 'You're babies!'

They ate dinner and talked about their attraction to one another. Suz didn't really date women, but she was bi-curious. Keston said Caron and Alexa were a good match. They all agreed to take a walk to the Orgy Dome together. Suz had been last year with Keston and a mutual friend from LA called Daryl, an ex-Google employee. Daryl and Suz had amazing chemistry, it turned out. Their threesome lasted one and a half hours. They tried double penetration, but it didn't really work out. *Hardly ever does*, said Keston wistfully, shaking his head.

In the long queue for the Dome, Caron looped her arms round Alexa and kissed the back of her head, lightly. They'd both caught the sun already and Alexa's neck was sore. They had thought about getting some beers for the wait, but they didn't want to get too sluggish. Keston sang songs by The Doors to keep them all going, but the mouth organ interludes sounded comical. When they finally got near the front, they were given the lowdown, along with packs that contained condoms, lube and baby wipes. Everyone was encouraged to give consent loudly and enthusiastically. There could be no touching without permission, but there should be no watching either, no 'lurking', as Suz put it, making ironic speech marks in the air with her fingers. Alexa stared past the tent at small silver points of light she took for lanterns at first, before she realised she was looking at the desert stars. There was a constant hum from the festival, drumming like a heartbeat.

Inside the tent, it was air-conditioned. It wasn't exactly an orgy, but lots of couples – mainly heterosexual – were having sex at the same time. Alexa wasn't sure where to stand or whether it was OK to sit down. Then Suz asked Alexa if she could kiss her and Alexa said *Yes* in a clear voice, the way she had been told. Suz was a gentle kisser. She flicked her tongue in and out of Alexa's mouth. Later, when Keston penetrated Alexa from behind, Suz bit down softly on her lip. It was surprisingly tender, his hands firm on her hips as he pulled her back towards him, Suz kissing and sucking her nipples. When Alexa came, she made a choking, hiccupping sound that embarrassed her.

She watched Caron straddling an older man with salt-and-pepper stubble and sculpted hair. She wondered how he'd stayed so neat in the desert. She observed Caron as if she was going to paint her, studying the small ripples in her flesh as she sank and rose on the man's cock, noticing the way she sometimes lifted a hand to her own mouth as if she was trying to hush herself. She watched the man's feet clench. She let out a small moan herself when he slid his finger inside Caron's arsehole. He pronounced it *ass*, the way Americans do. Later, she was aching and Keston seemed distant, spent but restless. Caron was between Suz's legs, spreading her thighs. They became an island somehow, separate from the rest of the bodies. Suz was lying down, her hair spread out behind her, moving as if she was swimming on her back. *Oh God*, she said. *Oh GodGodGod!*

That night in the RV, Alexa thought she'd sleep curled up with Caron like they'd agreed, but Caron took the far bunk and let Alexa have the comfier space on the mattress, where there was room to stretch out. *It's too cramped for two*, she said. Keston and Suz were entwined on the floor. Alexa dozed and dreamed about a scarecrow on fire, a huge model of a man with straw for hair and no eyes. At 4 a.m. she was woken by Suz softly moaning and she heard Caron saying something indistinct. Suz's moans grew softer, as if she had her face buried in a pillow. Alexa turned over, rustling the blankets and down jackets she was sleeping under. The noises didn't stop. Her pulse felt definite and quick. She could smell Caron's body, their mingled sweat. She turned her face towards the window, towards the desert. She imagined a small fox she saw in a documentary once when she was a kid, its reflective eyes and its body lithe between the cactuses. Outside, some guys were still awake. *Canada is just, like, whoah*, said one of them and someone laughed for no reason. They talked about Burning Man, the vibe of it, the best places to get drugs. One time last year a man's heart had burst in his chest. *Just like that. Literally burst.* One of the guys laughed again. The RV creaked like a house in the wind. Keston was sleeping soundly.

Brincliffe Edge

The empty branches and the empty pavements. The roots of trees dormant under the soil. Hollows in the tree stumps that fill with rainwater, cups of sky that dogs like to drink from by day. When the houses are silent, I come to life. A badger, walking the boundary between the tidy houses and the lip of soil where its den could be. Frogs beginning to crawl towards the gardens. Two adolescent foxes, fucking impatiently behind the last house on the road, behind the woodshed and the vegetable patches, the kale that grows all year round, the buried potatoes in the earth. A Siamese cat with a cruel face who stalks the road up to the woodland, pauses there as if, for the first time, he's not sure whether to enter, whether to join the faster creatures who tolerate the cold, who fight each other after dusk, blood and teeth and muscle. He has a velvet collar and a silver tag with his name engraved. He has elegant paws and grey ears. The mud under his claws. The worms in the soil and the woodlice teeming in sheltered places. The cry of something almost human, impossibly close.

Alexa

Everyone was expecting something to happen. Everyone behind their lines. The English Defence League with their home-made signs, all sunburn red against white, England flags and St George's dragons. The police holding their radios close. Some officers in black, some in bright tabards. And the residents lining the streets as well, crowding with their backs against the buildings. Muslims. Jamaicans. Eastern Europeans. Black and white.

And they felt watched by the rest of Sheffield, too. Even Alexa felt it. All morning the radio had been tacking it on at the end of the news: EDL march in Page Hall. They reported the background, too: rumours that an old pub was to be turned into a mosque, the far-right campaigners bristling with indignation, shouting about the spread of Islamism and Sharia law in the UK. The radio presenters did their best anxious voices, before it was back to 'Gold' and 'Changes' and the weekend weather report. Good, with a chance of showers.

Alexa thought the protestors looked strangely disengaged. She scanned the wall of pale T-shirts and raw, folded arms. Some tattooed. Some skinny. One man was wearing a black balaclava with a cross embroidered into the top of it. Two eye holes that made his eyes look like marbles. A small gap for his mouth. They carried placards with statements like 'EVERY NEW MOSQUE IS A NAIL IN BRITAIN'S COFFIN' and 'WE WILL NEVER SUBMIT TO ISLAM'. Mostly they were quiet, subdued almost. A few men at the back were chanting 'England till I die!' and 'We want our country back!', but it never spread more than a ripple. Everyone was hanging on, wondering what was going to happen.

Maybe it was the police presence silencing them, the sight of all those square bodies in line. Alexa didn't know how many of them were here or how much it was costing the force, but it had been planned to the letter. They stood like a single presence. A shield, from the kebab shop to the corner bus stop. Alexa thought of all the nights she spent in Page Hall alone or with Dave, doing the rounds. This was the first time in months she felt cocooned. Like she was in a pack.

A disembodied voice yelled 'EDL, go to hell!' and someone cheered. Most people stared straight ahead of them or at the ground.

Standing in line, Alexa thought of a picture she'd seen of Orgreave in '84, taken from above. One they always used in the papers, all monochrome. The straggled pickets on the right, groups of them bunched together or lined up one in front of the other. So small they hardly looked like people. And then, on the left, the police. Like a forest. Like that point on the beach where the tide can reach when the water comes in further than you thought it would and you end up running, running just to get away. You couldn't pick anyone out. It made her feel sick. She'd never been part of a line before. Not really. Not unless you counted match days, her and five others, facing the fans.

The EDL were too ragtag, too varied. They didn't look whole. If they were all wearing balaclavas it'd be different. Like a coal-dust Ku Klux Klan.

The whole thing was hard to take seriously anyway. The pub that was supposedly going to be turned into a mosque was now being turned into a fried chicken shop. What they wanted – what everybody wanted – was a pot for their anger. A name for what kept them up at night and made them swear over nothing and made them drunk and close to tears on a Saturday night, a night after a day like this. All the pubs round here were shut today. The EDL lot would have to go to the station tap on the way home, the yeasty back room full of day trippers with oversized bags who'd move away from them, lowering their voices for the sheer drama of it.

Alexa was so busy focusing on the line, on the still heads and eyes screwed up against the sun, she almost didn't see him at first: a man, near the turn-off to Horndean Road, squaring up to a group of Muslims. He'd broken away from his own side. He was drunk, red in the face. All of his movements seemed to come from his neck. He was mouthing off at one of the men, though he barely reached his chest. She pushed her way down towards the hubbub.

'Step back, please! Step away.'

'The fuck all you going to do about it?'

Alexa stood tall, tried to keep her voice level.

'Get back, please.'

His body sagged. He worked his pockets with his hands. He backed away, but swerved towards Alexa. She looked around her for backup, but for all their numbers, nobody seemed to be watching. She was away from the main line of the EDL now, on the fringes of the pack. He was hardly as tall as her, but she could smell his sour, savoury breath when he drew close.

'Ask me nicely, darling, yeah?'

'I'm not asking you. I'm telling you.'

His face darkened and his neck stopped bobbing for a minute. His voice tightened to a hiss as he leaned towards her, got right up in her face. He started as if he was going to touch her, grab her, take hold of her arms and pin them to her sides. She wanted to scream, but nothing came out.

And she wasn't in Page Hall any more. She was by the cemetery on Psalter Lane, ten years ago, only she couldn't move backwards any further, because of the wall. And the lad from the club, the friend of a friend of a friend who said he'd walk her home, he was so near she could see the clumps of gel in his bleached hair. And his body was pressing against hers, so it seemed like he was all around her. His erection against her thigh. His hand down the front of her skirt and then down the waistband of her thick, black tights. And the night getting thick and black, too, the silence of it oppressive, in her eyes and in her ears and in her mouth. And why weren't there any cars at the mini roundabout? And why wasn't anyone walking back from the pubs? The boy grinning and chewing his chewing gum, that sickly mint smell as his small hand worked at her, dry, with her legs clamped together. How she couldn't push him away. How she could, but she didn't. A siren somewhere else in town, getting quieter.

Alexa cried out. She'd stepped into another officer, a tall, thick-set woman she didn't know.

'You all right, love?'

'Sorry.'

She was in Page Hall. The afternoon was yawning out. The EDL looked like they wanted to go home.

The lad from the graveyard was called Simon Timperley. He joined the police after they left uni.

* * *

It was her date night with Caron and they were going to go down to The Riverside, away from the hubbub of the bars in town and the Saturday scent of West Street. Alexa liked it there: staring out across the water to the sombre apartments on the other side, drinking Brooklyn lager from the bottle, watching insects bother the reeds. She was gasping for a first beer, the way it made her veins all soften under her skin.

When she got home, Caron wasn't back yet. Just the open window and the breeze going through yesterday's paper. Upstairs, Leyton was stretched out on his bed trying to smoke away his cold, haloed by tissues. He'd left the door ajar and Roots Manuva was leaking out on to the landing.

She knocked and Leyton opened one eye. He exhaled and beckoned to her.

'How was the march?'

'Bit of a letdown really. Not much action.'

'All mouth and no trousers?'

Leyton was in his boxers and a black T-shirt that belonged to Caron. It was too tight for him and it made his neck look large. He hadn't shaved for days. Something about the musk of smoke in the room, the way it seemed to hug everything too close, made Alexa feel like crying. She wanted to hold Leyton's head in her hands, press his rough cheek against hers. Just that and no more.

They hadn't fucked for ages. It wasn't as if they'd grown apart, just got so close to each other they'd stopped wanting to. Maybe you can't touch someone when they live under your skin. Leyton understood her too well. But in a house where everything had to be put into words, everything explained for the benefit of the group, they'd had to find a simpler way of announcing it.

'You OK, Lex?'

She nodded and sat down on the end of the bed, kicking over a glass of water. She watched the stain spread over the carpet and didn't do anything.

'Where's Caron?' she asked.

'I think she went buildering.' That was the slang name climbers gave to scaling urban buildings. Alexa found the term ridiculous. 'There's a kid from the university who wants to climb a route up the Arts Tower at night. If you ask me, he's a bit of a twat. She'll be back soon. It's your date night, isn't it?'

Alexa nodded again. She'd always loved watching Leyton build a roll-up. The surprising delicacy. How he knew exactly how much Golden Virginia to pinch into the paper. The satisfaction when he licked along the seam and sealed it shut, looking up all the time.

Roots Manuva was saying *Left, right. Left, right.* Leyton's stereo was too small for the sound of it. It warped with the bass. Sometimes their whole house felt too small.

'Hard day at the office?' she asked.

He grinned. 'You know how it is. Still waiting for that sponsorship deal from North Face. It'll be folded into my next giro. Living the dream.'

Leyton lit up. It took several goes. Alexa felt like she was made of paper and he was made of bricks.

The night she met Leyton, he'd helped her break into her own room in Halls. Up the drainpipe and through the window. He'd had so much Famous Grouse he fell off when he tried to follow her. She'd watched him, lying in the bushes with his leg at a strange angle under him, still. But by the time she'd found her phone to call the ambulance, he was scrabbling over the edge of the windowsill, feet paddling behind him. He fell into her room headfirst and never really left. It was because of Leyton she'd met Caron. It was because of him she'd told her own dad who she was and how she wanted to live. It was Leyton who took her to the coast for the first time and showed her, showed her that view that made her feel like everything was running out, everything led to the sea if you looked hard enough and it didn't matter.

'Come here,' he said softly, without her having to ask.

She crawled up the bed and buried her head in his chest. He smelled of Caron and all the day's smoke.

'Is it her?' he asked and she shook her head into his hug and couldn't stop shaking it. He held her tighter. 'I know it's hard sometimes,' he said quietly. 'For what it's worth, I think she's keeping stuff from us. Me as well. I think you just pick up on it more than me.'

Alexa thought that if she could only hear one person's voice again, it would be Leyton's. His voice had always seemed better than him. She used to phone him up just to hear him answer. She wanted him to keep talking the way he did the first night when she'd said *Tell me about your name*, and it was after midnight and he'd made it all into a brilliant story, his dad and the football team that nobody else in the north supported. *Orient. He could at least have picked that part.* Afterwards, they'd moved like swimmers in the dark. He bit her neck and her nipples and left a mark.

'Tell me something,' she mumbled.

'What? About Caron?'

'No. About you. Tell me something you've never told me before.'

He took a breath. She moved with his chest. He said, 'I've told you everything.'

'No you haven't. Nobody tells anyone everything. Not even in this house.'

He laughed. 'Good or bad?'

'Bad.'

'OK ... When I was a kid, me and my brother painted a telephone box. Actually, it's not bad, but I'm going to tell you anyway. You know how all the phone boxes in Hull are white? Mum was doing up the front room with this emulsion stuff, sort of off-cream coloured. Browny-cream, really. Me and Max nicked the tin after school and went across the Avenues, down near the railway tracks. We couldn't reach the top of the phone box, even when he lifted me, but we had a go at the rest. The sides. All of it. We were dead careful not to get any on the windows. Whenever someone came past we hid, away from the road and then we'd go back. It was mad really, because it wasn't as if it even looked that different at the end. I mean, the paint were nearly white anyway. Cream, like I say. But we knew. Every time we walked past.'

She smiled into Caron's black T-shirt. She wanted him to carry on.

'Mum went mad when she saw the tin was missing. I blamed Max and he blamed me. I said he'd taken it and tried to paint the dog. They believed me, because I was older. Next week we did try to paint the dog, but with varnish. That was different.'

He'd made himself laugh and they shook together, one lumpy shape on the bed with the tissues and Leyton's fag butts all around them. And it was suddenly better, better than any time he'd ever held her before.

Hillsborough

I'm in the news again. Stills of banners that say TRUTH and JUSTICE FOR THE 96. Images of fans in black and white, scrabbling over the barriers inside the stadium. A picture of a woman, holding a photograph of her son out in front of her at arm's length like an offering. My name on everyone's lips, body parts excavated and damned. I see it in capital letters on tabloids and broadsheets, screens and T-shirts, documents held by politicians, passed over furtively. In 1997 Tony Blair picked one up – a call for a new inquiry, my name swarming over the page. He took a pen and scribbled across the top: 'Why? What's the point?' Now, everything is stirring. I feel it in the slim ribs of my fences, the arterial roads that split me. In the cafés and newsagents, people seem nervy. I see a man who sits for hours in the park some days, down by the tennis courts, thumbing through a sheaf of papers, scribbling in a notebook he's bought. He finds writing difficult – his tongue pokes out through his teeth and he hunches forward, crooks one arm round the Moleskine as if to protect it. I'm in the breeze that ruffles the treetops. I gently lift the pages and let them drop.

Leigh

'Get in,' Pete growled, winding down the window of the van. *Van* was a bit generous. It was a large sandwich tin on wheels.

The traffic in the village was gridlocked, the side roads cordoned off with blue striped tape. Outside the garage, two police officers were stopping drivers. There had been a bank robbery last night at the Royal Bank of Scotland and the early morning hillwalkers gawped from the bus stop, watching. The village was bristling, busier and noisier than usual, as if the robbery had brought the city closer to Hathersage. This was supposed to be the kind of place where nothing happened.

'Hurry up,' said Pete. 'I'm freezing my balls off.'

Leigh hopped in and slammed the door. The warm smell of sweat and rotting apple cores hit her. If you live alone for long enough, she thought, you stop caring what you smell like. Maybe she stank most days, too.

'What's this about? You know I'm at work in an hour.'

'Bollocks to that. Stretcher's in town. Heard he's going for something on Stanage.' Pete was turning the van round. He mounted the pavement and a red Fiesta beeped at them. He grinned at her. 'Don't worry, the boss'll just think you're wanted for armed robbery.'

'Apparently, they climbed in through the roof. They got them on CCTV, but you can't see their faces.'

'Wonder how much they got away with? Think what you could do with money like that.' He gave a low whistle.

The van lurched and Safi the grey whippet appeared at Leigh's shoulder, panting, flung forwards. She eyed her master with curiosity.

'Who the hell's Stretcher anyway?' said Leigh.

Stretcher, it turned out, was big in the Eighties. He'd put up a host of new routes in Stoney Middleton, climbed Welsh sea cliffs that were more debris than stone, then moved to the Highlands and reinvented himself as an ice-climber. Nobody had seen him for years. Someone reckoned he'd lost a finger in the Alps, but Pete didn't believe it. He told her all this on the walk up from the Plantation car park, gulping for breath.

'Why's he called Stretcher?'

'Because he's a tall bastard. And the last of his mates still standing. He's lost more climbing partners than you've had pints. Careless, really. The stretcher-bearer. Don't mention that. He thinks it's because of his height.'

They heard him before they saw him. He was belaying from the top of The Right Unconquerable, yelling down at a lad in a red waterproof jacket and vomit-coloured trousers.

'Take your time, pal! I've got all day!' His voice was high and thin. He had a Sheffield accent, but he went up at the end of sentences. He'd borrowed a Scottish way of saying 'day'.

The lad was puffing hard, struggling with a fist jam. His whole body seemed clenched.

'For Christ's sake!' Stretcher sang down.

'Hey, Stretch!' hollered Pete.

The boy on the end of the rope seemed even more nervous now he had an audience.

'Chuffing hell!' Stretcher's face creased with recognition. 'Look who's back from the dead.' He broke into a wheezy laugh and Leigh was worried he was going to let go of the rope.

'A little bird told me you were coming over.'

'A bird? Near you?' Stretcher liked to laugh at his own jokes. 'And who's this nice young lady? What did you put in her drink to get her here?'

'We work together,' said Leigh.

While they were talking, the boy on the rope had managed to wriggle and haul himself past the worst of the laybacking and was nearly at the top, though Stretcher hadn't taken in any slack. He returned to the routine of belaying, grunting with irritation. The lad hesitated and then flapped his way over the top.

'You'll love Stretch,' said Pete, cheerfully. 'Once you get to know him, like.'

When they stumbled down to join Leigh and Pete, Stretcher thrust his hand into Leigh's. He didn't bother to introduce his climbing partner, who was even younger than he'd looked when he was on the rock. Leigh asked politely if it was his son.

'You must be joking. This nesh bugger's not mine. Picked him up in Kinlochleven.'

He didn't care to elaborate and the boy wasn't saying much either. Stretcher's front teeth were missing. His face was threaded with thin scarlet lines. She thought his breath smelled of whisky, but she could have been imagining it. He reminded her of her Uncle Trevor, a red-faced fell-runner whose body always seemed too big for him, a man who couldn't sit still, who'd leave his pint untouched for half an hour and then down it in one.

'What's on the menu today then, Stretch?' asked Pete. Leigh could tell he was nervous, in awe of what Stretcher had done once, or said he'd done, what he thought him capable of.

'Ah, I'm taking it easy for the lad here.'

'Thought you might be gunning for routes.'

Stretcher turned away and started unclipping quickdraws from his harness, laying them out flat on his rucksack, one by one. He stooped like a much older man. The lad rushed over to return the gear he'd retrieved on the route. Stretcher patted him on the shoulder and muttered a kind of congratulations. *You stuck it out. You're a tryer.*

Pete was watching them together. He didn't say anything, but Leigh saw the weather of his face change. Envy. Or just wistfulness. Leigh felt embarrassed for him, ashamed he could be so easily read. She opened her mouth to break the silence. Black Car Burning. She itched to tell them about Caron and her plans, her strength, her wide shoulders and her delicate feet. But the words died in her mouth. She could hear Stretcher's laughter already. Some unknown girl on an E7? *Don't be a twat*, she thought. You could kill a dream with too much talk. She bit down hard on her lip.

Stretcher took a hip flask from his rucksack and offered it round. Pete's face became his again.

'See off the cold?'

As she picked her way back down to the Plantation, she could still hear them swapping stories. Stretcher had taken a big fall once. Stretcher had on-sighted something at Curbar when he was still pissed. Stretcher had climbed Quietus in the dark. Stretcher had run off with Dan McKay's missus and then dropped her off in a lay-by near Perth when she got on his nerves and couldn't keep up with the climbing. Pete was giggling like a kid. They both laughed in the past tense.

She was very late for work. But the boss wouldn't care. She turned back and glanced up at Stretcher and Pete and the boy, small under the lip of the rock. They looked like nothing at all.

* * *

When she finally got to the shop, there was no sign of her manager, but Tom was waiting for her by the climbing-gear counter. She saw the side of his head first, his slim profile. Elegant. She paused in the doorway and tried to take a breath. One of the spotty teenagers who usually did weekend shifts was showing him a selection of blue and orange climbing helmets. Marvine. Or Max. Max moved under a permanent curtain of hair.

'Thanks,' she said quietly, taking off her coat. 'I can deal with this customer.'

The boy darted into the stockroom and Tom turned to face her, half-smiling. He was wearing a grey wool jacket, tight black jeans and a striped shirt, buttoned to the neck. She thought about making a joke – *Has sir come straight from the mountain?* – but his face was drawn and tired under its suit of stubble.

'What are you doing here?'

'Missed you, too. Why aren't you answering your phone?'

Leigh took him by the wrist and pulled him behind the counter. It felt more private back there, even though they were in full view of the door. It smelled of Pete's dog. A dozen empty down jackets watched them. Above the jackets, a display of ice axes that Leigh had arranged last week, angled diagonally. She hadn't realised how sinister it looked until now.

Tom tried to grab her by the hips and pull her closer to him.

'I've been going mad without you. It's been a shit week. Shit students, shit meetings. And there's so much distance between me and Rach ...'

She turned her back on him and started tidying the stock, rearranging the expensive cams and brightly-coloured nuts.

'I'm sorry,' he said, 'that was a crap thing to say. I'm not looking for sympathy.'

'Good, you're in the right place.'

'Where have you been? I wanted to see you.'

'I've been busy.'

Tom's face tightened. She noticed the heavy bags under his eyes.

'Busy with who?'

'Keep it down. I'm late. I'm already in the shit if management catches me. And Pete's off climbing.'

He leaned in close to her ear. His breath tickled her neck and she felt the hairs on her arms stir.

'I am going to leave her, you know. One day. When things are simpler.'

Leigh turned to look at him. She didn't say anything.

'Leigh,' he hissed. 'I want to be with you.'

A customer was browsing the books at the far end of the shop, a fat bloke she recognised from the indoor walls in Sheffield. He had all the gear and none of the moves. She pushed Tom away, very gently, letting her hand linger on his chest.

'Look, this is a bad time.'

The fat bloke had sidled over closer and was thumbing through guidebooks to places he'd never climb: Squamish, Mont Blanc. He kept moving closer to the counter, earwigging. Leigh wondered if she and Tom looked like a couple or not, if a stranger would put them together. Tom and his girlfriend definitely looked the part. She'd known that the first time she saw them through the window of his flat. Tall, poised. Her fur-trim coat and his black leather gloves. Their matching small noses and long fingers. She could imagine their future wedding photos. Leigh had never even been a bridesmaid. The one time she was meant to be, her cousin had called off the wedding a week before and Leigh decided she was a jinx. Her school friend didn't want her to be her bridesmaid, because of her short hair and tattoos, the uncomfortable way she stood when she wore a dress, like a shop dummy.

Tom started buttoning his expensive coat. 'Let me see you. I could come out with you sometime, out here. I could even hold your ropes if you want.'

She laughed, even though she didn't feel like it.

'Let me hold your ropes, Leigh.'

'This isn't about climbing.'

He stood up straight. 'My mistake. I thought everything was with you.'

* * *

When Leigh used to go out with Tom in Sheffield and he saw someone he knew – one of his horn-rimmed PhD students with pointed shoes, or a colleague talking breezily into an iPhone, or the attractive receptionist from the faculty – they'd always nod to him, and she'd panic for a moment, expecting them to clock her and freeze her with a look, a full, suspicious, up-and-down stare. It was worse than that. They didn't really notice her at all. And she'd give Tom a forced smile, mid-sentence, and remember that the things that make you shudder or thrill in your own life are invisible to other people.

But by the time they'd reached the foot of Division Street, she'd have convinced herself that she was the invisible one. Their glances passed straight through. While Tom picked up the over-priced coffees and she waited outside, she was back at school and it was Valentine's Day in Year 11, and she was having a fag outside the back of the sports hall and trying not to look towards Jordan Richardson as he walked towards her, larger and larger in the corner of her eye. And her lanky, teenage self was ready to deny the card and the sparse poem. Ready to look him full in the face and turn at the last moment, turn back and smile, and they'd both know it was her, and he'd humour the pretence, but without saying anything he'd press against her and she'd feel the sheepskin collar on his denim jacket tickling at her neck, and his tongue slipping inside her mouth, and she'd drop her cigarette on the floor. Jordan Richardson, with his quiet kindness and solemn answers in English Literature and his worker's hands and his permanent headphones. Then, he was right in front of her, sudden, his face all eyebrows. And she knew as soon as he took her by the arm and squeezed that it wasn't going to play out that way.

'I'm really glad Faye asked you to do it. You know what I'm on about, don't you? I really appreciate you being cool about it. Discreet, I mean.'

'Sure,' she said. 'Sure.'

'To be fair, I've fancied her since Year 9. I just never thought … I weren't going to say anything. I knew right away it had to be from her. You're a good mate.'

And she laughed when he walked away. She laughed silently until the laugh became an ache in her stomach and her ribs. And she texted Faye from the back seat of the bus to say *Jordan really likes you*, like the good go-between she was, like the messenger she always would be. In revision week, she saw Jordan and Faye in the library, hands entwined, Faye wearing his jumper, and he winked at her and she tried to hide whatever she was writing, but he came over the way he always did now, making an effort to speak to her, and asked her what it was and she lied and said a script. *Great*, he said, *that's great. You'd make a good scriptwriter.*

People were always thinking Leigh was someone else. Or telling her she reminded them of someone. The people they named never had anything in common. Sinéad O'Connor. That girl from the news. They always grinned as if it was a compliment. A thin, sinewy woman with a perm stopped in front of the tills in the shop once and told Leigh she had a double, a woman who climbed at the bouldering wall on the south side of Sheffield. *She's the spit of you.* Another time, a gang of teenage lads started hollering at her at the interchange, asking her if she had a sister. One of them thought they knew her so-called twin, that she worked in a hairdressing salon in Rotherham. Sometimes she could sense the words forming before they'd been spoken. *You remind me of someone. You're just like …* It made her think of the man she slept with in a basement flat in Edinburgh who kept calling her Kirsty, who gripped her waist and pushed her face down into the pillow and shouted the wrong name, over and over, until she started to pretend she was Kirsty and she'd known him all her life and she was sick to death of him.

She and Tom only went away together once – a weekend in Whitby when he was meant to be at a symposium, and it rained for two days, the sea threatening the hillside – she'd woken up with him watching her, the hotel kettle steaming softly in the corner of the room. He'd been smoothing her hair while she slept and he smiled and asked her if she wanted to take the pirate boat trip out of the harbour for three quid, and she knew that he'd been thinking she reminded him of someone else with her eyes shut. Some ex he'd mentioned enough times for her to know it was more than a vague regret, the Romanticist who went to Iceland for a summer and only called him once, who cheated on him and made him feel that it was all his fault. And when he pulled her back under the duvet and licked a firm line from her navel to the base of her neck, she knew it was the idea of her that he wanted to fuck, the lovely, bittersweet notion of her, a woman who wasn't afraid to be alone, who kept something back, who didn't care about the morning after. The idea of a rock climber, a risk-taker. His own past and his own impossible future. She was just passing through. She had a message to deliver and then she could go. *Discreet.* And when he told her he loved her, it meant he loved someone she might become, someone he hadn't quite met yet. Someone she hadn't met either. It was perfect. Somehow, it was just what she wanted. To be unknown, even when he was inside her. The rain battered the sash window and they decided not to get out of bed all day.

Turning Stone Edge

I'm made-up with graffiti. Pink and bright green, smiley faces, giant cocks, signatures daubed by local kids. It's drizzling, the air's muzzy with damp and when the short girl settles down to belay, my new colours bleed into her clothes. I look best in bad weather, though – a dark thought, kept out of mind behind the agricultural fields and faint softness of Ashover, behind the beech copse and stone wall. I've never been popular. All day, nobody's held me or said my name but these two women who call to each other back and forth through the grey air. Sometimes they climb separately, traversing near the ground on juggy handholds and small ledges. But mostly, they're roped together. One tall and slim with cropped, dark hair, the other stronger, smaller, piercings glinting on her face. Between them, the yellow rope judders with movement, pulling taut and then slackening again. The tall one never takes her eyes off the other. She moves her feet up, and the things she carries on her harness chime and click together. I love their strange music. *Take in. Safe.* I love that one best of all. *Safe.* A word that locks itself shut. I like the way the shorter woman murmurs it first, as if she's talking to herself, then shouts it down to her partner. How *Safe* makes the rope go loose, the air soften, the day uncoil. Sometimes, she says it when she isn't quite safe yet – she's still near the edge, not yet anchored. From the ground, the other woman can't possibly know the difference.

Him

He couldn't stop looking at that poster of Jimi Hendrix. Legs apart, strangling the neck of the guitar. It had taken him a moment to place Jimi, like he was someone he caught the bus with every day and had just seen out of context, clutching a coffee in the Peace Gardens. He stared at him and Jimi looked out somewhere over his shoulder, at the bruise-coloured sofa with its out-of-date hippy throws and furry cushions, at the peace lily on the windowsill and the joint on the lip of the ashtray. Or perhaps Jimi was looking through the floorboards, down into the bar and the knot of regulars round the jukebox. Jimi could see through walls and walk through them. How else could he have got here, straight from heaven, leaving his small cloud to pose in a pub landlord's flat? Perhaps it was hell and there was a shortcut. *I want to go to hell, where the soundtrack's better.* Who said that?

Sandra the pub landlady was framed in the kitchenette doorway, holding two mugs of tea. It was sometime after two in the morning. She set one down in front of him, on the antique chest that doubled as a table, and sat down, holding the other. Her blonde hair was bigger than her. A mane. Watching her in the pub from his corner table, he'd always thought she looked like Stevie Nicks in the right light.

'You all right now, love?' Her hand on his knee. Jimi watching.

'You ever wish you could go back in time and see him?'

'Who?' She picked up the joint from the ashtray and took a drag. 'Hendrix?'

'Yeah.'

Passing the joint to him, she exhaled. 'Nope.'

The flat smelled stale and sickly. He wondered how his house must smell to someone who came back for the first time. There was a chest of drawers in the spare room and even now he thought he could smell Angela in it. He used to go in and open them, one by one, then sit on the edge of the single bed and breathe.

'I played guitar once,' he said, taking a drag. 'In a covers band.'

She snorted. 'You? Were it The Everly Pregnant Brothers? Something like that?'

He laughed and sang a line from 'No Oven No Pie'. Out of tune. The smoke filled his lungs. He could feel its tendrils in the quiet places of his body. Curling round the inside of his ribs. He took another drag and he could feel it behind his eyes. Before he could exhale, she was pulling his face towards her, coaxing his lips near, wanting him to breathe into her mouth. He got so close, the room went dark. There was a brief warmth and then she was pulling away from him. Then she was leaning in again.

'Sandra ...'

He was trying to remember if they'd done this before. The way she gripped his thigh seemed familiar. He had no memory of the room. There were nights in The Byron that he hardly knew at all the next morning. Times when someone helped him leave and he went back to his house and listened to old Bowie CDs and new, nameless things he'd picked up from Fopp in a fit of optimism and sang himself senseless, or walked along Brincliffe Edge until dawn, never cold, alive and restless and almost happy. He was never afraid when he woke up and couldn't recall anything. He never reached for the phone or cowered under the duvet, trying to put the pieces together. Why should it be frightening to forget? There were days and months he'd give anything to get rid of.

She was kind. He was fairly certain of that. She let him be the last to leave when that was what he wanted. Other nights, she wouldn't serve him when the mood was on him and he kept asking for whisky. It was comforting to touch someone after all these years. That was enough.

She had an old record player on the sideboard, the kind that hadn't been used in too long, not one of the new ones everyone was going mad for these days, and she got up and took an LP from the box, took the record from the sleeve and placed it under the needle. She had a neat way of doing things. Capable. 'All Along the Watchtower' filled the room. She sat down next to him and smiled, and he stretched as if he was yawning, then settled an arm around her shoulders, like a kid in the cinema.

'My ex-hubby hated this version,' she said, shaking her head. 'He always thought the Dylan one was better. I don't reckon much to him, not really.' She had a smoker's laugh. 'Dylan, I mean. Not my ex.'

The joint was going out and she re-lit it.

'I remember him trying to get Glastonbury tickets, years ago. He wouldn't leave the flat until it was done. He was just sitting there in that armchair, kind of rocking backwards and forwards with the phone under his chin. I was trying to make a sandwich or something and the sound of the knife on the chopping board was doing his head in. I was slicing a cucumber. He kept saying to me *Do you have to be that loud, Sand?* and I just laughed. And I must have kept on or something, because the next thing I know he's pinned me against the oven and he's got the knife up close against my cheek and he's holding the back of my head, winding my hair with his hands, and I remember I could see the blade of the knife was orange at the end, glistening, because I'd just started cutting one of those peppers. The yellowy ones, you know?' She lifted the joint. 'Have you got kids?'

'One.'

She nodded, holding the smoke in her mouth for a moment and letting it go.

'I like that about a person. You know, like my ex. You can live with them for twenty years and you know what they like doing, know what they sound like in the house and what they think about things. But there's always summat, isn't there?'

She passed the joint to him again and he stared at her like a complete stranger. But it wasn't her he was looking at. It was his own face in the glass of the cheap door, the one that looked as if it had been kicked in and replaced.

When he saw footage of Hillsborough in the newspapers, he stared at it as if it was the first time he'd ever seen the place in his life.

'You can never be sure of a man, that's what I think. Like them lot downstairs,' she nudged the floor with the black heel of her boot, 'when they're tanked up ... Paul glassed one of the lads from the bakery last week.'

He smoked greedily, letting his chest expand as far as it would go. She was talking about the bouncers and why most of them were teetotal, how some of them arrived and worked for a while and left, and you never knew what went off. A doorman from Hungary who never told her his name, a rectangular man with shoulders like bollards who she once watched in the car park, kissing another man, one of the regulars. She talked and he stared past her at the threadbare armchair, where he could see her ex-husband, holding the phone between both his hands, legs apart, swaying slowly, staring at the carpet, the anger boiling inside him. And he took his arm from around her shoulders and folded it across himself instead.

He must have fallen asleep like that, because when he woke up he was on the boxy sofa with a blanket tucked up under his chin and another mug of tea in front of him on the antique chest. He took a sip. It was cold. He could hear Sandra breathing somewhere in the next room. Her boots stood empty by the doorway. He had hoped this would be comforting, sleeping in the same house as someone again, but it was not.

* * *

He passed weeks without noticing where the days started and ended. He went to work, driving across the moors too fast, but taking the bends easily. He'd pull up in the car park without remembering how he'd got there. He had no recollection of traffic lights or junctions and wondered if he'd stopped for them at all. At work he spoke to people, or said nothing unless he was asked. On his days off, or when he finished early, he sat cramped in his corner of the library, reading until the place behind his eyes ached.

Sometimes he looked up and the huge municipal clock was showing a significant time. As if he knew when to pause. It was often 3.15 when he raised his head from the screen. 3.15. To some people, it meant the end of school or the mid-afternoon tea break, or the time when traffic started to clog the bottom of Ecclesall Road, down past the Botanical Gardens. To others, it would always be cut-off time. The end. The point after which no evidence would be considered. The second hand seemed to hover over the hour forever, and he wondered if it was a trick, or if the clock was stuck, if it was going backwards.

3.15. He stopped. Half an hour passed in silence before he went back to his vigil.

The crossings-out across the grainy print on the screen, the public access police statements. Pages of bad handwriting. Emphatic statements with large, curved ticks over them.

Struck through: *Still we received no information.* Written over the top: *We still did not know exactly what had occurred.*

Then the passages that reminded him of the way he'd write, the way he'd put things. Sentences he thought he might have said.

I talked with a London woman and her friend, they were the Liverpool club London section. They had chips and shared them. I joked about my diet.

Some of the statements were written on a typewriter, the lettering small and squat.

An Inspector appeared and ordered us to go and clear the bridge over the Don, which was packed with supporters. They were simply waiting. Twelve of us cleared the bridge, very diplomatically. The bridge filled up behind us with fans ... I felt that his decision to clear the bridge was totally wrong and that a riot could easily have started. I remained there until the last of the bodies had been removed.

Sometimes he would read something and hear the voice behind it.

I then saw several people pressed against the fencing obviously being crushed and to one side of the centre was a pile of bodies all blue faced white skinned clothing disarrayed apparently dead. It looked as if they had been stacked neatly at first resemblant of scenes from the concentration camps of WW2.

Often, he read things and they did nothing to him at first, or just made him feel like there was a cool stone lying flat in the bottom of his stomach. Then the words would come back to him, pulling up to the garage or waiting in line at the bakery while the girl – a daughter of a friend, he was sure – was splitting open cobs and buttering them. Like that, the rest of the world going quiet. A voice he almost recognised, a voice that might have been his own.

I said, 'We're going to have to do something, someone is going to die.' 'They'll die at the turnstiles,' he spoke. I can remember what he said.

In the library, he had to check himself, make sure he wasn't speaking out loud. Some days, his notebook stayed blank, open on the table.

Other times, he remembered everything he did all day. Too well. He walked down The Moor as if someone was watching him and ducked into the shops. He spent as long as possible in the back room at work, pretending to count the stock. He didn't go to The Byron or, if he did, he went when he knew Sandra wouldn't be on her shift, and he took a newspaper and held it high in front of his face. Crossing the street, he'd glance back, wondering if his route through the city seemed logical. He saw the same man – tall, thin, mid-thirties, with a long ginger beard – twice between the town hall and the roundabout, and he quickened his pace.

He visited the library café only once. It was a bare place on the ground floor with red plastic seats fastened to the floor, walls covered in posters about healthy eating – a large image of a green apple that looked plastic. There was one other man in there and he stared at the back of his head, a bobble hat pulled down over the dark, wiry hair. The shape of him, his rolling shoulders and the strange thinness of his arms, reminded him of a madman in a taverna in Greece, four or maybe five years ago, the one who steadied himself on the edge of their table and then sat down. He kept saying the same phrase over and over in Greek. His eyes were deep. Not piercing exactly, just vivid, as if they went a long way back into his head. Perhaps he was not mad at all, that was just a word the other diners used. The café owner moved him along, flapping a dishcloth after him as if he was a stray dog. When they asked what the words had meant, the owner told them: 'He is saying "They silenced me."'

Thinking of it now, he wished they had let him sit down.

In the café there was no sound, except the man who faced steadfastly away from him, slowly drinking his pint of tea. When he walked back upstairs to his computer station, his hidden place, the sign on the wall urged SILENCE in black letters. He began to read again, hoping nobody could hear him.

Sharrow Vale

I'm full of things that mattered to people once. Some of them were loved and some weren't. The yards and glass rooms of the antique shops that display them are jammed between converted garages selling coffee and sourdough and tiny art galleries. The girl always comes on her own. The woman, I mean. On Saturdays, when it rains, she walks past the open doors of The Lescar, the smoke and laughter of the beer garden, and steps into one of the yards. There are two Weimaraners keeping guard, impossibly blue eyes and alert, quizzical faces. She looks bored, but she fondles the brooches and bric-a-brac with care, asks what exactly the expensive paintings cost. She is small, built for strength, and she likes compact objects best. Squat vases, an ashtray in the shape of a frog. Sometimes she raises a hand to her face, touches her nose ring as if to remind herself it's still there. She stands for hours in an outbuilding that the shop owner had to open specially for her, stands beneath a huge painting of the Ascot horse races, a multicolour scene in which everything is happening at once, slanted bodies in bowler hats, the diagonal charge of the horses, bright tickets attached to the frame. She never buys anything. Sometimes she walks towards the till, but she doesn't commit to it. Hats and matchboxes. Things she loves, but can't justify. Behind her, impatient drivers go too fast down Hickmott Road. A child stands with her hands pressed flat against the window of a doughnut shop. The woman asks the antiques dealer to show her something, fetch something from the storeroom and when he's gone she slips out.

Alexa

If Alexa smoked, this would be the time to light up. Leaning against the fence outside Wild Walls, listening to her own breath. The windows of the ex-warehouse were open and she could hear climbers falling off and slamming into the plastic holds. Someone was shouting *Take!* Someone else was yelling *Hold me there!,* which could almost be intimate if you didn't know what it meant.

The girl had been missing since Friday. Her face was on every lamp post round here, all the way through Brightside and Atlas. For all the good it would do. She was thirteen. From Rotherham. She had a face that was older than her. Eyeliner. Crusty mascara. Her name was Maria.

Alexa stared until Maria's photo stared her out. Having MISSING printed under your face changes it forever. When the picture was taken, Maria was probably at home in the school holidays, smiling up at her mum and brother. But now she was missing, you couldn't help seeing it in her eyes. Maria looked like she was expecting someone else to walk into the photo.

Alexa watched the cars crawl down to the roundabout, indicators too bright in the twilight. Left to Meadowhall, right to the city. Being in the police was bad for you, she thought. It made you wonder who might be in every car. It made you listen for other people's silences through their windows and wonder if they were friendly silences or not.

She tipped back her head and exhaled her imaginary cigarette.

A slim girl with a severe haircut careered out of the entrance to Wild Walls and almost took Alexa out. She was about Alexa's height and build, but her face was rounder and her pixie crop made her look boyish. Her cord trousers were too baggy and her sleeves almost hid her hands – it was as if she didn't want anyone to see the shape of her. She got into a battered Micra and slammed the door. You could hear the tremble of the radio over the car's tinny engine. Alexa always wondered where strangers were going and who they were going home to. Maybe that went with policing, too. Or perhaps it was just her. She used to play a guessing game as a kid in the supermarket with her dad. She'd make up names for people and tell him what they were doing later. Her dad never wanted to play. He must have been embarrassed. The girl in the Micra looked like an off-duty nurse. Someone whose patience was always worn out by midday. The car was flecked with mud, so she must live out in the Peak. Somewhere beautiful. Somewhere that ought to make her happy but didn't.

While she was watching the Micra edge down the hill, Caron sidled out of Wild Walls with a bright green rope coiled over her shoulder and a pen tucked behind her ear.

'Boo.'

'You took your time.'

'Lighten up, officer. I was working on a bouldering problem.'

'What kind of problem?'

'The kind you can't solve in a night. A slab with no holds on it.'

She stood on her tiptoes and kissed Alexa's cheek. She'd started doing that in public recently. There was something oddly formal about it. Alexa never kissed back. It was OK to lean up to someone, but leaning down to peck someone on the cheek seemed somehow patronising. They walked out of the car park and turned right. Alexa was wheeling her bike along. It was miles into town, but she always liked walking next to Caron, keeping pace beside her, while she detoured to walk along low walls or took running leaps at puddles.

Caron gestured to the lamp-post pictures. 'That your doing?'

'Not mine exactly, but yeah, she's the concern of the police. She's called Maria.'

'Where do you think she is?'

Alexa shrugged. 'In a hotel somewhere in the West Riding. That's where they found the last one. She was with four different men.'

'How old is she?'

'Thirteen.'

Caron didn't say anything about her day and Alexa didn't say anything much about hers. They walked along the ring road, past the multicoloured Tesco and the empty office spaces and the empty warehouses, under the bridge that led back to the city centre, the small shops and buildings that were still used. By the Wicker, someone had stuck up posters about a missing cat. *Dennis. Black and White. Last seen being helped across the road on Tuesday.* Alexa wondered how you help a cat across a road. There were no posters about Maria in this bit of town. She was starting to feel faint, as if her head was in a bubble. Or her legs weren't part of her own body. The lights from the cars and the shops all stood out too much.

Caron stopped outside Bargain Booze.

'We should get some supplies. Party drinks.'

'Sure.'

'What do you fancy?'

'That Desperate beer. You know. The one with tequila in.'

'Desperados!'

Alexa watched Caron through the window of the shop as she paid, the way the cashier couldn't help smiling at the pen tucked into her hair, her hands still white with chalk from the wall. She liked watching her as if it was the first time and they were nobody to each other, as if this was Weston Park and the last year of uni again, Leyton and Caron flat on their backs in the short grass puffing out smoke and her approaching them, imagining for a daft moment Caron's hair was on fire.

Caron came out with two packs of Desperados and a bottle of Shiraz. Balanced on top of them was a pack of beef jerky.

'It seemed like a good idea at the time.'

* * *

The party was at a peeling terrace somewhere on Abbeydale Road. When they got close, there was a girl leaning out of an upstairs window, cackling, and a group of men in paint-stained fleeces huddled outside the front door, holding cans of Carling. The house belonged to a friend of Matt's, someone he worked with in Rope Access. Alexa had met some of his mates before. She liked them, but she thought they were nutters. She wondered what it was like to spend every day up a girder or a crane, high above the roofs.

You probably had to stop noticing the view after a while. Matt said some of them took coke on quiet days to make the work more exciting. They were always short men for some reason, strong and nonchalant. Most of them didn't meet your eye. As they walked up the garden path, Alexa was conscious of her scraped-back hair. She pulled the elastic band out and let it fall limp over her shoulders. She must smell of the police station, of stale sandwiches and instant coffee and Dave's sweat. He had the kind of smell you could catch.

As soon as they were in the hallway, Caron slipped away from her in the crowd, taking their booze to the kitchen. The stairs looked far too steep. There was a kid on the top step, dancing on his own to an imaginary rhythm. He kept stepping both feet down and then up again. He had his eyes closed, but he never stumbled. On the bottom step, two women who looked like climbers were passing a bottle of white wine back and forth, whispering about something that was probably less than it seemed. Alexa picked an empty cup off the hall table, for the sake of something to hold.

When she caught up with Caron, she was in the kitchen watching a huge man open bottles of San Miguel with his teeth. He'd done three already. Everyone was clapping. His face was flushed with effort. Caron winked at her.

'Beats a keyring. Take your pick.'

Alexa swiped a bottle and squeezed in next to her.

'I keep losing you,' she said.

Caron could pass through parties as if she belonged in every room. She never made a conversation last too long, never asked unnecessary questions. She gave the impression of being interested, even when she wasn't, of being surrounded by people even when she was making her own way through the house, more or less alone. They'd always separated from each other at these dos. Tonight shouldn't be any different.

'Your hair looks better tied back.'

Alexa shrugged. 'It makes me feel like I'm still at work.'

'I know. It's a turn-on.'

Parties like this always had someone who knew three chords playing guitar, while someone who could really play, but was too drunk, conducted from an armchair. A couple shouting requests and getting the song names wrong. Alexa thought she could hear banjo music from the living room. In the kitchen, someone was telling the large bloke it would be more impressive if he could open bottles with his cock.

It was at a party like this one that Alexa had first felt that twinge of compassion and excitement that was possible when you saw your partner animated by someone else. That faint stirring and warmth that started somewhere below your heart and seemed to move upwards through your body. Caron had told her that there was a man she was interested in and wanted to kiss at the party, to see what happened afterwards. Alexa had registered it in the abstract, but when she'd come to find the two of them and Caron was sitting on his lap in the attic room, Caron's eyes were shining and her face was alight. The man was attractive in the way tall dark men are supposed to be, his face and beard built for bad weather, his eyes incredibly green, his skin permanently tanned. But it was something about the way they sat together that started the feeling. Like their bodies didn't just fit around each other, they grew to fill the same spaces. She felt a laugh bubbling inside her, genuine and bright. That night, Caron seemed to hold her even tighter than usual in bed and she got that jigsaw-piece feeling again.

Alexa slunk off to the living room, leaving Caron with Matt's mates in the kitchen. One of them was demonstrating a hand jam in between two cupboards. The lounge was the darkest room in the house; someone had lit a few candles that teetered dangerously close to the edge of the table and they'd draped some sort of sheet or fabric over the window, giving everything outside an eerie red quality. Someone was playing cards on their own, cross-legged. Someone else was wedged between the sofa and the wall, squeezed tight in the gap, rocking slowly to the beat from the radio. The back of the room was entirely dominated by a group of older men – climbers, surely – laughing too loud; and Alexa recognised the girl from the climbing wall on the edge of the group, the one with short hair and a pissed-off look. Without knowing why, she found she was watching. The tilt of her face. The way the bloke on her right liked to punctuate his sentences by slapping her on the back. It was as if the whole room wanted to impress her, but they didn't know why.

Leyton appeared at her shoulder. 'You look like you need a shot,' he said.

It was slivovitz. Slovakian plum brandy. The taste of plums and then the afterburn, the dry heat. The first shot made her smile. The second made her shoulders drop. The third one made her throw her arms around Leyton and try and make him dance with her. The fourth made her irritable, scanning the house for Caron. She went to find the bathroom. She thought she saw her on the upstairs landing, laughing with a younger woman with blue hair in plaits, touching her shoulder, touching her face. But she was drunk.

By the fifth shot, she was on another side of the room, talking to a bloke her dad's age and the girl with the pixie crop and sarcastic expression about why climbers were shit. The climbers were all agreeing with her and the conversation was a muddle of anecdotes about forgotten birthdays, sick days spent at Burbage, doomed relationships with women who thought Sundays were for roasts and telly. The short-haired girl wasn't really joining in, but she cracked a thin smile occasionally. Alexa realised she was addressing her with all her slurred remarks. Leyton passed her another slivovitz.

'Climbers are shit?' he said. 'Did I hear that right?'

'Yeah. Cheers. Down the hatch.'

'What do you think? Leigh, isn't it?' Leyton was looking at the girl with the short hair, too. She shrugged.

'Shit,' said Alexa, leaning in to him. She nodded at the girl. 'You should ask my partner. Or my dad. He used to climb. Maybe still does.' She turned to Leyton for approval. 'Shit,' she said again, for effect.

He put his arm around her and helped her to the floor. Alexa sat with her eyes closed and let everyone else's conversation wash down over her face. She'd thought she was interested in the girl, in Leigh, but she knew now she wasn't interested in anything. All she could see with her eyelids shut was the poster of Maria. Her broad mouth. Her pink hairclip. Maria standing up and stepping out of her own photograph. Now she was walking down a long white corridor with a bad carpet and lights that were too bright. There were doors on either side of her, doors that opened and shut. A man in every room. Most of them looked at Maria and just closed the door. But at the end of the corridor, there was a darker panelled door and it was ajar. Behind it Alexa could see movement, bodies like shadows. Maria kept walking towards the end of the corridor, straight ahead of her.

She didn't look at any of the other doors, any of the room numbers. 8, 10, 12. The corridor counted for her. 14, 16, 18. The door at the end was the only one that didn't have a number on it. Maria walked slowly but purposefully. She reached the end of the corridor and stepped into the gap. And the wall closed around her, easy as a hand.

* * *

When Alexa woke up, her head was full of cotton wool and the street outside was booming.

At work, Dave told her Maria had been picked up. She'd been in Bradford, in a hotel with an older man named Ali who she called her boyfriend. She said his family had looked after her well. She was happy and didn't want to go home. Dave said they interviewed her three times and her story stayed the same. Maria hadn't seen her father for years and her mother wasn't interested in where she'd been. Slowly, her face was removed from the lamp posts round Brightside and Attercliffe.

Alexa walked her beat. With each person she passed, she wondered if she'd remember their face, if she'd be able to pick them out in a crowd. 1,500 Roma children. How many neighbours would notice if someone went missing round here? She had a crumpled poster in her pocket, Maria scrunched up, her face wrinkled by the folds of the shiny paper. When she was small, Alexa's dad used to keep a photograph of Alexa in his wallet. In the picture, one of her baby teeth had just come out and her hair was pulled into bunches. She wondered if he still had it. She wondered if he cared what her face looked like now.

When she passed Eva's house on Wade Street, she looked in through the kitchen window. Nobody home. The room holding itself still, waiting for her to come back. Alexa hoped she'd found the money for the plane ticket. That she was making peace with her dad.

The River at Froggatt

It's been months. When you first lower yourself down to meet me, I grip your legs like a child. But I'm ancient, bellyful of stones, slicked with moss, overgrown and grey. You've been away for a while. You've forgotten how cold I am, how fast I can move, how many I've swept away and carried close. Each time you come back, my touch is a little icier. Your friends say you should buy a wetsuit, but you always say you like the sting of me, the numbness, the shortening of your breath. I hear you gasp as you go up to your thighs. A quick, dark fish darts out of the weeds and away, riding the current. Today, I'm like the surface beneath a mirror. I'm the colour of dark rock or of worn metal. I hold many things deep and close. A bedded tyre from a farm truck. A lost hairgrip. The tins from a picnic, dirty with rust. And now I'm holding you. A chill wind passes, brief — ghost wind, ghost sigh. You pause before you slip down. When you enter me, I enter you and it's glorious. I'm in the fabric of your swimming costume, making it heavy. I'm stroking your neck at the nape, the back of your head, your soaking hair. I touch the riverbank and the grass shudders in the wind.

Leigh

Froggatt was unnervingly still. Night like a dustsheet over it. Leigh was used to the wind through the trees or buffeting you on the track as you approached, saying *You're not too big to be pushed.* Tonight, the rocks stood indistinct but proud. In the dark, Three Pebble Slab seemed larger than she remembered.

'Climbing,' said Greg's disembodied voice. Caron paid out the orange rope.

His headtorch shone a lame moon on the slab. It was lemony, sickly. The batteries might not last the route. Greg thought climbing by night was pure. The one last natural challenge: trusting your feet, blind, focusing on nothing but the circle of lit rock in front of you. He was going to climb Three Pebble Slab like a Zen master. He was young. He was entitled to his opinion. Leigh sank her neck down into her jacket.

Everyone was silent as Greg took his first step. Then he stopped, turned, shone his bad light on them.

'You getting this, Jonno?'

Jonno held his phone at arm's length like he'd never seen it before.

'I dunno,' he said. 'It's just a bit … dark.'

Caron turned to Leigh and smiled. She hadn't tried to put Greg off when he first got obsessed with night climbing. She'd just nodded and said she knew Three Pebble Slab, she'd hold his ropes. She'd helped him practise traverses at midnight in Sheffield City Centre. He'd done the left wall of the University Arms and the right wall of the Kelham Island Tavern. A crowd of drunk students had gathered to egg him on. Boys with T-shirts that said VARSITY SKI and MY GIRLFRIEND'S OUT OF TOWN.

Leigh wondered if she should switch her headtorch off. If Greg was a purist, he should really have asked them not to bring lights. But something sharp in her wanted to see him fail. He was moving again now, past the pocket where he'd placed a cam and up on to the main slab, angled like a roof. She could hear him breathing.

'It's thin,' he panted. 'Really thin.'

Caron could have shouted advice, but she didn't. She just kept holding the rope and watching him, coolly.

'Hey!' Jonno was suddenly animated. 'If you turn round again I can get you better. It looks good there. Kind of green. That's a great shot.'

Greg didn't reply. His body was a column of dark, haloed slightly against the slab. He was blowing hard.

'Watch me.'

Caron gripped the rope. As if that would make any difference when he was that high above the gear.

'I could be off …'

He had forgotten the darkness. He had forgotten everything except the shaking in his legs and his tight fingertips. Leigh realised with a jolt that she liked this, liked seeing other people's fear surprise them. The way it starts in your feet and crawls upwards through your body, rattling you. It was something she understood.

'Christ!' panted Greg. It was only then Caron gave Jonno the nod to bail him out.

Then Jonno was crashing through the darkness with a rope, his phone left somewhere in the bracken and mud as he beat a path to the rescue. Soon, he'd be at the top, throwing a bight down, feeling the rope go taut when Greg clipped it to his harness. Leigh knew he'd get there in time. People could always hold on longer than they thought.

When Greg got down, he started taking off his shoes and chucking his gear into his rucksack, silently. Caron crouched beside him. Then she took her boots off, unfastened the Velcro of her rock shoes. She stood underneath Three Pebble Slab with her headtorch glaring at it. Slowly, gently, she started to climb into the darkness.

'Greg,' Jonno was out of breath. 'You all right with this?'

Greg carried on packing his rucksack. The moon had gone behind a cloud. There was a faint breeze. Leigh inhaled sharply. Jonno scooped up his phone from the mud and held it in front of him, filming Caron, who was nearly halfway up already. She moved deliberately, planting her feet.

Leigh understood why it mattered. All the weeks of not saying anything. All the years of being told you weren't good enough or brave enough. That you climbed like a girl. This was show-not-tell. Her whole body yearned for Caron's. She stood on her tiptoes for no reason, as if that would send Caron extra reach and height. Remembered all the times she'd almost got the hold, almost fallen, almost committed to the move. Caron didn't deal in *almost*.

People said climbers looked like dancers, but this was no dance. It was martial arts. Turning the rock against itself. Making it accept your strength. Caron was at the top. Descending, back over the rocks, towards the woods. And the slab was suddenly empty. Greg sat on his rucksack, watching nothing and Leigh breathed again.

* * *

'Pete. Pete, wake up.'

She'd seen the shop light burning from the road as she walked back to the house, her face numb from Froggatt, her left hand slightly cold and her right hand warm from where Caron had held it.

'Pete, it's me.'

He had made a bed behind the counter, a pillow of this season's Arc'teryx jackets, a duvet of waterproofs. His breath smelled of red wine. Leigh took hold of his shoulders and shook him gently until he opened his eyes. She was frightened by the way he looked at her, his face hooded with confusion.

'Come on, you can't sleep here.'

'Leigh. Fucking hell … Can't a man have a nap?'

Safi was at his feet. She raised her solemn head and dropped it again.

'I'm taking you to mine.'

'I only closed my eyes for five minutes.' He sat up and all the windstopper jackets peeled off him. 'Where am I? Where's Stretch?'

'You're in the shop.'

'I can see that,' he slurred. 'Did that twat leave me here?'

'Probably. Let's get you a proper bed.'

She helped him to his feet and the dog reluctantly followed suit. He grabbed her earnestly by the shoulders.

'You're a good girl.'

His breath almost knocked her out. They walked to the front of the shop, joined and separate, like contestants in a three-legged race.

'You know, just then when I were still out of it, I thought you were my daughter.'

'I know.'

Back in the cottage, shivering, she tucked him in to the camp bed with its vicious springs and Carry-On sound effects. He snored all through the night, only came upstairs once, mistaking her room for the toilet. She stopped him before he pissed on the chair where she always slung her clothes.

Eventually, she softened into sleep, thinking about Caron and Three Pebble Slab, and feeling special because she knew Caron wouldn't tell Alexa about the night climbing. Caron wouldn't say anything, because Alexa would have had a hard shift clapping handcuffs on some petty thief or interviewing an abused woman or just walking a square mile of the city over and over and she wouldn't want to know. Or because Caron needed secrets the same way Leigh needed secrets, things to turn over in your mind at night, run your tongue around their invisible shape, stow under your pillow. And holding Caron's secret with her made up for everything, for the absences and the cold bed, for the picture she'd had since the party of Alexa's pale, hunted face, her beautiful mouth, the shape of her neck.

Burbage Edge

I'm elevated, but only just. I'm a child on tiptoe, straining for a better look. Mostly, the view's the same. The distant road, the squat shape of Fox House, the tended ground towards the Longshaw Estate, overflowing streams and boggy paths to Higgar Tor. In one direction, Stanage End, cut with tracks. In the other, Lady Canning's Plantation. Scot's pine. Japanese larch. Lodgepole pine. The lovely secrecy of trees, their privacy at twilight. I can't count them, but I know how much I have, what belongs to me and what doesn't. The mist comes down. Now you see me, now you don't: I'm hiding, counting to ten under my breath. When you look back, there'll be a glimpse of Ash Tree Wall beneath the grey; two women arguing at the foot of a route that traverses right, the only ones out in this weather. One of them shrugs and starts bundling her shoes and harness back into her bag, zipping her rucksack, movements exaggerated with aggressive energy. The other turns to the rock, glistening dark with water, then she turns her face towards the empty car park and the brook, back towards where they walked from. My only argument is with the sky.

Alexa

Alexa had never tried to coax someone down from a roof before. She'd never tried to coax anyone anywhere. The calm night. The car lights snaking out towards Barnsley. Concentrate. She tried his name.

'Tony?'

It rattled round her mouth. Try harder. Persuasion wasn't her thing. Her forte. Shut up. Tonight it would have to be.

'Tony, why don't you come back here where it's a bit safer?'

The lads outside the betting shop had told her casually. One of them was eating a fried chicken wing. *There's a bloke stood on his roof. On our street. Think he might want to … y' know.* Another bite of the wing.

This would be a gorgeous place in summer. A view of Sheffield in all its rectangular glory. Alexa didn't know there were rooftops like this round here, between the red-brick terraces and shops, but there it was – a strange, exposed flatness. The gap that led back down to the stairs and the flats. A few small weeds. And a man in a white vest and navy tracksuit bottoms, standing on the brink of it, staring out as if he didn't see the city at all.

'Mr Hanley?' She tried formality. He couldn't hear her through his thoughts. She took a step forwards, closer towards him and then hesitated. It was important she didn't get too close to the edge.

She tried to gauge the fall. Twenty feet, maybe. Enough to leave you broken. Presumably, he was counting on traffic. For a brief moment, she wished she was a climber. Calculating falls must be second nature. Or perhaps they never thought about it. Caron didn't seem to have any fear of falling, though she'd hit the ground enough times. Broken ankle, broken arm, a near escape with her back. Alexa remembered her grinning in A&E. *My life didn't flash before my eyes. I hit the ground and I thought, at least I can't go any further.*

Alexa didn't know how long she'd been up on the roof, but it was getting dark. She stared at the back of Tony's head, the thinning black hair, the wisps on the back of his neck. His vest looked like it had fitted him once.

'Tony, come back inside. We can get you some warm clothes. Get you a brew on. You've been out for a long time.' She hesitated. 'My name's Alexa. I'm a Police Community Support Officer and I've been sent up here to make sure you're OK. I'm here to look after you.'

Minutes dragged their heels. Was this what it felt like to be invisible? It was the kind of thing people said all the time, *I feel as if I don't exist*, but here on the roof above Page Hall, Alexa understood what it really meant. To be nothing. To be no one to someone. To be no one at all. She wanted to take her hi-vis jacket off and be part of the night sky. Then, in a fit of resolution, she did. She wanted to seem less official when Tony looked round. If he ever did. This was probably the wrong way of doing things.

She ought to run over and grab him, pull him back to relative safety, be a hero and put herself at risk. She ought to have phoned for backup ages ago. But nobody had prepared her for this. Nobody had told her what to do.

In the end, it happened very casually. She had been silent for what seemed like hours. A small crowd had started to gather down on the street, the lads from the betting shop and some others, girls mostly, more intrigued than concerned. Alexa was crouched down, trying to make herself very still. Waiting. And, slowly, Tony turned round with a half-shrug, like someone in a supermarket queue realising they've forgotten something or deciding not to bother with the wait after all. He walked towards her and past her and started descending the metal ladder that led up to the roof plateau. She heard faint clapping from the street. Something that sounded like a jeer. She followed him, sliding the hatch closed after her.

He let her come into the flat and put the kettle on and when the tea was ready he spooned four sugars into his and stirred and stirred. There was nothing on the walls. No plants in the hall. A small, old-fashioned radio on the kitchen worktop. Was this how her dad lived, too? Tony's arms were thick and he had a blue tattoo on his right, just above the hand. He answered all her questions calmly. Yes, he had seen his GP. No, he wasn't taking medication, not any more. Yes, he had relatives in Sheffield, but he didn't talk to them these days. A son. And when she nodded and said she knew what that was like, he snorted and didn't believe her. He was so quiet. So relentlessly polite. So unlike what she'd imagined him to be. So when she got up to leave and turned towards the door, his shout and his fist on the table was like a hammer blow.

'There's going to be a fight! Not today maybe, not tomorrow, but there is. There's going to be blood.'

He banged on the table again and the mug he'd been drinking from tumbled to the floor.

'Don't look like you don't know what I'm talking about. There's people round here that have had enough.'

'Enough of what, Tony?'

'Do you want me to spell it out for you?' His voice was high and whiny.

No. She didn't. The point was that nobody could spell it out. Not properly. They couldn't tell you why all their sadness and loneliness and bitterness was bundled into a lump the size of a stone and lobbed into the air. They couldn't tell you when the damage had started here or who started it. They sat, they stared, they became compass points around the city. They couldn't tell you what had gone wrong in their lives. She did what she wasn't supposed to do. She just closed the door and left.

* * *

Dave picked Alexa up on Hinde Street.

'You look like you've seen a ghost. I'm taking you back.'

She spoke to him without knowing what she was saying. The only thing that made sense was that she'd failed, she wanted to quit. She'd had enough of working for South Yorkshire.

Dave parked the car. She didn't know where. He told her to sleep, let him cover for her. She heard the door slam and she leaned her head against the cold window and closed her eyes. Felt that heaviness drop over her like a shroud, the heaviness she was feeling all the time these days, especially when she lay in bed at night. She felt Page Hall and Burngreave soften as they merged into the background.

As soon as the dreams came, she wished she could get out. But sleep was too heavy. She dreamt she was in a vehicle, moving very slowly. At first she thought it was a police car, but it was too big. And full of equipment. Oxygen masks and first aid. Ambulance, it had to be. Now it wasn't moving at all. In the dream, she didn't want to look out of the window, kept looking into the back instead. But it was as if she was a puppet and something kept turning her head, controlling her movements. Bodies in red shirts. Bodies with people crouching round them. The roar and the screams and the shouts for help. And other people, behind cages, behind mesh. A policeman running past, his face opened up with panic. She was trying to move forwards, the ambulance should be moving forwards, but it was stuck. She couldn't get on to the pitch. And nobody seemed to be able to get to her, either, nobody could carry the bodies that filled the ground. If she could move, where would she start? And she realised with a lurch that she wasn't even in the driving seat, she was a passenger. She tried the door and she was locked in.

She woke up and she was gripping the door of the police car, breathing hard. Christ. It must have been something on the radio. A testimony from one of the ambulance drivers at Hillsborough, something she'd caught early this morning as well. But why did it always feel like a memory? The stadium was in her, somehow. Poisoning her. It had got into her blood.

She didn't go back to sleep. Dave had a newspaper supplement in the back and she read about the seven things that happy people never do. *Happy people do not complain. Happy people do not compare themselves to other people. Happy people do not live in the past.* She read until she felt like there must be a great Tribe of the Happy that existed somewhere, an exclusive club that wouldn't admit anyone she knew. Happy people do not avoid mirrors. Happy people don't stand on rooftops until the afternoon's not the afternoon. Happy people don't always have the same nightmares.

When Dave came back, he had brought her a coffee and a doughnut, balanced on top of it so the glaze had almost melted. She smiled at him. She said *Thank you*, and meant it.

Alport Castles

I'd like to reach out to them, but I can't. I send a breeze across the grass in front of them instead and it shivers slightly, not like a person would shiver but like ice juddering when it enters a glass: shudder, pause, blink and you miss it. They're sitting close together, but not quite against one another. The tall one says the other woman's name a lot, *Caron*, and it always sounds like a question. If Caron touched her now, I don't know what she'd do. Touch like a jumper with static electricity in it. Touch like a cold plate that you thought was warm. Sometimes, they say my name, too, and Caron asks *Why is it called a castle?* I don't know, either. Some of my rocks are shaped like battlements, but others are just hunched, unremarkable. They are easy to read, these two, as easy as weather from the north-west, the patterned movements of the sheep. They both love the city, but they have to get out of it, again and again, drawn to places where no one asks questions. They both wake up at 3.17 a.m. with the urge to keep driving, past the all-night garages and service stations, dark lay-bys with emergency phones. Not silent places, just places without words, without people who want to describe them back. My trees twitch. A rabbit scuttles for cover. After a while, they run out of things to say to each other. They pick at the grass, only one of them seems unhappy. They sit together all afternoon until dusk.

Leigh

Leigh waited for Tom in the dark outside Pete's birthday party. She never thought he'd say yes, never thought he'd come. Perhaps it would be easier if he didn't turn up. The barn was on a hill above Hathersage, down a track that you could miss if you weren't local or if you were too pissed. By day, there was a sign that advertised ice creams from the farm in improbably bright colours. The door to the barn was open and she could hear Motown music and whoops. Pete's voice, which had a way of carrying through any room.

They'd pinned a sign to the railings outside, along with some half-arsed bunting. It said BRING BEER OR FUCK OFF. There were other signs, some saying 60 TODAY and some saying 21 TODAY, along with a balloon that read CONGRATULATIONS ON YOUR NEW BABY. Nobody really knew Pete's age.

She saw Tom's car pull up in the car park. Her heart skipped.

'What, did you think I was joking? Where's the party at?'

He unloaded a box of Carling from the boot, took one out and threw it at her. She grinned despite herself, despite everything.

'I hope you're ready to barn dance.'

'Always.'

She opened the ring pull and fizzy beer volcanoed down her arm and on to her jeans.

Inside, Pete was by the food table, eating a sausage roll. He nodded at them, gave Leigh a wink and kept his distance. Some lads were trying to climb up the beams of the barn roof. One had taken his shirt off. They were monkeying across the room, using just their arms and the occasional heel hook.

'Who invited Tarzan?' Tom was too close to her, she could feel her body responding to his. She pulled away.

'God knows. Pete probably got bored in the shop this afternoon and started asking everyone to come.'

'So when do I get to meet the birthday boy? It's weird, I've heard so much about him.'

'He'll be around. Soon.'

The room was divided. There was the usual clutch of climbers, a patchwork of blokes from Pete's younger days with beer guts and knackered hands, but some of them lithe and quick, still in the game, still climbing harder than men half their age. There was a small table in the corner with some of Pete's relatives from Wakefield, a tall woman in navy stilettos and a fur throw around her shoulders who might be his sister and who looked like the walk up the track had killed her. Then there was a bunched group of men whom she couldn't place, about Pete's age, sharing a carry-out of Hobgoblin. Their lumpy brown jumpers and tucked-in shirts gave nothing away. She looked for someone she recognised, for Stretcher and the boy who wasn't his son, for some of the staff from work, but there was nobody. She was a corner of Pete's world, on her own. Except

Tom was beside her. His hand hovering on the small of her back.

'Can I get you some food?'

She had never introduced Tom to her friends. She was used to bars where they made themselves an island, or anonymous, busy places away from Sheffield. They'd never been for dinner. She wondered, with a start, if he'd ever even seen her eat. She shook her head. She couldn't bear his reassuring smile, the firmness of his touch, the new certainty of it.

He disappeared and she stood on her own for a moment, feeling self-conscious in her short-sleeved T-shirt and denim. She hugged herself, but that only made her wiry arms stand out more, the thin muscles that ridged them. She caught her own reflection in the window and it shocked her, pale. Skinnier than she believed. Leigh didn't keep full-length mirrors. Never had. She could feel Pete's relatives looking at her, the stare of the women prickling over her from her wrong-angled hair to her dirty UGG boots. For the first time in years, she wished she'd made more of an effort. Lip gloss. Eyeliner. That thing you could do with it at the corner of your eyes, like a trick. She could hear her mum whispering *For Christ's sake, Leigh-Ann, you could try to look like a woman*. Feel her fingers gripping her arm.

She started. It wasn't her mother. It was Tom, cradling her elbow and handing her a whisky.

'It's Laphroaig. I got it from one of the cupboards. Don't think I was meant to find it.'

They touched glasses.

'Sláinte.' Tom always said it. At first, she'd thought he was saying *slang*.

'What does that even mean?'

'Cheers. Good health. My uncle taught it me. I'm half-Scottish you know.'

'I bet your uncle was having a laugh. I bet it means dickhead or something.'

They laughed, and the laugh turned into a kiss, him holding the back of her head, gently, his other hand on her hip. One of those kisses that feels like a dance. She breathed him in.

Sometimes she knew that this was what she wanted. To be half of someone else's life. To be in a spotlight she could duck out of. Having someone and not having them. When Tom talked about leaving his girlfriend, she got a stab of fear in her stomach. She didn't want the beam to be turned on her. Not all of it. Or she wanted it and she was afraid. Dazzled. It was easier, having a part-time heart. She thought about Caron, what it must be like to put your trust in so many people. Tell the world you loved each of them. Pledge your honesty, not once, but time and again. Whenever she thought about it, she was filled with something like admiration. Then she remembered that Caron had secrets, Caron was always ducking out of something, too.

Everyone was drunker now. There was some kind of ceilidh dance going on, rhythms stamped through the barn floor. People were being chucked around. Leigh and Tom stood on the fringe of it, tapping their feet and nodding in time, until a fat balding bloke in a leather jacket that would have suited him twenty years ago grabbed her and pulled her into the throng. The music was terrible. It sounded like 'Cotton-Eye Joe'. The man looped his arm through hers and skipped her round the room.

'Are you his niece?' he yelled.

'Who?'

'Gobshite's.' He nodded towards Pete, who had both his hands in the air and was wearing someone else's straw hat.

'God, no.'

'Good for you. You don't want to end up looking like that ugly bastard.' He erupted at his own joke.

'How do you know him?'

'We worked together. Police.'

Leigh tried to mask her surprise.

'South Yorkshire?'

'Yeah.' He was panting for breath now and they limped to the edge of the dance floor. Something in his face had darkened. He put his hands on Leigh's shoulders. 'You mean he's never mentioned his sexy ex-colleague?'

She shook her head, slowly.

'Good for him.'

A new tune started up. Before she had time to find Tom, Pete loomed over her shoulder and scooped her up, started boogying round the room with her. Everything she wanted to say got dropped along the way. He lifted her feet off the floor.

'Let me go, you daft bastard.'

'Light as a feather!'

'Happy birthday, Pete.'

'I'm glad you came,' he was shouting in her ear as he carried her. She could feel his grip slipping a bit. 'And I'm glad you brought him as well. He looks all right.'

They'd done a full circuit of the dance floor, he set her down at Tom's feet with a thump.

'Special delivery, sir.'

'You must be Pete. I'm Tom.'

'Hey, look after this one, won't you, Tom. She's a diamond.' He had his serious face on. He turned to Leigh. 'Good looking lad, eh? He'll do. You know, I always thought you swung the other way. Had you down for one of my daughter's lot.'

She was going to say *What?*, but her mouth didn't get the chance.

The door swung open and bounced off the wall. It was the lad from Stanage. The one with bile-coloured trousers. He shuffled in, poured himself a whisky and sat in the corner. Flushed and tipsy, she felt a sudden rush of compassion towards him, hunched over in his soft shell jacket. She remembered him shaking up there on The Right Unconquerable, trying to keep a lid on it. In a crowd, he looked even more like a child. Tom was laughing with some of Pete's relatives. The policeman was dancing furiously with a woman with a vertiginous perm, pivoting her round on one arm while she yelled *Behave yourself!* Leigh went over to the lad and pulled up a chair opposite him.

'All right?' she said and he nodded. 'Come from the crag?'

'Been soloing,' he muttered. 'Higgar Tor. Not long back from France, bouldering – can't get used to the rock here.'

'I prefer Burbage. Less midgy.' She tried to raise her glass to his. She realised she still didn't know his name. 'Cheers, anyhow. What have you done with Stretch?'

The lad turned his glass around in his hands. 'Stretch can't make it tonight.'

'Fair enough,' said Leigh. 'Still in the Alps?'

The lad wouldn't look at her. 'He's dead.'

'What?'

'Call came through today. His brother. Must have gi'd him my number when we were in Chamonix, his own phone never worked. When I left he was planning something on the Aiguille du Dru.'

He said it as if he was describing the start of a climbing route, or explaining new damage to his car.

She swore under her breath, then she glanced over at Pete. 'Does he know?'

The lad shook his head and shrugged. 'I wouldn't know what to say.'

Leigh remembered her last glimpse of Pete and Stretch at Stanage, leaning towards each other, wonky and familiar, like someone holding a lighter to a cigarette. She couldn't hate the boy for his coolness. There was a strange, half-logic to it, a survival mechanism. Move on or go under. Pete was at the buffet table, clinking pint glasses with Tom. She moved towards him and gently put her hand on his back.

Kinder

I can't tell you which way to go. In the mist, everything is featureless. You could run close to the edge and step straight off. Only the Woolpacks let you know where you are, lumps and curves, surrounded by boggy ground. They're unmistakable, but only when the fog lifts enough for you to spot them. When it snows, even the shape of Jacob's Ladder is hidden, disguised under a cold, glittering canopy. In winter, ice-climbers test themselves against frozen waterfalls on the west side and some of them shear off, axe placements failing. The ground and the sky are indistinguishable. There's a gathering darkness, a huge bulk to the north that might be a plateau, but might be the rusting body of an aircraft, sinking into the hillside, a flight that went off course in the night, decades ago. There's a man alone with a wiry sheepdog, holding a map. The dog is nervy and alert. On the approach from Hayfield, past the reservoir, there's another man in a coat too light for the weather. He has no map, no compass and no rucksack. He walks slowly, leaning in to the hill. The path vanishes and then he does – no footprints on the spine of the ridge, no proof, no breath in the air.

Alexa

Alexa was tired. Her eyes felt like marbles in her head. She was trying to make herself small in the staffroom, but she was heavy. Sue tapped her on the shoulder.

'Didn't you hear that? You're with me today, I'm afraid. We're on my beat.'

'Parson Cross?'

'Yeah. I'm kidnapping you. I'm at full stretch. With the Section 30 on Page Hall, they're running riot up there. Kids. I need all the help I can get. Come on, quick. Before Masterplan Apsley sees us.'

In the car, Sue turned the radio up. It was ABBA. Alexa stared out of the window at mothers pushing prams and women shouting into mobile phones and men with their hoods hiding their faces. She wished she had a hood today. As they turned off towards Parson Cross everything felt a bit greener and emptier, but it was a bleak kind of greenness, not the peace you associated with villages and rural places. Sue spoke only to complain about the Section 30.

'I mean, it's great for Page Hall and that, but what's going to happen when it gets lifted?'

'It's not great. Not really. Now we've got a Section 30 there, they're expecting miracles from us. The Asian community, especially. They think it means we can sort stuff out.'

'I'll tell you what it means. It means no one on patrol in Parson Cross. Just me, on me tod.'

The Section 30 was Inspector Apsley's latest scheme to calm things down in Page Hall. He'd got it approved by the District Commander last week. It gave them the power to break up groups who might commit anti-social behaviour and place a curfew on teenagers. But only for six months. Alexa had been charged with putting the signs up all around the area, fixing them to lamp posts with black wire. Nobody read them. Or if they did, nobody understood. They just walked past her and said things like *We want our streets back*. Some of the Roma couldn't read them at all.

They went past the huge, vacant pub and the small park. Sue swung the car towards a clutch of shops. Outside, a group of lads not much older than fifteen or sixteen were buzzing, listening to tinny music on a phone. Some of them were wearing baseball caps and some of them were wearing baggy jumpers and they were all in the same trainers. When they saw the police car, they started jeering. One of them pumped his fist in the air. Another threw a can at the windscreen. Sue's face tightened, as if someone was pulling her backwards by her hair.

Parson Cross was white. Working class. Parson Cross was full of boredom.

Sue got out of the car and slammed the door and Alexa followed her. The lads howled with laughter.

'It's PC Slag! Who's your friend?'

'We didn't think you'd got friends.'

'Your friend's fit.'

'I'd do her.'

One of them started making sex noises as his mate humped the air.

'Move!' yelled Sue. 'Now.'

'Where to?' The boy's face was still round with puppy fat, but his eyes were sharp. His breath smelled cidery.

'Anywhere but here. You're not supposed to be here.'

'What you going to do about it?' said a thin voice from the back of the group. 'You can't do fuck all. There's no Section 30 now.'

They all whooped and hollered at this.

'We've had complaints about you from the shop owners.' Sue sounded like she was trying to keep a lid on her voice. Her words were coming out strangled. 'You've been intimidating the customers. You're not supposed to be hanging round the shops. Come on, lads, don't make this difficult.'

'Where are we meant to go?' the fat boy said again. 'There's fuck all to do round here.'

'Try looking for a job.'

'Will your mate give me a job? Bet she's reet good at them.'

Alexa could feel her cheeks colouring and she hated herself for it. She hated herself for just standing there, rooted to the spot, while Sue spoke for her, standing there like a neon fucking bollard or a statue that people piss up. She folded her arms. As if that would help.

The fat boy leaned towards Sue. He was all sourness now. 'Yeah, you think it's funny, don't you? When's the last time you saw any work? Round here? It's a joke.'

'Don't argue,' said Sue. 'Just move. Go home.'

Every time Alexa tried to say something, tried to back Sue up, her mouth got dry. She froze. She was so tired. Last night, she'd just stayed up watching shit telly so she wouldn't have to dream. Not even watching it – she had the sound off so as not to wake Caron. Just looking at the colours. Cookery programmes, mostly. People making things she'd never eat. Dried, misshapen mushrooms with exotic names. Bulbs of fennel. People whisking eggs in big, open plan kitchens with shiny work surfaces. She drank cold cups of tea until it was morning.

The lads were all talking at once now, clamouring. They moved as one. Grudgingly, they started to shift towards the far end of the shops, kicking invisible things on the ground. Sue started the engine of the car. As they drove away, they could see the lads in the mirror, going back to their spot in front of the parade of shops.

'I can't do nothing,' Sue said. She switched the radio off and they drove in silence, back through the denser streets of East Sheffield.

As they got closer to the station, Alexa felt sweaty and feverish.

'Sue,' she said. 'Can I tell you something?'

'You're not pregnant, are you? You're not going on leave?'

'It's nothing like that.'

Alexa cradled her stomach with her hand. She wondered if she looked fat.

'Thank God for that.'

'I'm not sleeping.'

'I can tell.'

The bags under Alexa's eyes looked as if they'd been drawn on with crayon.

'I keep having these dreams, you know, recurring ones.'

'About what?'

'It sounds a bit mad, but they're all about Hillsborough. I don't know why. It's like I'm there. I can see all the bodies and the ambulances. Sometimes I'm driving one ...' She tailed off.

Sue didn't answer. She indicated and drove into the station car park. She pulled up next to one of the vans, yanked the handbrake on and switched off the ignition. She wouldn't look at Alexa at all.

'I just can't stop having nightmares.'

'You and the rest of South Yorkshire, love,' she said.

Rivelin

The afternoons are long and almost silent. I start where Crookes and Walkley peter out, and I get wilder as I stretch further from town. Past Rails Road, the allotments are neglected, except for retired couples who lift and stoop, lift and stoop, mopping their brows, holding up beetroot, spindly roots of vegetables they stack in wicker baskets. A dog with cotton-wool fur circles and circles into dizziness, lost in pursuit of a scent he can't quite follow, but can't drop either. There's always an unattended child on the monkey bars or the metal slide, a mother intent on something blinking from the screen of her phone. *Why aren't you home? Did you take out the chicken?* Deeper into me, the tracks are muddier, the walkers scarcer. There are great horses with shining, antique legs stepping out towards the dams, their steam-engine breath pluming in the air. Their riders sit proud and very upright, backs turned to the city, faces angled away from the suburbs, the high houses on the hillside. They are striking out, they won't turn back now. A couple who used to be happy are walking side by side out of habit, keeping their hands in their pockets and their eyes on the ground. One is tall and blonde, she watches the horses and she doesn't smile. There is no rain yet. They have been here before, but not like this.

Leigh

On Sunday Pete didn't turn up for work. Leigh watched the wooden clock with its struggling arms. At five past eleven, the phone rang shrilly behind the desk.

'Pete?'

'Not last time I looked.' Caron's voice was husky.

'What do you want?'

'Tell them you have to go home, you're sick. Today's the day. I feel strong. I want to try Black Car Burning.'

'No. I can't. What's wrong with tomorrow?'

'I need to do it before I change my mind. Come on, Leigh. I'm tired of fucking about.'

'So am I.'

She slammed the phone down.

* * *

Two hours later she was walking up from the lay-by to Apparent North, Caron's figure looming bigger, more solid in front of her as she got near. The rocks were growing, too. One of those days when she felt hemmed in on all sides. The sky was like a kid's attempt to shade in with a pencil, vague bits of white at the edges. It looked like rain over the Snake Pass. Her rucksack was heavy with gear neither of them would need: all her own stuff and some of Pete's she'd lifted from the staffroom. She wished Pete was here now, with his bad jokes and broken biscuits. It would lift the cloud of expectation.

If Caron was nervous, she didn't show it. She didn't hug Leigh when she arrived. She'd already laid her gear out on the floor. Too many quickdraws. Small cams. They looked almost delicate set out like that. As if you'd use them for darning.

'Need to get a move on before the weather changes.'

Leigh nodded. She was thinking about all the other times she'd been here with Caron, practising, debating the early moves. The days when they didn't even make it to the buttress at all, just hid by the fire in Fox House and made a cup of coffee last three hours. Too bitter. Not enough milk. Leigh always liked that feeling that you could sack things off, play truant from your own good intentions. It reminded her of cross-country at school, her and Gemma Robson legging it round the first playing field and then sprinting down the hill, listening to Gemma's CD player on the damp bank instead, while everyone else scissored off into the distance, white T-shirts against the green. Once, Gemma had pulled down the neck of her polo shirt and showed Leigh her first love bite. It was no bigger than a slug, purple and grey. Then Gemma bit Leigh, so she'd know what it felt like. She did it on her shoulder, where nobody could see. They'd always make sure they left enough time before they jogged back along the hedge to join the other runners – not too quick, or it looked suspicious. But Leigh always looked suspicious anyway. She had the kind of face parents didn't trust.

That was often the best part about climbing. The drive back from the crag at sunset, after the proving-yourself was done. The sweetness of sore knuckles and bashed knees. Or even a long drive out in bad weather, keeping up the pretence that you'd find somewhere to climb that day, the private joy at seeing it all rained off. It wasn't that she didn't love climbing. But some days you had to know you could let yourself off the hook.

Leigh opened her mouth and a vague sound came out. Not quite a word.

Caron turned to her sharply. 'Eh?'

'Sorry. Nothing.'

'Are you up for this? I'm going to need you with me all the way.'

She raised her eyebrows. Yes. She would belay Caron until her neck killed her and her shoulders felt like they were made of stone. She would watch until she couldn't. Belaying's an art. As much as climbing. You have to anticipate the climber's moves before they do, know when to give slack and when to keep the rope tight, a reminder of the lifeline, the link between you. You have to be as solid as a tree. And, at the same time, you have to know how to make yourself disappear. Like a road someone could pass every day and never think of taking. A sign you only notice when it's gone. Like a relative.

Caron had tied her figure of eight. She checked her gear. Once. Twice. Shook her arms out and rolled her shoulders back. She was ready.

'OK. Climbing.'

Even getting off the ground on Black Car Burning was hard. Especially for someone of Caron's height. The footholds were a bit lacking and the hands were high. Caron had to stretch out of her own skin.

Leigh held the rope and felt useless. She was a good belayer. If she was afraid for her partner, she never showed it. Leigh was superstitious like that – she thought fear could be transmitted through the rope, as if it was a telephone wire. When you climbed with someone, the rope was taut with everything that was between you. Leigh never shouted instructions, just matter-of-fact things, reassuring things. *Your gear looks good! Go on, you're there! Can you get something else in that break?* She kept the rope tight, but not too tight. Just enough so you'd know it was there. If you lost your nerve, you sent all your panic through the sheath and it nipped and pulled at your climbing partner, making them heavy. It made no sense, but she believed it. She wondered what was travelling through the rope as Caron climbed, what was between them. She was watching her, but she had to keep blinking with effort. She kept thinking about Stretcher. The last time she'd been to Stanage, he was there, talking bollocks with Pete, his laugh like a knackered engine echoing across the valley. He was there and then he wasn't. The boy at the party hadn't said much and Pete hadn't pressed him, just watched as he drank whisky straight from the bottle, passed him another when the Laphroaig was gone.

'Come on,' said Caron. She was talking to herself, not Leigh. She had hardly moved.

The boy told them it was an avalanche. That was about all he'd say. An easy route for Stretch. No one much out. He said that a few times. Then his eyes got that glassy sheen again and Pete patted him on the shoulder, told him to drink up. Leigh shook the thought out of her head. She had to be here, with Caron. Caron's movements were staccato. Even her way of hanging from the rock looked laboured. It made no sense. She was stronger than she'd ever been. She'd been climbing hard and she'd been in the gym. All the softness had gone from her. Even her face looked more angular than before. She kept trying to make a reach and stalling. Leigh got ready to pay out the rope and then took it in again. Caron's breath escaped in a hiss. Then she said something Leigh had never heard her say before.

'It's not happening. It's not going to go.'

She was hardly off the ground. It didn't take her long to step back to earth. She took her shoes off, crouched over with her back to Leigh.

Leigh didn't ask questions on the way back down to the lay-by or in the car. She just drove without intention, past the Popular End car park, filling with walkers and amateur photographers who didn't mind the weather, past the Plantation with its scruff of woods, across to Dennis Knoll, where the road turned its back on Stanage.

'Turn right,' said Caron and she did.

They passed Bamford Edge and started the steep descent towards Ladybower. Leigh's car juddered all the way down the hill, her foot shook on the clutch. By instinct, she turned right on to the main road and, soon, the reservoirs opened up on either side, bright and impassive. You weren't supposed to swim in them, but she did, often, after dark. Somewhere under the water were the remains of Derwent village, the streets the flooding took. The old church spire that used to poke above the waterline like a beckoning finger wasn't there any more – blown up – but there had to be something at the bottom of the reservoir. Cobbles. Crossroads. Leigh always thought about sinking down through the black water until her feet met something solid.

At the traffic lights she turned right, heading back towards Sheffield. She could take Caron home. She'd never been to her house. But as they turned, Caron told her to stop. She pulled into the car park opposite the pub. The beer garden was already full of hikers, dogs chained under the tables, bikes propped up against the far wall.

'Ladybower Quarry,' Caron said. 'We can do something there.'

'Why?'

'It's sheltered. The wind won't matter.'

'No, I mean, why do you want to?'

Caron opened the passenger door. 'Because I'm pissed off.'

'With me?'

'With myself.'

The track to the quarry seemed disappointed in itself, too. It rose a quarter of a mile from the car park, then stopped abruptly. One minute they were walking on shapely stones, then they were vaulting a fence and scrambling down through bracken, over hidden clefts and holes. Leigh tripped over a tree root and swore. She ducked under a branch and her rucksack got attached to the tree, so she was almost hanging from it. Caron was happy now they were moving, trying to guess where the best part of the quarry began. She scrambled on ahead, looking at her guidebook and zigzagging through the foliage. They had gone too high and had to clamber down, through bracken and roots that trapped their shins.

'Did you pack a chainsaw?' asked Leigh.

Once, Caron slipped and came up clutching a handful of thick grass. It was still in her hand when they reached the bay they were looking for. From below, the quarry looked forbidding. It wasn't particularly high, but it was slightly overhanging, punctuated with greenery. The rock was a sandy colour, rough. The cracks and breaks were damp with old rain. All the most obvious lines were smooth and wet, parallel cracks just a bit too wide for a hand.

'Doesn't look like it's been climbed this century.'

'Exactly.' Caron grinned. 'Adventure climbing.'

Caron had started unpacking her gear. Leigh noticed she hadn't even taken her harness off since they left Black Car Burning.

She picked up the guidebook. 'What are you doing, the corner line? It looks a bit wet.'

Caron shrugged.

'I'm making it up as I go along.'

She was standing underneath the main wall of the quarry, the only part that wasn't scored with cracks and obvious lines. At intervals, there were squares and pebbles of rock jutting out. It was drier than the rest, a vertical slab at the start and then a slight overhang. At the top there was a spindly tree that might take a belay. Silvery, watching over the face.

'Not the slab?'

'Why not?'

'It looks loose.'

'I'll be careful,' said Caron. 'And I'll be quick.'

Leigh fed the rope through her belay device. Caron had to kick her way through a rubble of stones and a tangle of bracken just to get to the start of the climb. She was happy and purposeful.

'Hey,' she said, 'if it hasn't been climbed, that'd be a great name.'

'What?'

'Fast and Loose.'

Leigh had no time to reply. Caron was off, making short work of the slab, whistling quietly through her teeth. She placed a small nut too far out to the right and clipped into it. Better than nothing. Then she hopped her feet up, too absorbed in the movement of climbing to look for any other gear. She was fluid again, enjoying herself.

'Anywhere for some more gear?' Leigh tried to keep her voice flat and level.

'I guess.'

There were two jutting squares of rock, angled out from the face. Caron whacked one of them with her palm and, seeming satisfied, slotted a small friend between them.

'OK,' she said.

She was almost halfway up the face now and the slab had steepened. Leigh watched water running down the crack to her right, slow in the darker grey of the quarry's seams. There was something book-shaped about the place. Caron was in the centre of a page. Leigh let herself relax into her stillness, knowing she was the only one standing for miles. She felt small in the privacy of the quarry, contained by it. And, holding Caron's ropes, she felt important. This could be a new climb. A sliver of history. Even if it meant nothing to anyone else, it would mean something to them.

When it happened, it happened quickly. Caron's feet were in a good break. She reached up to one of the nubbins of rock on the steeper wall – a big hold, almost a chickenhead – and it came away in her hand.

Leigh had no time. She didn't hear her cry out. She didn't see anything but movement, Caron's body in flight. To her, the quarry was still silent. Then the whip of the rope in her hands. Leigh trying to run backwards, taking in. The rip of gear coming out.

She ducked as another lump of rock sailed past, close to her head. Caron was crumpled on the ground. She didn't move.

Ladybower Quarry

Somewhere in my still heart, a goshawk drops the squirrel it was carrying in its talons – inexplicable, momentary lapse – and it falls into the leaves with a papery crash. I understand letting go. You might say I'm an expert. Every morning I release the sun above me like a child who's clung to a balloon too long, watch it rise over the Derwent Dams and the flat reservoirs. I let the sparrows and geese go easily, throw them like paper aeroplanes. They move as if they weigh nothing. Sometimes I let stones go, a hail of them, small parts of myself that dice-rattle down into the bracken and debris, little tooth-shaped bits of rock. I've been quarried and shaken. Every year there's less of me. As each piece falls, I breathe out – like this. When frost decorates my edges, the grass and hard ground, I hold it as long as I can, then I let it melt. When the downpour starts – a drop first, then a smattering, then a riot – I let it run down and away from me. I only drink what I need. I am not jealous: I let the evenings go, let the long afternoons darken and pass. With practice, it becomes easy, inconsequential, not loss exactly but something lighter. So when the woman moves against me, higher than she should, metres above the slip of metal she's worked into me, when she reaches out to her left and shifts her weight to her feet, I feel as if I'm stepping backwards gently. A slow withdrawal and release. I begin to lessen, crumble under her touch. I let her fall the length of the rope that holds her. The metal pops out, hardly making a sound. I let her go further, then. I let her fall the whole length of me.

Alexa

Dave removed the clammy mask of his hands from Alexa's face and the world became bright again. She blinked, twice.

'Surprise!'

It was an icing sugar and sponge bike, the wheels more spiderweb than spoke. The frame was studded with striped candles. She tried to count them, then stopped. Nobody knew her age anyway. A crowd had gathered around the cake. Sue was there. Big Paul was there. The attractive PC with corkscrew hair was there. Even Darren, the new PCSO who addressed everything to your shoes, was standing at the side of the table with his arms folded.

She let her face soften into a smile. She hoped Dave hadn't smudged her eyeliner. The moisture from his fingers seemed to film her skin. She realised, with a start, that the room was loud with singing. *Happy Birthday*. They were on the last *to you*. Dave had one hand on his stomach as he sang, the other was held out as if he was ushering someone through a door. How had she not noticed the sound of it? It was her thoughts. They were getting too loud.

'Make a wish.'

'You daft twat,' hissed Sue. 'You've not lit the candles!'

'Anyone got a light?' Dave patted his pockets.

'I've got an e-cig,' said Darren.

'Oh well, Lex. Better wish for a lighter, then!'

She made a show of closing her eyes and inhaling from her diaphragm. Then she bent forwards and blew the imaginary fires out, one by one. They all whooped and clapped. Then Dave chopped the back wheel in half with his knife and scooped it up.

'You snooze, you lose.'

It was the first cake she'd had in years. With her eyes half-shut and the room suddenly far away, it was too easy to remember the last one. A birthday without her mum. Two years after the accident. She was short, only just big enough for the table, so the cake seemed very close to her face. A toadstool. Red with huge, white spots, like the ones in illustrated books. Her dad must have daubed the icing on himself, the blobs were uneven, but it was Auntie Maggie who lifted the foil away and lit the candles and nudged her dad in the ribs so he would remember to sing, and Alexa thought he must have been proud of it, whoever did the baking, because he had touched her on the arm for the first time in weeks and ruffled her hair, and he even said something about the colours being Sheffield United and maybe she'd turn out to be a Blade after all. And everyone laughed too hard, except for her cousins, who just wanted to sink their fingers into the toadstool and didn't understand about Alexa's dad and his silences and his days on the sofa and the new rows of bottles in the porch that let the sun through. One of them even said it wasn't as good as the cakes Auntie Angela used to make and Maggie knelt down and shook him harder than she should have. His face turned the same colour as the cake.

After she had blown the candles out and made her one, obvious wish and worried that she'd wished it so hard that all her cousins would hear it, they cut the cake into cubes and wrapped it in white tissue paper, so everyone could take a piece home. Alexa ate hers in her bedroom later on, when it was dark outside and past her bedtime, but her dad hadn't noticed because he was watching TV. Not even programmes on TV, just the TV. The sound didn't work any more, so it was just colours and images. From her room, she could hear the electric buzz of it, a high-pitched noise a bit like a dog whistle, and nothing else.

She left the icing because it was too sticky. She wiped her hands down her bare legs and then they were sticky, too. That was the last time her dad got her a cake and she never asked about it again, because she didn't like sweet things anyway. It was her mum who used to love chocolates and neon jellies and things that made your teeth glue together. Dad used to pack them for her in a plastic tub when she was out instructing all day; he said she needed them to keep warm out on the rocks.

Back in the room, the real room, everyone had dispersed, back to their conversations and jobs and fag breaks. Dave and Sue were having a hushed conversation about the lads in Parson Cross. Darren nodded to Alexa as he left the room, just once. He had spent all of yesterday shadowing her round Page Hall, while she explained, between breaths, what the situation was like since the Section 30, the ways he could get groups of people to move on. He nodded, but he looked as if he was permanently underwater. The others were already calling him Smiler.

Alexa was left holding her three-quarters cake. She would save a wheel for Caron. Cut around it and put it on a clean plate. Stick jelly beans on it in the shape of a grin and two eyes. Caron would be back late. She was always leaving or arriving at the moment, overfilling a bag with climbing gear before dawn, coming back at midnight with sour breath, and pinching cigarettes off Leyton so she could smoke out of their bedroom window before bed, letting the cool air from the street into their room.

'Thanks for the bike,' she said to the room and turned to leave.

'Pleasure, love,' said Sue. 'Doing anything nice with your fella tonight?'

'I'm working late,' she said, quietly.

'Don't work too hard,' said Sue. 'I mean it.'

She didn't work hard. Her hands felt as if they were made out of sponge. On Hinde Street she realised she had been standing next to the same lamp post for half an hour. The pavements were eerily quiet today and all the houses seemed to have their curtains drawn against an unlikely afternoon sun. Everything was happening behind closed doors. She heard a young boy shout his friend's name and then the sound of feet slapping down a ginnel, but she never saw anything. Page Hall was hiding from her. The peace made her suspicious. She and Darren stood like gargoyles, letting the day run its silent film. She thought about a story her dad used to tell her when he was pissed, about a snowfall during the miners' strike. The pickets built a huge snowman, finished it off with a scarf and trimmings. An officer told them to knock it down and, when they refused, said he'd do the job himself with his shiny, fast car. He got into the driver's seat. Her dad would always get animated at this point, slam his glass down on the carpet, spilling some of his beer on the floor. In the story, the officer turned the ignition and revved, then accelerated towards the snowman. It was only when he felt the jolt and heard the crunching sound that he realised the snowman's heart was made of stone. They had built it around a bollard. Sometimes, when he repeated one of his stories and she didn't laugh hard enough, her dad just used to get up and go into another room. He had a particular way of turning his back that didn't seem cruel, only hopeless.

The last time Alexa saw her dad walk away was the year before they went to Burning Man; it was summer in a pub by Devonshire Green. Not the kind of place he would have chosen, too many wines by the glass and bar staff with single hoop earrings. Too many varieties of handcrafted burger. He took his pint with him when he went out of the door and none of the staff tried to stop him. Alexa only watched him from the corner of her eye. She stared at a couple at the next booth who had their legs intertwined under the table. She was trying to work out where the man's jeans finished and the woman's jeans started. And her dad was gone and Leyton was gripping her hand and repeating something over and over, saying she had done the right thing. That it was her way of life and her dad had to accept her for who she was or not at all. And, after a year of match days and birthdays and Christmas and the anniversary of mum's accident, she had known it was going to be not at all.

Caron wasn't with them then. She'd stayed away in case it was too much for Alexa's dad. Caron was good at staying away. But when she got back to Ranmoor in tears, Caron had come over and held her face as if it was a bunch of flowers to be kept alive, and had done tequila shots with her and put the lime and salt across her nipples and made Alexa lick it off. She'd licked the salt from Alexa's face, too, the lines that stained her cheeks and her white T-shirt, then pulled Alexa's shorts to her knees. When Alexa came, it was like the end of a long sentence, something she'd been trying to say all afternoon. *This is who I am. This is my family now.*

It took her several minutes to realise that Darren had been talking to her in his flat, accentless voice. His eyes were screwed up against the sun, but he was looking at her.

'I mean, it seems a shame you've got no plans. I know this new micro pub down Eccy Road. It's … it's meant to be good. It was in the paper. I could pick you up, get there for last orders.'

His voice was getting louder, as if he was talking to an elderly relative.

'You're all right, thanks.' She squinted back at him. 'I'm going out with my girlfriend.'

Before he had chance to respond, she walked very slowly away from him, back towards the main road. The sun was setting over the ragged back gardens; its light on them was concentrated, but it gave nothing away. Her phone buzzed in her pocket. Probably a late happy birthday from someone she used to know. She pulled it out. Three missed calls from Matt. A message from Leyton:

Come home. There's been an accident. X

Burngreave Ward

If you look down from above, I'm right where the city's heart should be. I beat with a steady rhythm: day, then night. Day, then night. It's almost dawn and lights are going on in houses, slowly, so every part of me has a star, small pinpricks of electricity. Pitsmoor and Osgathorpe, Grimesthorpe and Fir Vale. Shirecliffe shines best, because its name comes from *scir-cliffe* – my body is a bright, steep hillside. The Don Valley lies flat, an ellipsis, orange street-lamp sheen. Night-shift workers are coming home, shutting the doors of their cars quietly, taking their shoes off in the hall, draping coats on bannisters. In Pitsmoor a man steps from his shirt and it falls open to the floor. A woman folds her skirt carefully on her chair, takes a cup of tea back to bed. At Wincobank there's an early dog-walker, head-torch lit, climbing the old hill fort the way his ancestors might have done if only he knew them, if only he knew who they were. He stoops and bends to nudge the dog along, an ancient terrier. When he's spent, he stands on the top of the hill and becomes part of a chain, a ghost border, a defensive line running through to Carl Wark and Scholes Coppice, on to Roman Rig, the ancient dyke north-east of Mexborough. Somewhere, long ago, somebody might have called him king.

Alexa

On the way to the hospital, Alexa shouldn't have had time to think, but she did. Leyton was driving Matt's car, badly. The exhaust made sniper noises and people stared at them as they sped past. He didn't say much to her, so she didn't say much back, just sat and thought about the only time Caron and Leyton had taken her climbing.

It was a day she'd put off for weeks, exam term in their final year. The sky over Stanage was blue beyond denial, and she'd almost felt happy as she watched Caron from below. The chosen place was near the Popular End of the crag, a route called Flying Buttress. Caron had already climbed the direct version of the route, up and out on a forbidding overhang, but she hadn't bothered to place any gear, the rope trailing behind her like spider silk as she levered her body up, silent and effortless. So when she got to the strange nest of rock at the top, she could sling the rope down the easier route for Alexa. From where she stood, Alexa could just see Caron's face peering down over the edge. A head without a body.

Leyton stayed at the bottom of the route and helped her attach herself to the rope, a series of twists and loops she knew she'd never be able to repeat. She was wearing his shoes and they gaped over her feet, too big.

'Climb when you're ready!' hollered Caron.

She would never be ready. She wished there weren't as many people around, groups in matching jackets swarming, one after another, up the routes to either side of them, urged on by a barrel-chested instructor. She wished she could stop the sweat trickling down her sides and beading the back of her neck, and the midges prickling her scalp.

'Say "climbing",' said Leyton.

'Climbing.'

But she wasn't climbing, not really. She was glued to the slab. The first part was easy-angled, not steep at all, but she couldn't work out where to put her hands and feet. There were small scoops, almost toe-sized all the way up the rock, but they seemed smooth, glassy. She imagined her feet slipping out of them, her body rushing back to the ground.

'Trust those feet,' said Leyton. 'They'll stay.'

She managed a halting walk up the slab, her movements wooden. Foot, foot, hand, hand. Hand, hand, foot, foot. She realised she had been holding her breath. When she reached the top of the ramp, a ceiling of rock forced her to move awkwardly to her left until she was in a dark corner. She could see handholds above her, a ledge quite high up, but to hold and pull on it would force her body backwards, away from the rocks. Leyton was out of view on the ground. She couldn't see Caron, either.

'Alexa?' Leyton's voice was level and loud. 'Are you at the crux?'

'I'm in a corner. I'm trapped.'

'OK. This is the difficult part. It's just one tricky move and then you've done it. Can you reach the hold for your left hand?'

She didn't say anything. She felt like Caron's and Leyton's weird child. She wished her parents had taken her with them climbing, just once. Enough for her to know she never wanted to be high up again. Her hands felt damp, but she didn't dare take them from the ledge she was gripping. Her arms were becoming knotted and warm.

'Alexa, can you hear me?'

'Half the crag can fucking hear you!' yelled Caron from above.

'Trust me, Alexa. Just this one move, then you're home and dry.'

And she did trust him. Back then, she trusted Leyton and Caron about everything. They made her life softer at the edges. They kissed her and kissed each other in public and didn't care who looked. They told her it was OK to be sick of the bullshit and choices other people wanted to make for you. She listened to them talk ten to the dozen about climbing and sex and books she should read and music she should listen to and they always turned out to be right. She trusted Caron most of all, because Caron never said *perhaps*, she just said *yes*.

Alexa softened her grip on the high hold slightly. She moved her feet up and tried to lean backwards into the movement, as if she was half-falling, letting someone push her down on to a bed. And she was held. Up and away. She was past the hard move and she was still breathing, and the blood was flowing back down her arms the right way and Caron had her snug on the rope, so she knew she couldn't fall even if she slipped.

'Nice!' Leyton couldn't mask the surprise in his voice.

'She's a natural,' said Caron.

And, just for a moment, she was. She traversed right, looking down now to notice how high up she was, and the steps were easy, like walking. She padded confidently until she was directly underneath where Caron was perched, framed by sky and floss-thin clouds that shifted behind her. But the last few metres were steep again.

'Where do I go from here?' She was very close to Caron now and she was embarrassed to be so out of breath.

'You climb up to me.'

'It looks very smooth.'

'You'll be fine. I've got you. You're not going anywhere.'

Where Caron sat, the edge of the rock was shaped almost like a crown or that red part chickens have on their heads. Caron looked as if she was in an eyrie.

'I've got you, Alexa,' she said again.

'I don't think I can do this.'

The old tightness was back. The feeling that there was something in her chest that was too big for it and she couldn't keep it in, but it couldn't get out either. The weight. She got it in lectures when other people asked clever questions. She got it in stairwells, sometimes. On crowded buses. She used to get it every time someone held her hand, until she met Caron and Leyton and holding hands stopped feeling like a loose chain, a thing that bound you.

She realised Caron was looking her right in the eyes. She hardly ever did that and when she did it was like being wrapped in someone else's coat.

'You can. I know you can.'

'How?'

'Don't think about it. Just come towards me.'

The first time Caron had looked at her like that was on the first day they met, when they'd walked the perimeter of Weston Park five times at dusk and ended up in the near-deserted library when it went dark, sniggering and sharing a bag of Doritos and a bottle of wine that Caron had in her bag. They were chewing and talking too loudly for the only other person on the top level, a mature Chinese student with a skyscraper of books piled on his desk. They sat down on the floor by one of the shelves like mock bookends, and at some point Caron turned to fix her with that look and said *Don't you think it's ridiculous? All those soaps and shit pop songs where someone has to make a choice. The big love triangle. Do you think pop culture would die if they knew you could have both?* And Alexa burst out laughing, not because it was funny, but because it was the truest thing she'd ever heard and she thought that too, exactly that, but she hadn't known it until now. And afterwards Caron dragged her into the lift and kept pushing all the buttons and took her clothes off and pressed her mouth to her while the lift went up and down. Once, it stopped and the doors opened on them, but there was nobody there, just Alexa's reflection in the dark window until the lift closed over it.

'You won't fall, I'll hold you.'

It wasn't the words. It was the way Caron looked. Alexa breathed out, the way she'd done before, and launched herself up at the handholds at the edge of the crow's nest and the rocks let her scramble over them, up and over and into Caron's brief world, the tangle of rope and her shining eyes and the scudding afternoon behind.

She would never climb again.

* * *

Alexa didn't realise she was angry until she got to the hospital. She walked slower than usual through the maze of corridors, a

211

metre behind Leyton. One of the long walls had writing printed across it in a sombre font. It was a bad poem, something about the wards of the body.

Caron was propped up in bed, her auburn hair tousled, sticking up. She was reading a book with a black and red cover.

'You selfish bitch.' The words didn't seem to come from Alexa, and she found herself glancing at Leyton as if it was him who had said it.

Caron's face creased. It was the first time Alexa had ever seen her look afraid.

'What were you climbing? Was it that route you can't shut up about? Was it Black Car Burning?'

The elderly woman in the bed opposite had started singing. There weren't any words, it was a musical kind of moan. Her voice was deep for an old woman's.

'No,' said Leyton, softly. 'She fell in a quarry.'

Alexa wished she didn't feel guilty about the missed call last night, about barely even noticing that Caron didn't sleep at home. It wasn't unusual. She stayed out all the time. Why would a Sunday be any different? The remorse was bitter, acidic in her throat.

'Who were you with?'

Caron's lips were a tiny seam.

'Well, who were you with?'

'A friend.' Her voice was hoarse.

The woman's singing got louder, more despairing. Then, there was another sound, a gulping, sobbing sound and Alexa realised with surprise that it was coming from her. Her body dropped and the chair by the bed caught her, so she was half-sitting, rocking forwards over the bed as she cried. Caron put her arms round her and held her tight. The book slipped to the floor. Leyton shifted at the edge of the bed.

'I'm sorry,' Caron said into her hair. Then she said, 'Happy birthday.'

Alexa wasn't sure when the crying stopped, but she knew the old woman wasn't singing any more, either. Now she was chanting something to herself in a deep mutter. It sounded as if she was saying *later*. Alexa tried to arrange herself upright. Caron nodded to Leyton.

'Don't just stand there,' she said, gruffly. 'You're making the place look untidy.'

'I need a fag,' Leyton replied.

'Me too.' Caron had taken her blue nose-stud out. Alexa stared at the tiny hole at the side of her nose. It was the first time she'd seen it. Caron didn't smell like herself, either. Too soft. Talcum powder, maybe. She was wearing pale green hospital pyjamas.

'What's the damage?'

'Fractured pelvis. It isn't as bad as they thought.'

Pelvis. For some reason it took Alexa a moment to recognise the word, to work out where the pelvis was. She thought about Caron's small hips, the lamb-chop shapes her hip bones made when she lay flat on her back, as if they were pushing their way out of her skin.

'Do you need anything?' asked Leyton. Nursing didn't suit him. He was fidgeting like an addict.

Caron gave him a shy smile. 'Gin,' she said. 'Gin and sympathy.'

Caron wouldn't look at Alexa directly, even though she gripped her hand. Alexa wondered how long it had been since she'd looked at her properly. She tightened her grip.

'I'm sorry, chuck. You'll have to wait for your birthday present.'

Alexa bent down to pick up the book from the floor. It was a paperback, something pop art about the illustration on the cover. The writer had a surname she couldn't pronounce. As she went to place it on the table, she thumbed through the pages, as if it was one of those flick books, as if the corners of the pages might give something away. Just words. *Westerly. Doorway. Star. Elsewhere.* The title page at the front caught her attention for a second, though, because it wasn't blank.

Caron, Don't eat this all at once. L. xxx

She shut the book and skimmed it on to the table.

'I should be at work.'

Her chest was filling with wet sand.

General Cemetery

They are never here at the same time, the young woman and the older man, but they're both regulars. She prefers the top section, the descent from Psalter Lane. He likes to follow the line of the Porter Brook. I am vast enough to hold people at a distance. The gravestones are my teeth – important and unremarkable. Students in their first week of term wander in by mistake from the bustle of Ecclesall Road and stay, transfixed by the privacy, the extent of bramble. They step through the entrance, the gatehouse stern over the river, a symbol of crossing the River Styx, engraved with stone snakes – coiled, holding their tails in their mouths. Uphill, the neo-Gothic Anglican chapel, places where the grass hasn't been tended, tries to claim the graves back. Moss and silence. A butterfly trembling low, afraid to settle.

Leigh

Leigh watched Caron's girlfriend leave the hospital and stand outside the entrance for a moment like a kid at a swimming lesson. Her honey-coloured hair was scraped into a high ponytail. Her face was very drawn and pale. Strong cheekbones. She was wearing her police uniform, the neon yellow jersey with silver seams. She checked her watch, then started down the slope, past the car park. She walked more confidently than she stood. Seeing her from a distance, Leigh realised for the first time how tall she was.

Leigh didn't intend to follow her. She had a plastic bag full of digestive biscuits and grapes, things you're supposed to take someone in hospital. But here she was, keeping a steady distance in the scant shadow, away from the road. From time to time, Alexa glanced over her shoulder and Leigh flinched, but she was only looking for a gap in the traffic. At length, she crossed. A double-decker bus careered down the hill and Leigh had to wait for it to pass. Four blank faces stared out of the windows at her. When it trundled on, Alexa was revealed again. Leigh crossed, too, stuffing her bag of food into the bin next to the bus stop as she went.

At the police station Alexa scanned her card and pushed the glass doors and Leigh slunk behind the bushes, feeling like a stalker. She could see rows of faces lit behind the windows, hunched in concentration over their computers. It was a more bureaucratic place than she'd expected. She heard Pete talk about the police. *Pigs. Scum.* How could he have worked for them? She tried to picture his body in the uniform and couldn't. She expected police headquarters to give off an air of safety. A fortress. But all the faces behind the glass looked harassed and worried. They were next to a busy main road and it seemed like the traffic hemmed the place in.

It occurred to her that Alexa might not be coming out again, but as soon as she'd thought it, her shape appeared. The bright jacket had gone and she was wearing olive, skintight jeans tucked into knee-high boots, a grey wool coat buttoned to the top. Effortless. Smart. Seeing her like that made Leigh feel ashamed of her own clothes. She followed at a safe distance, down the arterial road, over into the red-light district, where the night hadn't started yet. Alexa glanced into every pub she passed and Leigh smiled privately, because she did that too. It wasn't that she wanted to go in, it was just the idea that she could. The overly warm room. Bar staff who would make you feel like they wanted to talk to you, even if they were just being polite.

By the time they got to Ecclesall Road, Leigh was walking in a trance. She couldn't remember what Alexa's voice sounded like. Hearing it at the party wasn't enough. She didn't know whether she smoked or not. She didn't know if she was close to her parents; if she grew up in a house with a neat lawn and flowers sprucing the path or a flat above the train station with eye-socket windows and walkways you could fall from. But she knew what she'd studied at university. How she hated to climb. What she drank. The trouble she had getting to sleep at night. How she liked to have her wrists tied and what with. How many sugars. Caron's speech dripped with details. And everything Caron said about her filled Leigh with a strange curiosity. Almost a yearning. It wasn't like when Tom talked about his girlfriend at all.

When Alexa turned off the main road towards Brincliffe Edge, Leigh hesitated. But she still found herself turning round at the top of the small hill, past Alexa and Caron and Leyton's house. She stood for a moment, breathing hard. What was there left to do? Ring the fucking doorbell? As she moved away, she couldn't help glancing back to the terrace with the lit window, where a woman was undressing, taking off her buttoned-up coat and her smart clothes, one by one, then remembering, facing the window, reaching wide to close the curtains.

When Leigh walked back down Ecclesall Road South, she realised how hungry she was. She stopped outside a small, well-lit Italian restaurant, family-run, flags on the wall and a large woman wrestling with a bottle of champagne behind the bar. The menu was short and predictable. Her eyes travelled from the board to the glass. There were only two couples in the place and, with a jolt, she took in Tom's best coat, slung across the back of his chair, the close-cropped hair on the back of his neck. Tom's girlfriend was leaning across the table towards him. Her strapless dress looked new and her thin, gold necklace caught the light. They touched glasses and, even though she didn't hear it, the sound stayed in Leigh's head. She turned back towards town again.

* * *

When Leigh lived far north for a year – her first and last attempt to get away from Sheffield – a woman was found dead in the lake. Everyone called it The Last Village. It wasn't the last, or even the most northerly, it just felt like there couldn't be anywhere further to go afterwards. Stuart the sheep farmer saw the dead woman, swept by the current under the bridge, a glimpse of raincoat and black hair and then gone. Instead of reporting it, he went straight to The White Lion and drained three pints of Guinness, mumbling into his tankard. He reckoned she was in her fifties. And he swore she'd looked right at him as the water dragged her away. His hands almost broke his glass. It was the landlord who phoned the police and made it into some kind of story.

When they found her, she was washed up by the shore of the lake, next to the flat green stones, and she wasn't fifty but twenty. Leigh didn't see the body, just the police cars blocking the main road and the team dredging the beach. But she couldn't help imagining it. That night in The Lion, Stuart invented more and more details. He had seen her wristwatch. He knew it had stopped the moment she died. She was haunted. She was beautiful. By the end of the night, the dead woman might as well have been Stuart's wife. At quarter past twelve, he slunk down off his bar stool, raised a hand and left the others to settle his tab.

When Leigh had got home that night, she was swaying and the house was very cold. She phoned her mum anyway, phoned her to tell her that she wasn't the body in the lake. Her mum was half-asleep. Leigh didn't explain herself very well. She was trying to say that she swam in that water every day, swam out under the reflection of the mountain and didn't turn round until her bones contracted with the chill. But she was OK. She wasn't the lost woman. She just got frightened when she swam sometimes, that moment when she turned around and had to turn her back to the mountain. She had to keep looking over her shoulder. None of this came out. Eventually, Leigh's mum passed the phone to slick Derek, who made clicking noises with his tongue. *This isn't the time to be calling, Leigh-Ann. Your mother and I have a christening tomorrow. In West Didsbury.*

He put the phone down and Leigh fell asleep with the receiver next to her ear. It was still purring when she woke up.

* * *

The Monday morning after the quarry, Leigh had packed a bag straight away. Hip flask. Jumpers. Swiss Army knife. She was paring things back. The knife was a gift from her ex. He had sent it in the post with no explanation a year after they split up. It had her name carved into the handle, in cursive script. Leigh slung the lot over her shoulder and let the cat out of the back door to fend for himself in other gardens, and walked out, clenching her face against the drizzle.

She walked to Bamford and the crossroads, the place where lorries trundled past to Manchester. After an hour, she started to feel like a tree. Her thumb was heavy. After two hours she was picked up by a tyre delivery man called Moonlight Barry who was shipping a load over the Snake Pass. Barry never explained the Moonlight part. He ate a whole tub of Jaffa Cakes and asked her detailed questions about her job. He started every sentence with *The thing is, Dee.* They were crawling past Ladybower Quarry.

'I crashed my car last night,' Leigh said, flatly. 'After my friend fell off a route, in there.'

'The thing is, Dee, a new car doesn't come cheap,' said Barry.

'It was a piece of shit anyway.'

Barry had been a champion cyclist in his day. Everyone was a champion at something, he reckoned. Or could be. He flipped a Jaffa Cake in the air and caught it with his mouth.

'I don't miss it,' he said, 'not the early mornings.'

He ate three Jaffa Cakes in one go. His T-shirt kept riding up over his stomach and he was taking the bends too fast. The road doubled back over itself the further they got from Sheffield, as if it had forgotten something. Somewhere past Peak Forest, she stopped talking to him.

It had turned out Barry was only going as far as Glossop. She scrambled out of the van and started to walk in the rain. Barry beeped and gave her a thumbs up as he revved away. The street was too busy for a weekday and she felt lost. She saw a man wearing three hats – two woolly ones and one flat cap – one on top of the other. A woman walking a cat on a kind of string leash. Two executives in pencil skirts, moving with the same tightly bound steps. She went into the nearest pub and had a lukewarm half, then she walked back out into the day and, after a moment's hesitation, stood at the side of the street that said BUSES TO SHEF-FIELD. She would go to the hospital. She had the name of Caron's ward scribbled on her hand. She owed it to her.

Instead, she got back home and went out. The Leadmill was all jostling and pushing under green lights, the whole room bob-bing to something by The Pixies and she didn't know why she kept thinking back to The Last Village and all the other places she'd ever lived and why that same train of thought swerved with every new track the DJ put on.

Leigh was sober and she was on her own and that made her unique. She worked here for a summer years ago and still

222

recognised some of the harassed bar staff, the tall guy with dreadlocks and thick eyebrows who was trying to explain to a fifteen-year-old that he couldn't serve her without ID. The girl was wearing toothpick heels and a white mini skirt. She stood out amongst the students in their plain vest tops and Converse and unbrushed hair.

She could have called Tom tonight. She could have gone home. But she wanted to be in a club, to be too warm, to overhear other people's conversations and pretend she was in a crap film about Sheffield, the kind you'd make on a hand-held camera and zoom up too close to people's faces, get shots of the bouncers flicking you the Vs.

A sweaty man with a sculpted beard shimmied over to her, leaned in and asked her if she wanted to buy any pills. She thought about getting off her head. But she might wind up knackered and emotional, thinking about Caron's crumpled shape and the stretcher and the journey to the hospital. The drive back, the swerve into darkness by the bridge, her matchbox car folding in on itself. She needed to be clear. The strobe lights were tripping her out enough anyway. It was as if each flash froze the dance floor for a second, captured everyone mid-gurn and mid-drink and mid-grope.

She didn't recognise the man with the close-shaved head and stubble at first, just became aware of the heat of him as he danced in her part of the room, the old baccy-and-lime juice smell. Then she saw he was looking at her. Not just looking, staring her down. She glanced around, but she was hemmed in.

'You've got a fucking nerve.'

'I know you, don't I?'

The song was some kind of high-pitched electronica and they had to lean in to each other.

'It's Leyton. Need me to jog your memory?'

She shook her head.

'Leyton, I – '

'I reckon Caron might appreciate some visitors. It was you, wasn't it? You she was with?'

Leigh wanted to defend herself, to say she'd almost gone to the hospital today, but she knew *almost* wasn't good enough. She just nodded.

'Of course it was,' he said.

'It wasn't my fault she fell.'

She could feel his breath against her ear now. 'Sort yourself out. Someone's going to get hurt.'

Leigh pushed her way towards the door.

Derwent

This is the drowned world. You think you want to touch me, but you don't. Under the water, the flooded village exists only as a blueprint, a patterning of silt, thick over the remains of what once stood. Where the Derwent Valley joins the Snake Valley there's engine noise and birdsong, signs of the living, cars driving west over the Snake Pass to blind bends and bad weather. You aren't allowed to swim here. You aren't allowed to hold your nose and duck your head under the surface. Below, there's nothing like Atlantis. No skeletal architecture. No lingering church spire, no rusted bell. No school, no sawmill, no bodies cut adrift from the churchyard when the flooding began. No ghostly hymns, no spectral fish. Nothing to dive and reach towards. Just the end of flooding, the dredged aftermath, the settled ground. Thin weeds that brush you. A cold current and a warmer one. The memory of footfall.

Leigh

Next day Leigh did nothing. She stayed in a café near the Peace Gardens all afternoon, nursing an empty cup. When she dragged herself home, Pete was sitting in her garden with a bottle of cheap whisky in one hand and a camera in the other. He took a picture of Leigh as she walked up the path.

'That won't come out well,' he said.

As Leigh opened the back door, the woman from the next cottage twitched her curtains, then darted back into the room. She was middle aged, kept her hands busy, bolted her windows shut. She didn't think much of Leigh and her visitors.

'Where you been?' Pete asked casually. 'I came round yesterday.'

'Needed to get away.'

'I'm only asking to be polite.'

'You're never polite.'

The living room was musty. A faint scent of bark and chalk. Was this what she smelled like?

'It was a good party. Good do. Just like Stretch to spoil it, though.' He laughed a hoarse laugh.

'Sit down.'

Pete sat on her climbing rucksack instead of a chair. She'd slung it by the fireplace the day of Caron's fall. He poured two large whiskies into old mugs.

'To Stretcher. Rest in peace.'

Leigh downed hers in one. Overtones of malt vinegar and lighter fluid. Pete refilled the glasses.

'I keep thinking it's one of his jokes. I keep thinking I'll be out on Stanage tomorrow and he'll stick his head out of Robin Hood's Cave.'

'Did the boy stay around?'

'He went back to Kinlochleven. Leigh, do you believe in the afterlife?'

She thought about it. 'I believe in being haunted. Don't know if that's quite the same.'

'It'd be nice if the old bastard could come back and explain himself.' He leaned back on Leigh's rucksack and almost toppled into the empty fireplace. 'You know, he got me through a difficult time in my life. We climbed together for ten years. And I knew fuck all about him. Just a few stories. Never even knew where he was from.'

Leigh drew her lips into a thin smile. Who did that remind her of?

The cat came in through the flap and announced itself with a thin, pathetic cry.

'Pete, were you really in the police?'

He didn't look at her.

'You been talking to Dave? At the party?'

She nodded. 'I never really had you down for that. Was it for long?'

'No.'

'Why did you leave?'

His harsh laugh turned into a cough. He took a long sip of whisky.

'Hillsborough. One of my first jobs was Hillsborough. I was a lad, really. Naive.'

He looked as if he was about to go on, his mouth stayed open slightly, but he didn't say anything more. She wondered how many times his silences were down to that. Times she thought he was thinking about his empty house, the daughter he mentioned, never saying her name, the one he didn't speak to. Times she thought he was just lonely or hungover or contrary. Maybe he'd been thinking of Leppings Lane, whatever happened to him there. She couldn't even picture it. Hillsborough to her was something from TV, from the newspapers; her parents putting down their cutlery at the dinner table when the news broke. The 96. Justice for the 96. She remembered the numbers. The measured voices on the radio and telly. She couldn't think of Pete in the middle of it, Pete in a uniform, Pete not knowing where to turn.

Leigh could hear the woman next door vacuuming. It was a bit late for that. She was always cleaning, trying to put her house in order.

'Are you cold, Pete?' She was ashamed of asking him about the police now.

'Save your heating bill,' he said. 'Have some Famous Wren or whatever the fuck it is.'

'Sorry it's so nippy. I've been away a bit.'

'Where?'

'Here and there.'

'This, that and the other?'

'Something like that. Good health.'

Their mugs collided. Pete leaned across the table. Whatever had gripped him seemed to have passed.

'Did you hear about the accident?'

Leigh didn't freeze, but she stalled slightly, mug just above the table. 'Which one?'

'Caron Rawlinson. The pretty lass that comes in the shop. Broke her pelvis in Ladybower Quarry.' He crossed his legs as if in sympathy. 'Why anyone would want to climb there is beyond me. They reckon she made a right mess of herself.'

'I know.' Leigh said, pouring more whisky into her glass. 'I was there.'

'What?'

'I was holding her ropes when she fell.'

'For fuck's sake, Leigh.' Pete buried his head in his hands.

Leigh nodded. She felt as if her eyes were very wide, but she couldn't be sure.

'She's a fucking maniac.' Pete was on his feet now.

'I thought you said she was special, a great climber.'

'She's bad news.'

'Stretcher was bad news.'

'Don't speak ill of the dead.' He slumped down on the sofa next to her. His eyes were slightly bloodshot and his forehead was crumpled, dented with anger. He'd never really raised his voice to her before, not in all the years they'd worked together. She'd never seen real passion in him, just disappointment or a flicker of fear as he climbed. For a moment, she imagined him with a baton in his hand, wrestling someone down, holding a man still, shouting his rights. Imagined him pushing his way through a crowd, fighting to survive.

They both stared at the broken fireplace.

At length, Pete spoke. 'How did she fall?'

'Loose rock. It just broke off in her hands.'

'Ladybower's notorious. What were you doing there anyway?'

Leigh hesitated. She felt as if she owed Caron less and less. 'She was in a bad mood. She wanted to climb Black Car Burning and it didn't work out.'

'Are you shitting me?'

'She'll do it, Pete. One day. She's really strong.'

'I didn't think that were serious.'

'I've never met anyone like her.'

'Oh, I don't know.' Pete got up and walked over to the window, away from her. Then he sat down heavily again. 'Seems to me you keep meeting people like her all the time.'

'You what?'

'Unavailable. Not interested. Out of reach.'

Leigh shifted her body further into the sofa. The cat leapt up and mauled her leg for a while, then shuffled in between her and Pete and lifted its back leg up, started grooming its arse.

'I thought he was all right, by the way. Your fella.'

'Tom?'

'Good looking. Good hair.'

'He's not my fella.'

'He loves you, though.'

The thought struck her that the first time Tom ever came to her house she'd sat exactly where she was sitting now, and Tom had sat where Pete was and they'd talked awkwardly for hours, a bottle of whisky between them, better than the one that perched on the table now. It was the long night after a long evening in the pub. Leigh remembered her brief incredulity that he was here,

231

in her cottage, this man she'd watched on stage only a few hours earlier, talking about what the Peak District used to be like, the things people used to die of, saying every place name with an alarming tenderness, so that she seemed to hear all these familiar words for the first time. She'd learned that the Goyt Valley coined the word *goyter*, from the large growths people used to sprout on their necks there from vitamin deficiency. She'd learned how many people died in Eyam during the Plague, and shivered despite herself at the tale of the woman who buried her whole family in one week. She'd stayed until the end, even though she was only there as a favour to a mate at the university, a skinny goth called Melissa who worked in admin and had organised the talks. She watched how the speaker kept his hands folded in front of him as he talked, as if he didn't trust them. She noticed the slight judder in his left leg, even though his voice was level and warm. And afterwards she found herself next to him at the bar, asking a question about Bradwell she didn't care about the answer to, then finding that she did care as he talked, her map of Derbyshire suddenly fraying at the edges.

When he sat on her sofa that first night, Tom looked like a captured, exotic bird. His blazer was too smart for the cat hair and charity shop furniture in Leigh's living room. But he unbuttoned the top of his shirt and took his shoes off and leaned back into it as if he'd always sat there, and he topped up her whisky glass and asked her so many questions about climbing she started to remember why she loved it, why rocks were strange and fascinating. He was obsessed by the terminology she used. *Fist jamming? Sounds filthy.* Nobody had ever asked her why she climbed before. And she got self-conscious from talking and kept putting her hand to the back of her neck, until he put his hand over the top of hers and placed it in his lap and said *You seem nervous* and she nodded and he moved her hand higher and moaned softly and started loosening his belt. And it wasn't that that made her breath quicken, but the moment when her hand slipped under his shirt and she could feel the heat of the blood under his skin, circling from his heart and it felt more private, more intimate than anything she'd done before.

Even in the morning, when he held her body crooked into his and stroked her hair as if they'd been doing this for years and told her about his girlfriend, he had a way of speaking that made everything seem natural, inevitable. He said his partner's name the way he said the names of all the places in Derbyshire, making it seem round and three-dimensional. He even said Leigh's name like that, eventually. He was good with words. He never lied and said *This won't happen again.* He kissed her on the forehead when he left. His blazer was still slung over the sofa. She tried it on and hugged it around her.

'Leigh?' said Pete. He was tapping on the side of her head with his fist. 'Anyone home?'

'Sorry.'

'What do you say to it, then?'

'To what?'

'Brid. Tomorrow morning. Get away for a bit.'

'Seriously?'

'Change of scene. No rocks. Do us both good.'

'Can't hurt.'

She put her whisky mug down on the table. When she straightened up, Pete was pointing a camera in her face. She flinched, despite herself.

'What are you doing?'

'Photos. It's my new thing. I should have started sooner. Do you know, I don't have a single photo of Stretch. Not one.'

The camera clicked. Leigh shivered, involuntarily.

'I hope you're not anticipating my death.'

Bamford Edge

The best part of my face is the short shape of Wrinkled Wall, a perpetual frown. Elephant skin, shallow grooves and indents, ruched and pleated, the weather folded in. In places, the gritstone is spotted, starred with old blood. Rock that has lived, beyond imagination. I'm a maze of levels, high and low spots. On the slant of Bamford Rib a young woman has frozen under the final moves; her friend is throwing a loop of rope down to her. She swears and sweats. There's a place where the edge juts out towards Ladybower; walkers reach the end and stand there, looking out, poised, as if they're walking the plank, ready to topple down into Derbyshire. Today, there's a man with his dog, the animal running too close to the edge, then veering back, careering into his legs, her mouth open, panting, but the man hardly noticing her. Below where he stands there are routes named by men like him, named for wives and girlfriends, softness in the syllables. *Angela's Ashes. Lovely June.* A fistful of heather moving in the wind.

Pete

The first time it happened, Pete was on Wrinkled Wall at Bamford, traversing left across the creased rock. He was about to place a small cam. He looked behind him and realised his leg was shaking uncontrollably. Not just a slight tremor, the kind of judder that could have you off in a moment if you didn't get it under control. He glanced down. Stretcher was holding the rope and, as usual, had his eyes fixed somewhere across the Hope Valley.

It was his breathing that went next. He felt as if his lungs were filling up with something solid, something hard. It crept up his chest and then started to line his throat. He felt like a jug, a jug held under a tap with the water rising to the brim.

It seemed to go on forever. But he didn't fall. He didn't move from his stance at all, even though his body was quivering. He was there for so long without letting go that he started to wonder if he was part of the rock itself. A stone giant. When he finally moved, he wasn't aware of it. It was as if he was in one place for a year, and then it took him a second to get to the top. Stretcher didn't notice a thing.

The doctor asked him if he was sleeping OK. She offered him anti-depressants, another course of bereavement counselling. It was only a year since Angela had died, after all. And not much longer since the day of the match, the aftermath, his resignation. Even when you think you're over the worst, the doctor said, these things can creep up on you. It was natural, she said, that he would get these feelings. Every time he climbed, his body was imagining his wife's accident. Imagining the stadium at Leppings Lane, too. The stands. She recommended some time away from the crag. She asked him if he had any hobbies. Asked if he'd thought about meditation.

'That's my hobby,' he said. 'Rocks.'

The doctor looked down at her file.

Pete refused the drugs, packed the nipper off to stay with his sister for the summer holidays and went to Greece with Stretch. They climbed from dawn until the midday sun melted them. Long routes. Multi-pitch routes. Scratchy rock that tore the skin off your knees and made your hands red and made you sweat. Big, jagged holds called chickenheads and long, slender tufas. And every day Pete got the same feeling, halfway off the ground. Frozen solid. No way up or down.

If Stretch noticed, he was too polite or too afraid to say anything. They finished every night drinking grappa and brandy in a bar on the main drag, flanked by huge palm trees. Stretch thought the barmaid had the hots for him, he kept asking her questions she didn't understand. One night he got her to reel off the name of every drink they sold behind the bar, just to keep her standing by their table in her tight white blouse and pencil skirt. The night before they were due to fly back, they stayed out until 5 a.m. They'd been necking red wine, because Pete thought Greek wine didn't give you hangovers – something about the tannins – and Stretch went to put his glass down and missed the edge of the table and it shattered to pieces on the floor. They got kicked out after that and walked the wrong way down the beach for ages, trying to get back to their grubby apartment, the slim moon winking at them overhead.

Out of the blue, Stretch had turned to him and said *Do you ever think about it, mate?* And he said *What?*, even though he knew full well what Stretch was on about, and Stretch spelled it out for him. And he said *Yes*. And he remembered, there on the beach, he remembered when he'd had that frozen solid feeling before. He was at Gate C, the turnstiles, by the Leppings Lane terrace and everyone was jostling around him. And they'd just been given the order to open the gates, but he didn't want to move; he just wanted to stand there as if he was a rock in a river and let everyone go around him, go around and past him and keep going as if there was somewhere they could go. Ten to one in the afternoon. He'd looked at his watch. And then there were more and more fans from every direction. And there was nowhere that any of them could go. As he remembered it, there on the beach, he had this feeling that him and Stretch were standing in the water, up to their knees, even though the tide was metres away. And he let himself go forwards, into the sea, and found himself crouched down on the shingle with wet sand in his hands and tears wetting his face.

Pete told Leigh this as they stood on the front at Bridlington, not looking at each other, the wind carrying his words away from her. Safi was tear-arsing it up and down the beach, trying to herd the small waves. Her tongue lolled from the side of her mouth, astonishingly pink.

'I love Brid,' he said. 'Came here on honeymoon.'

Leigh was remembering how much she hated the seaside. The sound of the gulls that seemed to tear straight through her. The long afternoons. The smell of vinegar. The kids letting go of balloons and crying for dropped ice creams. When she was a kid, before her parents split up, her mum used to take her to Skeggy, while her dad was in Scotland, walking. She would cry the day before he left and try to hide herself in his rucksack. Skeggy was all disappointing helter-skelters and candyfloss her mum wouldn't let her eat.

'I'm sorry,' said Pete. 'I'm sorry for telling you all that.'

Leigh put her arm round his shoulder and didn't say anything. She gave him a squeeze. Then she felt embarrassed and let her arm fall limp to her side.

'Was your wife a climber, then?' she asked.

He nodded. 'Outdoor instructor. Before it was trendy. She knew Stanage like the back of her hand.'

'How did she die?' The bluntness of her own question surprised her.

'Avalanche. Same as Stretch.'

Leigh's throat was parched. A seagull screeched low over their heads and she ducked instinctively, expecting it to shit on them.

'Angela was from Liverpool,' he said. 'It used to make me so fucking angry, all that shit in the press. I was glad … I was glad she wasn't there to see the way it carried on, all those years. What they said about the fans. It was disgusting.'

The gull settled on the railing behind them. It was unnaturally large. Close up, its beak and eye looked prehistoric.

Pete's voice was hard. 'You know he never apologised, don't you?'

'Who?'

'Duckenfield.'

Safi was racing back along the sand towards them now, her ears alert, kicking up plumes with her back legs. When she got close to them, she swerved off course. A tiny girl with blonde pigtails was building a huge sandcastle with her dad. She had a red plastic spade and a yellow bucket. Safi slowed, trotted over to them and ceremoniously pissed on the sandcastle, trampling it down. The child crumpled into tears.

'That's filled the moat,' said Pete.

Safi came back eventually and flopped at her master's feet. The three of them were statues. Leigh wondered if the sea could reach them if they stood there long enough.

One summer in Sheffield, someone had stolen a blue sign that said TO THE BEACH and planted it in the underpass, near Bramall Lane. In the weeks that followed, people brought things to leave by the sign – a bottle of suncream, a half-deflated beach ball. It was there for a month and then it was all gone. Sheffield-on-Sea.

'Do you like water?' she said to Pete, realising how stupid she sounded.

He paused. 'Take it or leave it.' Then, he added, 'I can't swim.'

'Really?'

'Can't type, either. Not properly. There's a lot of things I can't do.'

'You can climb.'

'That's what it'll say on my gravestone: HE COULD CLIMB.'

They walked back to the high street, past the karaoke bar with its 2-4-1 Jägerbombs and pink lighting, and bought a bag of steaming chips from The Top Plaice and ate them on a wooden bench.

Before they left, Pete took a photo of Leigh with the beach and the sea stretching away from her, like a long road.

* * *

On the drive home, they filled the van with the voice of Julian Cope. Pete turned it up as loud as it would go.

> She's flying in the face of fashion now,
> Seems to have a will of her own.
> She's flying in the face of fashion, yeah,
> Seems to have it all chromed.

'Do you ever wonder what he's on about?' asked Pete. 'All that Reynard the Fox stuff as well? I do. But then I'm very closed-minded. I'm starting to realise that as I get old.'

> The time was going, so frequently,
> She said if I try harder again.
> She's flying in the face of fashion now,
> Sells the world annually to a friend.

'There's a lot I don't understand,' said Pete. 'I should have fucking tried harder.'

Leigh wanted to say something about how you didn't always have to understand, sometimes it was better to accept something than understand it. But instead she belted out the chorus and Pete joined in with her:

> World, shut your mouth, shut your mouth,
> Put your head back in the clouds and shut your mouth.

The lanes turned into the motorway. The coast was just an idea now. They didn't talk to each other for the rest of the journey, but Pete winked at her in the mirror and she winked back.

They went the slow way, the roundabout way, through the town that Leigh grew up in with its derelict pubs and new community centre and multiple roundabouts and lingering, Tudor shop fronts. Leigh saw a girl she went to school with pushing a buggy. There were people dancing outside the Sports Bar in short-sleeved shirts. Pete had gone this way because he was going to drop her off in the village, but when they got to the winding roads and stomach-dropping hills that led towards Leigh's she said, 'Drop me off in Sheffield instead. There's somewhere I need to go.'

Julian Cope was going round for a third time now. Neither of them minded. Let him sing. As they crawled down Eccy Road, Leigh noticed all the joggers in neon zip-up tops and thermal leggings, all glancing anxiously at their Garmins and picking up speed. All the joggers and then all the women who could hardly walk in their pin-thin heels, sculpted black dresses that pressed their legs together. The women had perfect hair, which they smoothed down in the wind. The joggers had contorted red faces and kept their heads down. Leigh wondered what it was that made everybody try so hard all the time. What were they all working up to? Maybe it was because there wasn't enough danger in life any more. Or people didn't want to see it when it was there. None of them know, she thought. None of them know what it's like to climb so hard you put all your breath, all your hope into one small movement, one step that might not matter, but might be everything. At the bottom of the road, by the supermarket, two men in shorts were trying to outsprint one another. She couldn't tell who was winning.

* * *

When Pete let her out by the converted Brewery Works, she banged on the van door for luck and waved him off. The buildings were patterned with blue panels and an appropriate amount of glass. They were embossed with gold lettering. Hop House. Sheaf House. She checked her face in the shiny door window.

Rachel answered the door in a black leather jacket with fur collar and Leigh realised she wasn't as prepared for this as she thought. Rachel had a lot of hair. It spilled over the top of her jacket, framing her face.

'Is Tom around?'

'Sorry, do I know you?'

'Sophie. I'm a new Associate Lecturer at Hallam.'

Rachel's face softened. She had a kind face, Leigh thought. Brown, forgiving eyes.

'He's upstairs. I'm just off out, actually, but please come in.'

'Thank you.'

It was a room you felt you'd entered too suddenly, straight from Union Jack doormat to leather sofas. They had a widescreen telly fastened across one wall and a Klimt painting on the other. The coffee table was covered with newspapers.

'I'm sorry to be so rude, Sophie. I'd love to stay and talk to you, but I'm running *so* late.'

Leigh heard the toilet flush upstairs, then the gush of the tap.

'That's fine. I'm not going to keep him long. Just a question about the new mark scheme.'

'God, I know.' Rachel rolled her eyes. 'Head of Department sounds like a nightmare. Listen, must dash.' She squeezed Leigh's arm. She smelled of sandalwood. 'Come round for drinks sometime, yeah? Be lovely to get to know you.'

She slammed the door. Leigh sat down awkwardly on the sofa. The leather felt cold. Rachel's boots and shoes were lined up neatly by the radiator. Some had impressively pointed toes. She tried not to look at the shelf below the TV, but her eyes kept being drawn to it. Tom's head and Rachel's head were angled together in every photo. They wore matching smiles. Rachel always stood on the right, she noticed, and Tom on the left.

'Jesus fucking Christ, Leigh.'

He was framed in the doorway, topless, in a pair of loose jeans. He was gripping a white towel very tightly in his left hand.

'Your girlfriend let me in.'

He was holding the towel in front of himself now, as if he was suddenly frightened of Leigh seeing his skin. Panic seemed to make all his features bigger. His chin seemed uncannily large.

'Don't worry. I said I was a new AL. Sophie.' She laughed. 'I don't know where that came from. The only Sophie I can think of is Sophie Dahl.'

He came and sat opposite her and looked at her very intently. She couldn't work out his expression. It was a bit like pity, but there was something else, too.

'I'm glad you came. In a way. We need to talk.'

'We've always needed to talk.'

'I'm sorry I haven't called, since the party, I mean. It's been a strange week.'

She smiled at him. 'Tell me about it.' She was surprised that she didn't feel angry with him, that she couldn't. She knew that for certain, now she was looking at him, now he was within touching distance. She felt like she'd been walking into a strong breeze and it had suddenly lifted.

'Are you OK? Did something happen?'

'No more than usual.'

Tom on the mantelpiece watched Tom on the sofa. She'd never understood why people would keep photos of themselves.

'Leigh.' Tom sounded like he had too much breath in his chest. 'There's no easy way to say this ...'

'Go on.'

'We're going to make this work. We're engaged.'

Leigh wondered if he wanted her to look surprised. She could try, but most of her facial expressions just made her look anxious. Everyone said so.

'And she knows about you.' He paused. 'Well, not you. Not what you said you were just now ... I mean, she knows about Leigh.'

Leigh thought how curious it was to have herself referred to in the third person. How funny it was to have Tom address her like that. And yet how natural it felt. *She knows about Leigh.*

She reached across the coffee table and took his hand. It was very unlike her. Very unlike Leigh.

'Of course she knows,' she said. 'She's probably known all along. People do. It doesn't stop them from loving you.'

Her voice was cracking a little bit. There was something in the corner of her eye.

'I'm happy for you,' she whispered. 'I am. Honestly. That's what I came here for. I was going to tell you to do the right thing. It's been coming a long while.'

She squeezed his hand. He wouldn't look at her.

She laughed. 'At least this way we can be friends. Instead of getting bored and bitter.'

'There's no one like you, Leigh.'

She looked at Tom and Rachel, joined in their photograph, her hair curled round the back of his head, caught by the wind, a white sky behind them. When Leigh was small, she used to stay up late reading books about girls at boarding school, straining her eyes by torchlight. The girls wore knee socks and they were always having midnight feasts with chocolate and marshmallows and ginger beer, speaking properly and playing lacrosse. Their lives were so unlike Leigh's she could read about them forever. On the cover of one book was a girl with soft, black hair and eyes that weren't exactly blue but lilac. Violet, wasn't that the word for it? She was called Helena. Len for short. Leigh used to draw pictures of her at school, getting her gingham dress just right. Eventually, she tore the cover from the book and folded Helena under the pillow. In the playground with her pleated skirt uncomfortably high, showing her scabby knees, Leigh'd imagine she had black hair over her shoulders and a rosebud mouth.

Tom was still speaking to her earnestly, as if he wanted to make sure she had heard. 'No one,' he repeated.

'Good job,' said Leigh. 'One's more than enough.'

Sheffield-on-Sea

I'm the city that doesn't exist, the place you laugh about, imagining the long stretch of The Moor as shingle and groups of lads surfing in the Peace Gardens. Big waves, dwarfing the cathedral and jellyfish stranded on Fargate. In the Nineties, when you were still a kid, someone took a sign and planted it in the underpass near Bramall Lane: TO THE BEACH it said, white letters on blue. Nobody shifted it, not for weeks. One morning, the first offering appeared at the foot of the sign: a pink plastic bucket and a spade. Then people brought shells and scattered them. Somebody dropped an ice-cream cone – might have been an accident, might have been on purpose. Girls started posing next to the sign, making peace signs in their sunglasses and bikini tops, tongues stuck out for the camera. Men sunbathed topless on the way back from The Rutland, staggering up to the sign and pointing at it, then collapsing to the ground, rolling their trousers up the way they would in Skegness. By September, the council had placed a cordon round it as if it was the scene of an accident. By October, it was gone – they left the bucket and shells behind. One day, you'll find me. You'll step down an alleyway and the water will rise to meet you, salt and seaweed. You'll be lifted then, you'll know how to swim.

Alexa & Leigh

Alexa waited until the bread and miniature olives had been cleared away and the waiter had topped up their wine glasses, filling hers nearly to the brim. Then she said:

'To what do I owe this pleasure, Dave?'

Dave had tucked his napkin into the top of his jumper. This wasn't the kind of place where you did that, not really. It was a smart chain, branded bread sticks and silver embossed menus and cutlery that shone your face back at you, curved and ruined in a spoon. Dave belched quietly and looked around to see if anyone had noticed.

'Belated birthday treat,' he beamed. 'Got to look after my best co-worker.'

His nervous smile meant he wasn't telling the truth. Their waiter was back too quickly with the mains. He placed a doughy volcano in front of Dave, an Italian flag on a cocktail stick impaled in it. For Alexa, he shaved tiny flecks of Parmesan over a plate of carbonara, then produced a huge, phallic pepper-grinder and doused the pasta with black flakes. She was losing her appetite. It looked sooty. Alexa had trouble with food, sometimes. She pushed the pasta round her plate as Dave shovelled his calzone. She placed a hand on her stomach. She could feel a lip of skin bulging over the band of her tights. She took a large gulp of wine instead.

Dave didn't say anything until his plate was scraped, smeared with oily residue, his salad neglected in the corner. He clattered down his knife and fork.

'Belting. Mind if I go to the little boys' room?'

She shook her head. While he was gone, the waiter came back and asked her if everything was OK.

'Great, thanks. I'm just not very hungry today.'

He swooped away with the plates and left Alexa gripping her wine glass, turning the stem round and round. When Dave got back, he knocked the table with his knee. A drop of wine spread across the tablecloth. It was only a small stain, but she couldn't stop looking at it.

'That's better,' said Dave. 'Got to make room for dessert.'

'Are you going to tell me what this is all about now?'

The restaurant was emptying. They had booked late. The staff were joking around behind the till, hitting each other with napkins. A teenage lad was being escorted out, propped up by two of his mates. Dave looked over his shoulder, as if someone might be watching them.

'I've been concerned about you Alexa. I spoke to Sue ...'

Ever since their outing to Parson Cross, Sue had been kind to Alexa. Cups of over-sweetened tea. Smiles in the corridor. She had left her to her usual beat in Page Hall.

'She told me about your dreams. About, you know ...'

Alexa had hardly been sleeping. She wondered if it showed. She'd thought it might be easier while Caron was in hospital, no 3 a.m. cigarettes with the windows open, no late-night reggae from Leyton's room, but in truth, it was as bad as ever. She woke up every hour, on the hour. Or she drifted straight into the same dream, the steering wheel and the gear stick, the equipment that gave away the ambulance. The bodies. The people she needed to help. Sleep was something she had come to fear. She had started wearing more make-up, sculpting the hollows of her face with tinted moisturiser and concealer and two dots of blusher.

'Do you remember Keeley, who used to work in the force?'

Alexa wasn't sure she did.

'Doesn't matter. She left years ago. She's changed her whole life around. Got into all this clean-living stuff. Green tea and physiotherapy stuff. And then she trained to be a kinesiologist. Have you heard of that? Holistic healthcare. Linking the body and the mind. All of that. To tell you the truth, I thought it was all hippy crap at first. Sticking pins in people's backs. I mean, what good will that do? He's got a pain in his back. Whack a needle in it! Do you want some more wine?'

He waved his hand and the waiter came over.

'Same again please, mate.'

Alexa drained her glass. There was something gritty at the bottom of it. Residue. Dregs.

'Anyway, Keeley. I started going to see her when I had that trouble with my heart last year. Thought it couldn't do any harm. And she was really good, actually. Taught me loads of stuff to do with my breathing, diet and all that. And we just got talking. About life and stuff, about the police. I just kept going because, if I'm being honest, I could talk to her easier than the missus. She was interesting. It was nowt like that, don't get me wrong. I just like to talk to her.'

The waiter stooped to fill their glasses, first Alexa's, then Dave's.

'Where's this going, Dave?'

She noticed that the restaurant was empty now, except for them. A waitress was arranging knives and forks on a far table, inconspicuously.

'I'm getting to the point.' Dave shot Alexa a reproachful look. It made his face briefly childish. 'The thing is, she's learning all the time. Keeley, I mean. She's into a bit of everything. Druidism. Psychotherapy. Reiki. I don't know how she does it, how she finds the time, but she's just so in touch with all these ... ideas. And at the weekend she was telling me about trauma. Bear with me here, I want to get this bit right.'

He took a gulp of his wine for luck. They still had most of the bottle to get through. Dave folded his hands into a steeple in front of him on the tablecloth.

'You're going to think this sounds daft, but Keeley reckons we all carry these memories in our bodies. Memories of things that didn't necessarily happen to us, but they happened to people close to us. Family and that. Friends, even. Sometimes, it's a physical thing. She was telling me about this man who had really bad neck trouble that he couldn't explain, not properly. It bothered him for years and years. He hadn't had an accident to set it off. No.' Dave leaned in over the table for effect. 'It was only when he started doing some family history, looking at the family tree, that it all made sense. His mum had a twin she'd never told him about. Twin brother. He hanged himself in their house when he was twenty-five. Same age the bloke was when his neck pains started.'

Dave seemed agitated now, twitchy. There was a vein pumping on his temple. His nerves were infectious. Alexa found herself shifting in her chair.

'Have some more wine,' said Dave.

'Thanks.'

'Anyway. It's not just a one-off. Keeley's got loads of others like that. Clients of her own. People she knows about. She says we carry these stories around in our bodies and we hardly even know it. Summat like that, anyway.' He paused, more dramatically than he had intended. 'It got me thinking.'

'Of course it did.'

Alexa felt nauseous now. She'd hardly touched the carbonara, but she could feel what she'd eaten curdling in her stomach. She could taste the heavy cream.

'Alexa, has your dad ever talked to you about Hillsborough?'

Alexa wanted to look to the sky, but there was no sky. She looked at the floor instead. A constellation of breadcrumbs.

'Dave, my dad doesn't talk to me, full stop.'

He knew that. Dave knew that, even if he didn't know why. He was humiliating her, dredging this up.

'Look at me, Alexa. It's OK.'

Alexa raised her chin slightly. She didn't want to cause a scene. She didn't want the waitress with her neat chignon and pinched waist to think they were having some kind of argument. To think they were involved with each other or something. He was still talking to her. He had lowered his voice.

'Alexa, did he ever tell you about it when you were a kid? At the time, I mean? Did he ever say that's why he left the force?'

She tried to think. She tried so hard she wound the tablecloth into her fists. She couldn't remember him talking about anything at all. After Mum died. After her last good birthday party. When she thought back, she could see the shape of him, but she couldn't hear his voice.

She pushed herself away from the table. Her vision was blurred.

'Alexa? You all right?'

She got up.

'I think I'm going to be sick.'

She realised she had no idea what her dad sounded like any more. None at all.

* * *

Leigh was running down from Higgar Tor. Not faster than she'd ever run before. Not harder. But running with her legs free-wheeling underneath her and her arms low by her sides and her breathing coming from somewhere deep in her stomach. She didn't know how long she'd been going for and she didn't care. For the first time in her life, she really couldn't give a fuck. Not about Tom, not about Caron, not about herself. It wasn't anger. It was just the absence of feeling. It was a kind of freedom, if freedom was something you could feel in your shoulders and the small of your back and your hamstrings and calves.

She reached the steep descent, the track littered with rocks as if a giant had slung them there, and she let her body turn to putty. She didn't try to brake. She looked at the bottom of the hill instead of the rocks in front of her and she let herself drop. Good fell runners always talked about this, the way you should let go on the downhill. It had never made sense until now. She didn't mind if she tripped. That was the key. She wasn't afraid of hurting herself.

Leigh didn't know how long she had been running and she didn't know how far she was going to go. The sun was sinking in the valley. It was her favourite time of day, the clear, orange light, the point in the evening where everything seemed possible.

The path sunk into a dip, a jagged kind of trough with large, ragged stones raised on either side. Leigh hurdled it and her feet smacked down into old bracken and water. She sprung away, towards the woods. This was faith. Trusting your body. Trusting your aim. Not forgetting other people, but putting them out of mind just long enough to think about yourself.

The road broke her stride, but briefly. She made short work of the woods and the tended edges of the Longshaw Estate. Then, she was leaning into the hill that climbed to the plateau of White Edge, mud clinging to her heels. She hadn't got the right kind of shoes on. It didn't matter. She could run. She thought about Joss Naylor, the shepherd who used to sprint up the Lake District fells after work. Legend had it he once finished a race with a broken ankle. She thought it was a tall story at the time, but tonight she could almost imagine running so long, running so completely you wouldn't notice one part of your body any more. Your body couldn't hurt you if you didn't let it.

All the same, at the top of the hill, she stopped for breath and leaned over with her hands resting above her knees, gulping the air. There were no ramblers out at this time. No dog-walkers, even. Just her. It felt like this must be the way it had always been. She looked to her right, over towards Surprise View. Somewhere down there was her house, silent, idling for her to come home. She had forgotten to lock the door, but nothing would happen. Her empty house, waiting for her body to fill it again.

The thought made her so brilliantly and briefly happy she almost missed the deer. Two or three at first, tall against the skyline on her left. Then, she could pick out more of them. In this light they looked almost purple. They were very slender, alert. She started towards them and they didn't move at first. She broke into a run, and they startled away from her, so even though she was behind them it was as if she was running with them, too, at the back of the herd. Running across White Edge, only to weave a way back again. Only to stand still, then stoop to taste the earth. Leigh ran and, just this once, her body kept up with her.

Abney Moor

I'm holding everything lightly today, balancing the still, sharp morning, not spilling a drop. There's an eggshell in the long grass, a plover's egg, speckled yellowish and brown, flecked with spots like rust on a railing. I touch it and I touch a clutch of sheep's wool, marked with dye. Even the curlews with their liquid call and swoop are held above like kites. My control is fingertip-light. Sheep shit. Rabbit pellets. A man with neat binoculars who doesn't know where else to go to be at peace. The muddy patches that suck at his wellingtons. The standing stones where a gate once stood, keeping distance safe between them. In autumn, the violet heather, the violence of its grip across the moor. A young woman who walks with her secrets in front of her, leashed and straining like a dog. Maps lost and carried in the air and dropped again, the shape of me traced on them, or something like me, what they take me for.

Alexa

From above, it must have looked as if the whole of Page Hall was on fire. The city had a burning heart. Clouds of smoke clogged the sky and the length of Robey Street was lit viciously by the flames. Alexa wondered why people ever called them plumes of smoke. Plumes made her think of feathers, of delicate things. There was nothing delicate about this. There were no good descriptive words for smoke. It was just frightening, engulfing, blocking out the moon.

They stood at a safe distance and she held two of the children close to her as they shook. Sue had her arms around the mother. They were a tight-knit ball. The woman was saying something in her own language and Alexa wished she knew what it was, so she could answer her, comfort her, say anything at all. Sue was making hushing sounds.

The firefighters were spraying jets of water through the smashed windows and roof of the terrace. Imagine doing that job, thought Alexa. Her jaw clenched of its own accord. Imagine only ever dealing in death and rescue. They were shouting to each other, a calmness in their voices, even when they were raised.

Nobody was hurt. You could call that a miracle, if you were the kind of person who believed in miracles. Alexa wasn't. Sue was. The Roma family, the people who lived at Number 12, were coming back from the shops when it happened. They stood, stock-still, and stared at their own, smoking house. Now, they had to watch the destroyed building be salvaged.

The murmurs had started already. Arson. A sign. They'd been pushed over the edge and this is what they were giving back. Torching their own streets. Burning the Roma out of the houses. The thought made Alexa dizzy. She remembered Tony in his sickly yellow kitchen, beating the kitchen table with his fist. A warning. A ritual fire. *There's going to be a revolution.*

The crowds were massing at a distance, not sure how close it was safe to go. Two teenage girls were gripping each other tight at the end of the street. Alexa wasn't aware of the elderly couple until they were right behind her. Mr and Mrs Jones from Lloyd Street. She sat in their front room nearly every week, listening to Mrs Jones cluck like a spooked bird, complaining about the noise, the kids and their football.

'Dear Lord,' said Mrs Jones. 'Dear Lord.'

'What happened, love?' Mr Jones touched Alexa on the elbow.

'It's too early to say. But the family are safe.'

Mrs Jones's face was like shingle, soft shelves and ridges around her eyes. She looked up at Alexa and her eyes were clouded with alarm.

'That poor woman.'

'It's a rum business,' said Mr Jones. 'Something not right about it.'

'There's no reason to think – '

'Oh, there's every reason. There is now.' He tried to straighten himself up to his full height. 'This place is finished. It is, really. I'm not saying it's nobody's fault, but it's gone to the dogs.'

He said this to her every week. She knew his speech by heart. *We've lived here for fifty years.*

'We've lived here fifty years,' said Mr Jones.

We've nothing against the immigrants. There's all sorts of good people here.

'We've nothing against the immigrants, against these good people here.'

But there aren't enough houses any more.

'There's just not enough houses any more.'

'I understand how you feel, Mr Jones.'

'Of course you don't, love. Of course you don't.'

This part was unscripted.

'When we first moved here, you knew your neighbours. You helped each other out. I could have told you the name of everyone on our street. But nobody trusts each other any more. That's the thing. There's no trust. None at all.'

'Why should there be?' said Mrs Jones.

And Alexa knew he was right. People didn't know what to make of each other any more. People didn't know what to make of themselves. And you couldn't explain that away. You couldn't say that this was a bad area. You couldn't blame unemployment. You couldn't blame the EDL with their march and their rootless anger and their banners. You couldn't blame the small houses and the narrow streets. Eva was right. People see what they want to.

Inspector Apsley was always talking about trust. It was his favourite word. Rebuilding trust. Creating a police force we can all trust in. Fostering trust in the communities of East Sheffield.

But trust was something you lost in a day. Quick as a fire. And even if you ever got it back, would you know about it?

She watched the old couple walk slowly to the top of the street, helping each other quietly, their path lit by the blaze.

* * *

Alexa heard the front door shut quietly. She was sitting on the side of the bed in the dark, facing the window. There was a brief struggle as Leyton tried to help Caron up the stairs and Caron tried to push him away. Alexa registered the heavy feet, the raised voices, but everything was muffled by the soundtrack of the fire, still filling her head. When Caron came in, she didn't turn around.

'They've let me out.'

That crumpled sound, like wrapping paper, newspaper in a fist.

'Good behaviour. It's as if I'm on bail.'

The house collapsing, very slowly from the inside. The sirens and the shouts.

'Don't you want to talk to me?'

She was still in the doorway. Alexa couldn't look at her, the way she couldn't look at the fire. The way she couldn't look at Tony when he stood on the roof in Page Hall, so she stared at something just beyond him until it was over and he came down.

'It depends what you've got to say.' Her voice took her by surprise. It was parched, broken.

Caron came over to sit on the bed. 'How about "sorry"?'

'What for?'

'For keeping secrets.'

'I want to hear you say it.'

'Alexa. Come on.'

Caron took her chin in her hand and turned Alexa's face towards hers. She felt her body prickle, her muscles stiffening. That was what had always made her lean towards Caron. Her confidence and certainty. The easy way she took control, making her climb or pinning her down, filling her glass, taking her hand in public, the first time, then every time after. Telling her what she should say to make people listen, walking ahead of her, walking a step ahead. Caron had something she couldn't catch. Now, for the first time, she had it, whatever it was. Caron was level with her, willing her to stop, asking her to stay. But Alexa was exhausted and confused.

'Alexa, look at me. Nothing's changed. Nothing about us.'

Caron's eyes were large, the pupils dilating as she stared at them. She searched them for movement, the flicker of attention that let you know Caron was there one minute, gone the next, carrying you with her. She searched for the brightness that obsessed her. But she could see only her own body, dark and small, framed by the window. And when she took in Caron's face, it didn't seem like Caron's, not hers alone. It made her think of any face. The boys twitching the curtains in Page Hall when she walked past. The angry strangers on the EDL march. The Roma men, thronging the pavements after dark. The girl at the party. The women she'd kissed at Burning Man.

When she spoke, she had to say it quietly for the sake of her voice.

'Nothing's changed for you, you mean. You just do whatever you want. Same as always.'

Caron wouldn't fight. Caron had never needed to before. She let Alexa's chin fall. She lowered her hands.

Alexa closed her eyes and the burning street was there, the hunched figures of Mr and Mrs Jones, clinging to each other for comfort. It made sense now, the question the old woman had asked. Why should people trust one another? What made it so natural? You gave your word. You shook hands or kissed. And that was meant to be enough, across Page Hall, across the wide street at night. Across a pitch of rock. Or a room, a bed.

Caron was clutching herself, her arms wrapped tight around her.

'You know where I am,' she said. 'If you want to talk.'

But Alexa didn't.

Redmires

Come and sit by me and skim your thoughts like gathered pebbles across my skin. I'll accept each one. You left your bike by the road and continued on foot. You stared at my three tiers, as if you'd never been here before, all the years you've lived in Sheffield. Your whole life. I welcome you, tolerate you, the way I tolerate the shadow of Stanage Edge, the rain from Hallam Moors, how the Clough enters me so casually. I accept your stare the way I let Wyming Brook Farm and Redmires Plantation watch me. I am man-made. A contained staircase of water. A solution to the cholera epidemic. I have endured; the city's hold on me has loosened. I love all leased and stolen things. You dawdle here as if the chill doesn't bother you, wrapping your waterproof jacket tight, folding your arms. In the trees, a cuckoo moves with gentle confidence, metallic plumage, laying eggs in the nests of other birds, calling sweetly, small god of unrequited love.

Leigh

'Fuck. Jesus. Are you trying to kill me?' The woman's voice carried across Burbage.

Leigh paused on Triangle Buttress, just above the first break, looked to her right, watched the woman's hunched body. She reminded Leigh of a beetle. Her partner tried to mutter something reassuring from the top. All Leigh could see of him was his feet.

'I'm trying! My feet are at forty-five degrees to my body!' the woman panted.

As she watched, Leigh suddenly became aware of her own exposure, the moves she still had to make to get to the top, the well-worn holds. A moment ago, she'd thought of nothing except the blue air, the still woods behind her, the freedom of being out on her own with her bare shoulders and her scabby hands. The woman's loud voice was making her nervous. On a Severe, a route she'd climbed more times than any other.

'Jesus, Dan. Dan! Dan! I'm off!'

The woman did not fall off.

'I'm falling, Dan!'

She clung to the rock. She was large, something buoyant about her.

'I swear to God, Dan, when we get back. I swear. I'll bloody murder you.'

Her grunts seemed to propel her upwards at last and she flopped over the edge like someone clambering out of a swimming pool. Leigh watched her disappear. She wiped a clammy hand on her jeans and carried on climbing, focusing on the rock again, keeping her grip relaxed. She was back where she fitted. She saw the valley as a stranger would, noticed how pronounced the paths were, how ramshackle Higgar Tor looked from a distance, the punched mouth of it.

It was a busy day, the clearest in months. People were towing their families along the path in lines. A young man with an impossibly chiselled jawline and an incredibly clean windproof jacket was leading his blonde daughter by the hand. *Isn't it beautiful?* he said to the girl. His voice was well-oiled, Home Counties. *Aren't we lucky to have this on our doorstep, Edie?*

Leigh wanted to hate their easy happiness, but she couldn't disagree with him. They were lucky. She was lucky. The holds on Triangle Buttress were all there and she knew exactly how to hold them, exactly which way to reach. Like the niches of a familiar body, like pleasing a lover without even having to try. She closed her eyes and trusted the movements. She would pick her way down to the bottom and then she would climb again. Over and over until her shoulders turned pink in the freakish sun and her forearms ached. She would not stop. It was always a matter of repeating things. Doing them until you got them right. The way Pete's words had rattled round in her head until she knew what to make of them, figured how to put things together.

And she knew what to do. When she got down from here. If she ever got down from here. If she could ever drag herself away.

* * *

In The Robin Hood a man set a pint down on the table in front of her, so hard some of the warm liquid slopped over the sides.

'Thank you,' he said, 'those pants have been great. We went up Kinder Scout yesterday, up to the plateau, and my wife made it, no bother. She loves them.'

Leigh nodded at him, raised the pint and smiled. She'd sold them some Rohan trousers in the shop, weeks ago, helping his wife get the right fit, the right leg length. Not even her department. But there had been something about the pair of them, her greying, him unshaven, both East Coast American, picking things up in the shop and hollering to each other across the floor, something she'd warmed to. The man sank down beside his wife in a mock-comfy chair, the stuffing spilling out of the lining where Barney the pub dog had gnawed it. *Cheers*, said the wife, across the room, lifting her Chardonnay. It let all the light through.

She didn't like this ale. Nobody had bought her a drink unbidden before, not unless they wanted to pick her up. She gulped it down. The glass tasted unwashed.

Outside, gold light was making a show of the small church, the lift of the road out of the village, the rusty moors on either side. Pete was somewhere out there, walking to Apparent North with Safi, thinking about the routes dormant under the lip of the edge, sleeping, with nobody to climb them. Black Car Burning, quiet and still. Benign.

The American couple leaned into each other, their heads bowed, and she smiled. When Caron entered the pub, holding the door with one of her crutches and groping the other in front of her in a small circle, Leigh saw her as she was, the way she used to in the shop when Caron wasn't looking, when Caron was going about her business, head down. Her hair seemed disappointed with her scalp, stood out in dark red wisps and clumps. Her shoulders could hold the world. Her eyes were dark already, but darkened more when she got the measure of a room. The tall American started to his feet to get the door. Leigh sprang up, putting her drained glass down.

'It's OK,' she said. 'We're leaving.'

In her house, she made Caron tea and toast and let her flick through all the books she'd never bothered with before, the ones she'd only picked up and pretended to read. Caron sat bunched in the armchair. Leigh wanted to put her hands over her bare shoulders. Instead, she lent her a jumper and cleared space for her on the living-room floor and helped her through her physio exercises, manipulating her body gently. Afterwards, she got a chair up to the bathroom, knocking paint off the walls as she manoeuvred it and sat Caron in it and ran the water so it was just a bit too warm and leaned her back, holding her head carefully and soaped her hair, big, deep movements that lathered everything at once. Then she dried her neck and wrapped a towel around her head and the cat came to the door and yowled at the water on the floor, the strangeness of Caron in her white headdress.

Leigh left her to it for a while, giving her the empty bedroom. She went downstairs and took her cold tea out into the garden where it was late, as if it had been late forever, and the stars she didn't know the names for were bright as normal over the terrace, and the woman next door twitched her curtains and watched Leigh watching them. Leigh stared at the cluttered sky, the faint outlines of trees, darker than the surrounding air, and somewhere behind it all, Stanage. She sat back and tried to invent new names for climbing routes. It was a game she and Caron liked to play, trading their favourites from the Peak District: Tequila Mockingbird, Oedipus! Ring Your Mother. Caron was better at making up names than Leigh. Because Leigh came from Chesterfield, Caron suggested Death in Chez Vegas, a pun on the local nickname.

Behind her, Caron clicked the bedroom lamp off and her house went dark. She drew herself back inside the kitchen, closed the door and walked quietly upstairs, the landing striped with moonlight or starlight, whichever it was. She stood in the doorway.

'Night,' she said. Caron grunted.

'You know, you can stay as long as you like. Here.'

There was a long silence.

'Thanks,' said Caron.

'This place is yours. I mean it.'

'Why?'

'I thought you might need some space.' She paused and swallowed. 'And that's what friends do.'

An owl gave a high, melancholy call outside and nothing answered it. It called again. Leigh was always trying to work out how close it was, which tree behind the house it roosted in. They said you never heard one owl alone, it was always a pair of them. But this one was different. Solitary. She was sure.

She trailed the spare duvet downstairs after her, like a bridal train.

Hathersage

Before the weddings and the slanting tea shops and the vintage cars, I was unbalanced, teetering underneath the moor, looking up at Stanage, waiting for the gritstone to topple and wind me. I was full of millstones and hard labour, men who drank their wages, farmers who worked me properly. I'm trying to be polite. I don't mind the coach parties and ramblers, the tourists weighed down by cameras, the day-trippers who come without walking boots and trudge up to the Plantation, tiptoeing over the muddy parts, the bogs where runners lose their shoes. But some days I watch the would-be climbers queuing up for gear in the outdoor shop or shovelling bacon butties down their necks in the upstairs café, comparing lightweight coats and brand-new guidebooks, and I want someone to hurt me, rattle me, pick me up and shake me, so they all topple out like coins from a pocket. I want to be cut, the way the edges cut the violet heather and divide the land from the sky. I want the wind to batter me so hard my stone houses start to creak and shift in their foundations. I want someone to drink my swimming pool dry, then turn, unsatisfied, and ask *What next?*, crunching the pubs between huge yellow teeth, leaving less and less of me, an empty place where Little John's grave should be, gaps along my ribcage streets. I'm trying to be honest. I know it's tough. I know you thought I was nice.

Alexa

Alexa had slept badly again. In the morning, she'd just drifted off when Leyton pulled the covers off her.

'Get dressed. We're going to be late.'

'For what?'

She tried to pull the sheets back over herself, suddenly self-conscious, aware of her nipples showing through her tank top, her unshaven legs, the chipped varnish on her toes. How long since they'd seen each other naked? She had forgotten the real shape of Leyton's shoulders. She could only guess them through his T-shirt. His face was set hard. He was an unfinished sculpture. Leyton rattled his keys.

'There's someone you need to meet.' He pulled a roll-up from behind his ear and lit up. Then he changed his mind and stubbed it out in Caron's ashtray.

'No time. Come on.'

His eyes were serious. She'd always thought they were the colour of gritstone. Now she couldn't decide if that was quite right. She believed him. She always had. She pulled on a pair of Caron's jeans. On her long legs they looked like pedal pushers. Leyton looked and snorted.

'Might as well wear these,' she said. 'Don't know if she's coming back for them.'

When they got to Shalesmoor, she knew at once where he was taking her to. Her favourite hill, utterly nondescript and beautiful, off the road just before Pitsmoor, behind the ex-foundries and climbing walls and new restaurants on Mowbray Street. The first time she'd found it was by accident, a wrong turn on the bike after work. It was a long, thick slope of badly tended grass leading down to a bridge where people went to dump rubbish. But when you stood at the top of it, you could see the whole of town, the vivid red of the modern university buildings, the cranes swinging above everything. Standing here now, she thought with a lurch about Tony's roof in Page Hall, the long view and how she'd stared into it, willing him down. She walked a step behind Leyton. Neither of them spoke. The sun was trying to rise above the city, but the city was holding it down. There was an underwater feel about everything. They sat on the grass and Leyton lit up.

'Do you remember when I first brought you both here?' she said.

He nodded, exhaled.

'After the Kelham Island Tavern. Caron rolled all the way down the hill.'

A smile bothered his face. Then it was gone.

'It's where I come when I want to get some space.'

Leyton nodded again. 'I know. I know you better than you think.'

'Better than you should.'

Then Alexa saw her, a shape in the corner of her eye at first, then something more like a shadow. She was approaching from the east, from the scrappy parking bay by the road, the place where only dealers and dog-walkers ever stopped. Her walk was hesitant at first. Leyton got to his feet and waved. She raised a hand in return.

'Lex, come on,' he said. She trusted him. She got to her feet.

The woman held out her hand and Alexa didn't know how to take it. She was saying Alexa's name.

'You don't know me,' the woman said, 'not really.'

Alexa remembered her at the party. Her head slightly tilted to one side. Her way of nodding before you'd got to the end of your sentence. Her thin hands and long fingers. Her interested eyes. Her way of smoothing back hair she didn't have, tucking imaginary strands behind her ears. She remembered the back of her neck. She felt as if she must be drunk. The woman was still talking.

'There's no reason why you should like me. But just hear me out.'

Alexa was listening. She didn't know what else to do.

'There's someone who wants to talk to you. A good friend of mine. He's waiting in the van. He'd like to say hello if that's OK.'

She gestured back towards where she'd approached from. She did it nervously, something superstitious in the movement.

Alexa turned to Leyton. He was still smoking, looking down at the ground, at Sheffield, spread out. The sun was higher now, everything was fake gold. Cars were teeming up from Hillsborough. The city was so awake. She blinked and it did no good.

She hadn't said anything, not yes and not no, but the woman had backed off; she was loping off up the incline. She watched her get smaller. Leyton seemed a long way off. She thought about reaching for him, but she didn't quite know why. She thought about reaching for Caron and then she remembered she wasn't there.

A bird landed on the grass a few metres away from them and pecked at nothing. It was dark and quite large, some kind of crow. There was no breeze and she wished that there was, something to lift the bird away. At the foot of the hill, down towards the bridge, an old man was walking and stooping, picking up old cans and litter and putting them in a black plastic bag. Now Leyton's hand was on her shoulder. Now it wasn't.

She thought about Caron and all the hours they must have spent in this place, hours lying down over their own shadows on the grass. Summertimes. Nights when it was too cold to sit out, but they wrapped up and sat on the hill anyway. Caron's broad face. Caron's hair. Caron kissing someone else; Caron laughing for someone else; those nights when she didn't come home until early morning. Caron kissing the woman with short hair – this woman who was holding back now, hovering somewhere near the van, while a tall man walked in front of her, hands in the pockets of an oversize khaki duffel coat. Now he was near them. Now he was close enough to see. And now, only now, he was close enough to hold out his hand to her, hold out his left hand and leave it there. His hair was greyer. He'd lost weight. His eyes were slightly hooded, but they were very clear, very blue. He held out his hand and, without thinking, she took it.

'Hello love,' said Pete. 'It's been too long.'

Pitsmoor Road

I watch the girl as she takes the old man's hand and holds it. I am below them and above them, the yellow grass and the thin sky. I'm cluttered these days, decorated with the things people leave behind. Bicycle tyres and copies of *The Sun*, polystyrene cartons from the chip shops down by Kelham Island. People who come to look down at the river. The two of them an unsteady bridge across me now, their touch uncertain. The others slink away, back to the road, and it's just the two of them, facing each other like partners at a dance. As if there's never been anyone else. You can see the family resemblance. It's obvious. The same ears. Same delicate noses. Same curvature of the spine. She is a part of him, in her stance, in the things that can't be seen: the way her patient blood moves, the way she says *shouldn't* and makes it sound like *shunt*. Her thin hair and her unfinished sentences. Their shadows overlap on the ground, taller than they are. From up high, they are a kind of dash, punctuation, a small pause in the day. Neither of them wants to move, but he turns away first and begins to walk and – though she hesitates – she starts off up the slope, following his stooped walk until she's beside him. I let them pass, out of my shade and shelter. I'm left with the crows, how they pick up cigarette packets, shake them and let them drop, the world so much less than they thought.

Leigh

Autumn was in Leigh's blood. It was in her hair and thigh bones and shin bones. On her lips. Her fingers were like dry leaves. She rode the bus back through the city, noticing the burnt toffee colours of everything, the cloaked pavements. She had always hated that feeling, that new-school-year air hanging over the city. September always smelled like unopened exercise books and patent shoes. Students in the climbing shop. A faint dread you had to drag yourself through. Knee-high, dying bracken.

Today was different. Today was the start of something. She'd slunk away from Pete and Alexa on the hill, resisting the urge to look back. Leyton had offered her a lift, but she'd refused, preferring the stop-start of the bus into town. A plump woman looked up from her newspaper and glanced at Leigh. She smiled a full-lipped smile. It made the woman uncomfortable.

When she got off the bus outside The Crucible, Caron was already there, small next to two black holdalls and three cardboard boxes, bursting at the seams. The sun cast a long line across her body, sideways.

'How'd you get those here?'

Caron shrugged. 'Taxi.'

She fumbled a set of keys from her pocket. Shoppers pushed past them, on their way down to the Interchange or the tram stop by the old hole in the road.

'Do you want to come in?'

'Where?'

It was like a hidden door in the high street. There was a painted-over sign, cream and purple. If you squinted, you could read the words *Mulberry Tavern* in cursive script. Caron shouldered the door and they plunged into blackness, Leigh dragging the holdalls behind her.

The staircase was unlit, steep and narrow. Caron had to haul herself up by the bannister. They left the boxes at the bottom and inched up in the dark, feeling their way slowly. The stairwell was silent and their feet dragged loud. The smell of stale beer got stronger as they approached another double door. It gave way to a deserted bar room, scrunched John Smith's towels underneath empty optics, the pumps in their orderly line. The carpet was almost bald. Even in this state, you couldn't shake the feeling that someone had just left the room, that a long lock-in had only just been abandoned. There were faded squares on the walls where the pictures used to be. One of them showed pencil graffiti: *Wentworth College, Class of '94.*

Caron led Leigh slowly past the bar and round the back, through another entrance. A corridor with a pale rectangle of light at the end of it. Suddenly, the flat began to take shape, make sense. A box room. A slim bathroom. A room with just enough space for a bed. And last, the living room, full of upturned beer crates. But that wasn't the remarkable thing about it. The surprise was what it led to, the sliding doors and the open plateau of rooftop, dressed with scrawny bunting. Caron stepped out first and beckoned her, steadying herself against the doors with one hand.

It was like walking out into a Lego world, the small, exact buildings below. The sky was very white with cloud, a washed sheet on the line, a sheet you could get tangled up in and never see anything else again. They were right above The Crucible. If the snooker tournament was happening, you could almost reach down through the roof and steal the black ball. The buildings that screamed Sheffield to Leigh when she was growing up were laid out, all present and correct, within jumping distance, gobbing distance. She could see Park Hill Flats and the station, the trains pulling away with their short and long promises.

'Is this yours? Is it all yours?'

'Yeah. Until they decide to do something with the building. As long as I'm here, it'll stop squatters moving in. Matt tipped me off. It'll do.' She grimaced. 'They could at least have restocked the bar, eh?'

'It's beautiful. This is what I thought Sheffield was when I was a kid. All this.'

She wanted to leap off the edge towards the Winter Gardens, fall down through the glass and the wide, exotic leaves, land between a couple on a bench, knocking them like skittles.

'Why do you think it is,' she said, 'that things only make sense to people like us when we're above them, looking down?'

'There's no such thing as people like us.'

'There might be.'

Caron picked up a pebble, smaller than a ten-pence piece, and lobbed it in the direction of The Lyceum. She just missed a teenager with high-waisted jeans and an armful of shopping bags. The stone sailed out of sight and landed somewhere they couldn't see.

'Unlucky,' said Leigh. 'Next time.'

'There's always a next time. That's what I've been telling myself anyway. You always get another chance. Until you don't.'

Leigh was almost dizzy with happiness. She thought about the last time she felt like this. She was on top of The Chief in Squamish on a day so hot the granite was a skillet. Whistler and Powder Mountain somewhere out of reach, topped with snow. She spent her days climbing routes and eating fried bread and pancakes in the lonely cafés. She was filled with the sudden compulsion to emigrate. Her fingers were sanded down and her fingernails were black and blunt. She had not even considered the possibility that the feeling would pass. That her life would be full of moments like that, moments of looking down and thinking everything was simple. Until you had to climb down.

Caron was leaning against the wall. Leigh hadn't even noticed she was crying.

'I've fucked up so bad this time. I've been playing a game. And I don't even know why. That's the stupid thing.'

Leigh walked backwards until she was leaning up against the wall next to Caron.

'Have you talked to any of them?'

'No. I left Alexa a note.' She let out a ragged breath. 'I stopped talking months ago, didn't I? That's the problem.'

'Maybe things happen because they have to.' Leigh knew she sounded pretentious.

The cobbles of the square looked so neat you could hopscotch on them.

'What do you mean?'

'Like ... I don't know ... you've got to learn to trust yourself before you can trust anyone else.'

Leigh expected her to laugh. But she didn't. She just nodded, her mouth set in a thin line. Leigh looked away from her. She wasn't in love with Caron, or Tom, or anyone. She was in love with this city, the guts and grime of it. The tenderness of its spaces. The people eating sandwiches in the Peace Gardens. The man holding a paper cup outside Wicker Stores with a blanket over his knees. The early drinkers in The Brown Bear, making the afternoon shine. The cyclists going nowhere fast.

'You got time to help me shift these boxes?' Caron's tears had stopped. Her face looked clean, washed-out.

The sun had started to sink. It was perched above Caron's new roof like a piece of fruit, something fancy on the edge of a cocktail glass.

'All right. Come on.'

Division Street

I'm full. I don't know what to do with so many people. There are students in the pared-back cafés, sipping macchiatos and nibbling croissants, queuing up at cashpoints to withdraw crisp tenners. The boutique shops bustle with paper bags that smell like unworn boots. The Frog & Parrot is full of early drinkers. I can't entertain them all. I was built for trade and footfall, the distant rumble of trams. I was made to roll gently into the city. To be a concrete river, a stream, pooling around Devonshire Green, the meeting point with West Street. I watch the amber bubbles in a woman's pint. How her hand warms it, how condensation forms on the cool glass. How quickly the liquid disappears. How her throat moves as she swallows, a furtive shift, like a small animal. How she places both hands on the bar stool and closes her eyes. How her pockets are empty and her bag is forgotten on the floor. On the street, a child lets go of a unicorn balloon and does not cry as it rises, like water, like fever, like blood to the head. It lifts above the City Hall and the bodies, the people seem to move in formation. He kicks an empty can down the pavement and for a moment it gathers momentum, then it slows and slows and stops under the wheels of a car. In the bar, the woman orders another.

Alexa

Throughout the 1980s there was considerable ambiguity about South Yorkshire Police's and Sheffield Wednesday FC's crowd management responsibilities within the stadium.

There was so much Alexa should have been thinking about, so much she should have been doing, but instead she was frozen in her dad's spare room, going through his papers, reading things she couldn't put down.

The management of the crowd was viewed exclusively through a lens of potential crowd disorder, and this ambiguity was not resolved, despite problems at previous semi-finals. SWFC and SYP were unprepared for the disaster that unfolded on the terraces on 15 April 1989.

'You all right, love?' The house was smaller than she remembered. His voice from downstairs boomed.

'Yeah.'

Not only was there delay in recognising that there were mass casualties, the major incident plan was not correctly activated and only limited parts were then put into effect.

'Thought you might be lost.'

'Won't be a sec.'

It is not possible to establish whether a more effective emergency response would have saved the life of any one individual who died. Given the evidence disclosed to the panel of more prolonged survival of some people with partial asphyxiation, however, a swifter, more appropriate, better-focused and properly equipped response had the potential to save more lives.

He had printed out the lot. Highlighting and lines and scribbles everywhere. Alexa felt giddy. She'd been like it all day, as if she was floating an inch above herself. She put the papers back on the desk and made her way downstairs. She realised she was walking very slowly, because she didn't want to get to the bottom.

Eight years after the disaster it was revealed publicly that statements made by SYP officers were initially handwritten as 'recollections', then subjected to a process of 'review and alteration' involving SYP solicitors and a team of SYP officers.

Review and alteration. She took the stairs carefully, as if she was drunk.

Some 116 of the 164 statements identified for substantive amendment were amended to remove or alter comments unfavourable to SYP.

Her dad was in the living room with a tinny. The walls hadn't changed. The wedding picture, him all sideburns and tash. The picture of them all in Brid, when Alexa was very small and very blonde. Next to the door, with a jolt, she noticed her graduation picture. He'd kept it after all, kept it up all this time. She posted it to him, without a note. She'd written something, torn it up, written it again. In the end, she sent nothing, just the photo with its huge mortar board and insipid blue background.

'Drink?'

'No ta.'

She felt like she should sit on the floor, but she drew up a chair at the small wooden dining table. He'd hung a large clock above the telly, plastic with big red hands. United colours. It ticked very loudly. She wanted to say something. Where did all the things you wanted to say in your head go when you opened your mouth?

'So you've been OK? I mean, things are OK?'

'Yeah.'

Review and alteration. Review and alteration.

'You must have thought I was a right bastard. All this time.'

She shook her head.

'Come on. You must have.'

The carpet was brown and scuffed at the edges. There was a cigarette burn by the table leg, but Dad didn't smoke. Never had. She looked up.

'I never expected to see you.'

'I know.'

'What made you come?'

'Leigh. She talked me round. Recently, I ...'

Of course. It was her. Meddling. Putting things together. Trying to patch things up. Alexa felt angry and sad at the same time, and nothing for any good reason, nothing she could explain.

The panel's access to all of the relevant records has confirmed that the notion of a single, unvarying and rapid cause of death in all cases is unsustainable. Some of those who died did so after a significant period of unconsciousness, during which they might have been able to be resuscitated.

A significant period of unconsciousness.

'Fuck it.' He put his beer can down on the floor. 'Does it matter why I came? You're here now, aren't you?'

She nodded. Her head was very heavy.

'I want ... ' he said. 'I want to make up for lost time.'

She spoke, but her voice was hardly anything now. 'You don't know anything about me any more.'

He was in front of her, kneeling, trying to get down below her level.

'I do. I do. I promise. I just don't know what I can do to make you trust me again.'

Review and alteration. A significant period of unconsciousness.

Alexa leaned backwards into the chair and let the room take her weight.

* * *

This was her childhood bedroom. She remembered the crack in the ceiling, the one she always thought was the leg of a thin, giant spider. He hadn't changed anything. The bed that was too short for her now and felt too short for her then. The magnolia wallpaper that she wanted to change for purple stripes. The Michael Owen poster on the wardrobe doors, his face discoloured by sun. He looked as ill as she felt. The window where she used to plan getaways those evenings when Dad sat downstairs on his own. Down the drainpipe, onto the porch roof and next door's shed, taking a spotted bag made from a handkerchief with her, like Dick Whittington. Alexa closed her eyes and she could see red shapes in front of her. Reddish brown on black. The shape of a woman. No, the shape of a man on a roof in Page Hall. Now there were lots of them, small dots that spread and became larger, and she was caught in a crowd again, the hot, sticky day of the EDL march. Or the dream she had about the ambulance.

She sank into a fitful sleep. The same scene, the one she had on repeat. The stadium and the mesh of the fences, the stadium she'd never been into except like this, at night. The impossible way she knew it by heart. The gear stick and the windscreen. The medical equipment. The rushing bodies in front of her and then all around her, like a sea, or something less contained. A moving landscape. And her white hands on the steering wheel. The ambulance going nowhere. But this time, there was a woman right in front of the vehicle. She was trying to get away, jostling through the crowd as if she needed to get to someone, needed to save someone. And as if she could tell Alexa was there, she turned around and looked over her shoulder. And the face was Caron's. And she was startled, caught. Deer in headlights. Thief in the night. She looked right into her eyes and through them. And Caron carried on pushing away.

'It's all right, Lexie, you're safe.'

She was bathed in sweat and the sheets were pulled tight around her. Her dad was beside her, leaning down. Michael Owen's face was huge on the wooden doors behind him, making him look mad, two-headed.

'You need some rest.'

'What happened last night?'

'You just dropped. Like a brick. I reckon you fainted.'

She didn't have the energy to nod.

'Place hasn't changed, eh?'

She managed a weak smile.

'I know it's mad. I always had this idea that I should keep everything, in case you were ever coming home. I know how that sounds.'

Outside, Fat Billy was mowing his lawn. He did it on Sundays in all seasons, whether the grass needed cutting or not. Something about the drone was comforting. She remembered hangovers when she was a teenager, how the sound would split her head.

'Noisy twat,' said her dad. Then his face clouded. 'Marge isn't well. I think that's why he's out so much. She had breast cancer.'

'I'm sorry,' murmured Alexa. She remembered Marge taking her to the corner shop for sweets. She loved the smell of them more than the taste. When she hit fourteen, she found it embarrassing. Marge was always trying to be motherly to her. Lending her magazines. When her period started, Marge took her to one side and offered her paracetamol and to make her a hot-water bottle and Alexa shrank with shame. As if she didn't know everything anyway. As if she didn't read or have friends at school. When Marge called round, she'd sometimes hide in her room and try not to make a sound. The thought shamed her now.

'I made you some toast.'

He held out a plate of cold, thin slices. The white bread was undercooked and pale, the way she liked it.

'No, ta. I'm not hungry.'

'Do you want me to leave you in peace?'

She almost nodded.

'No. I want you to stay, Dad.'

It was the first time she'd said that word to him since she'd seen him again. He swallowed, sat down.

'Tell me if I'm boring you. I've become a right boring bastard, Alexa. Ask Leigh.'

'I don't know Leigh.'

Her face had tightened and he sensed it.

'She's a good kid. She wants to do right. Put things right. I would say that, wouldn't I? I mean, I trust her with my life.'

'Climbing?'

'You can tell a lot about someone by the way they hold a rope.'

Alexa tried to remember how she'd felt when Caron belayed her up Flying Buttress Direct. Tight. Held. Not safe exactly, but anchored.

'What can you tell?'

'Whether they're watching you. Whether they're bored. Whether they're willing you on. You can tell without looking. Well, I can.'

'What was it like climbing with Mum?'

He didn't look at her when he answered.

'Sometimes I loved it. Sometimes … it was too much.'

Something about illness, something about being sick that means people can talk to you. And you can listen. Something about being trapped in bed. No, not trapped – contained. Kept in the white softness of the duvet and propped up by pillows. Alexa wondered why she hadn't tried to talk to Caron when she was in hospital, when she couldn't walk. Leyton had visited more than she did. Somehow, that didn't matter now. She didn't feel angry any more, not with Caron or anyone. She just felt blank.

He talked and she listened. Or she talked and he nodded at her, and it wasn't the nod of someone who wants to be seen to be paying attention, but the unbidden kind. He was taking it all in, hearing her voice for the first time in years, its flattened accent, softer than his, blunted by university. She told him about work and Dave and how bad things had got in Page Hall. The Section 30 and the trouble in Parson Cross. He talked about what the area used to be like when he was growing up. His life after the police, the knobheads and show-offs in the climbing shop.

'A lad came to try some shoes the other day and I said he could mess about in them for a bit, see if they suited. I caught him doing chin-ups on the doorframe, arms pumped to buggery. His girlfriend was pretending to watch. Leigh's good with the TOTs.'

'TOTs?'

'Top-off Twats.'

She giggled, a spontaneous, snotty kind of laugh. She was embarrassed. He handed her a tissue.

'It's good to have you back.'

'Who says I'm back?'

'I mean, it's good to see you again.'

'I'm just messing.'

'If you knew how many times I'd thought …'

'It's all right. You don't have to apologise.'

As soon as the words were out of her mouth, she realised he never had. She couldn't remember her dad saying sorry, not to her as a kid, not to anyone.

He turned his face to hers.

'I am sorry, though. You know I am.'

So he could look her in the eye.

'Dad, can I ask you something?'

'You know you can. I've got no secrets.'

'What is it about the Hillsborough Inquiry? All the papers and notes …'

He had broken her stare. He wasn't speaking any more, he was mumbling.

'You know what it is. I was there.'

'I never knew that, though, did I? Not properly. Not back then. Because you never said.'

'What was there to say? You were a baby.'

'I don't mean then. Later. When I was older.'

'You were still too young for that.'

'Don't patronise me.'

He laughed a harsh laugh. 'Well, maybe I was too young for it then.'

She knew she should drop it, but she couldn't.

'You've underlined it all. All the findings.' She'd never seen so much writing. When she was a child, her dad never wrote anything down. Not even a shopping list. Seeing his cramped-up letters had been strange, intimate, a kind of trespass. 'It's like you're obsessed.'

His face was red. She was sick with the memory. Times he used to look at her like that. Times he was angry and silent.

'I am fucking obsessed,' he spat. 'Because it was the worst day of my life. And when I thought it was over, they made us write it all down, what we'd done. And then they reviewed it. They made us change the fucking lot.'

His eyes were shining and his mouth was wet.

'Worse than the day Mum died?' she said quietly.

'It was the day your mum died.'

She looked at him, her face clouded with hurt. She didn't understand. She didn't understand anything.

'It was. Because it was the day I came back from it. Because I tried to be the same and I couldn't. I'd had it knocked out of me. Pride or whatever. And there was never an end to it. Months and years. Not the same. That's what pushed her away. That's when she started going on more trips.'

He was half-pleading, looking at Alexa as if she might remember. But she didn't remember. Not those things. Not those subtleties.

She remembered Mum's rucksack in the hall. The ice axes she always wanted to pick up and swing. She remembered Mum and Dad kissing and how she felt like she should look away. And she remembered the weeks of waiting.

'That's when she took more work in the Alps. Because I was good for fuck all.'

Alexa felt like there was less of her than before. She was very light in the bed in the room she grew up in, the room where she must have been half a person all along, not seeing and noticing anything that mattered, being happy when the sun came through the high window and sad when the rain hammered the roof and sad when Mum was away and Dad was quiet, and not thinking there could be anything else to it, nothing past that window and that white room.

'You know, I always thought she was having an affair. Do you know that?'

'Dad, I don't want to hear this.' She felt sick again.

'No, you have to know. I thought she was with someone else. Lucy, the woman she climbed with. I thought she was going to leave me, Alexa. And I've always been so fucking old-fashioned. You meet a girl and you marry her for life and you don't piss about. Neither of you. Like my mam and dad, I suppose. It was this fear. And it ate away at me, at what I'd got left. Every time she was away. That jealousy. Looking at my mates when we were in the pub. Wondering what they thought of her. If they would. I wanted things to be simple.'

She nodded. She was biting down on her lip very hard.

'There's no point being jealous.' He was hitting his fist against his leg, as if he wanted to hurt himself. 'It only makes it happen. What you're afraid of.'

'I know,' she said. 'I know.'

'That's why I couldn't take it. Not at first. What you were ...'

'What I am.'

'I can't think of a right way to put it, can I? I'm in the fucking Dark Ages here.'

'What I chose.'

'I've never understood it, love. If you feel for someone, I mean, love someone. If you love someone the way I loved your mum, why would you want anyone else?'

She wished she had the words. She wished she could unfold them like a long scarf made of wool. She wished she was clever like Caron or confident like Leyton.

'Trust,' she said. 'It's about trust. It's about putting it into words.'

'I've thought about it a lot, you know. Thought back to the way I was. Things I got wrong. It makes more sense to me now than it ever did.'

'It's not about sense.'

'I just don't see how it can work.'

She'd fallen quiet again.

'It depends.'

'On what?'

She paused. 'On the people.'

He laughed a hoarse laugh. Fat Bill's mower cut out in the garden.

'So we're all as bad as one another? Is that what you're saying?'

'Something like that.'

'The bottom line is we're all screwed.'

He laughed and rocked back and forwards. He laughed until he was almost crying with it and they clung on to each other, and the day was almost over before it had begun and Fat Bill started his mower up again, and she thought about Billy, outside, going over and over the same patch of bald grass, trying to get the measure of it.

'Now,' Dad chuckled. 'Tell me how the hell you've stuck it out in the police.'

'You,' she said. Then, hesitantly, 'I thought it was the one thing in my life that might make you proud.'

He shook his head and buried his face in his hands.

'Good God.'

The Don

There's always someone on my banks, lost in their own drama. Angry phone conversations. Gestures nobody else can see. A woman rocking back and forth with her knees hugged to her chest, surrounded by the rubble of other people's lives – a fingerless glove, a Durex wrapper, copies of used car magazines. When it's all over, I'll carry on as I always have, beautiful, between the ghost shapes of mills, the outflow and the empty factories, the spoilt and unspoilt pubs, threading between the washed-up children's shoes and the crushed Stella cans. I'm a seam through the city, gleaming like melted-down cutlery when the sun shines on me directly, a memory of knives and brightness, polished usefulness. Sometimes the light makes me spark. My movement is slick as a machine. The engine of me pulses, fired by the Loxley, the Rivelin, the Sheaf, the Rother and the Dearne, powered by Great Grains Moss, Winscar Dam. I push through Penistone, Deepcar, Oughtibridge. I enter the edges of town like someone coming home. Leppings Lane. The Hillsborough Footbridge. I've seen weeping and anger, men throwing off scarves, couples holding one another tight. Hillfoot Bridge. Steelbank Weir. The disused footbridges. Kelham Weir. Wicker Weir. The places that stood for industry once: Owlerton Rolling Mill, lost to fire. The remnants of fig trees by the banks, from when they quenched hot metal in the water and made me warm enough to germinate new life.

Leigh

The first time Leigh went to meet Alexa in Nether Edge she was neurotically early. She sat outside the café on a wooden slatted bench, sheltered by a canopy of plants, and watched a man in a long leather coat feed crusts to his Akita. The creature was remarkably placid, but when she went to stroke it, the man didn't look up from his crossword, his frown deepening. The glass windows behind her were steaming up, coffee and wet coats. She saw Alexa approaching – tweed jacket and high ponytail, a slim efficiency of movement – and pretended she hadn't.

'Have you been here long?' Leigh shook her head.

Inside, Cafe#9 was unnaturally comfortable. There was a casual eccentricity about the customers – some with conspicuous hairdos, jackets decorated with ironic badges and others in paint-spattered overalls, unshaven, red-eyed. As if they belonged in the café and nowhere else, fixtures as crucial as the small wood-burner and the corner piano. Back on the street, they'd be shifty and nervous, slightly stooped as they walked. Here, they took their shoes off and talked loudly to strangers and ate gooey flapjacks and scattered the crumbs. There was a guide to trees and how each wood burned pinned on the wall. The tables were shaped like lungs. Two teen-agers were playing chess next to the bookstand, calling out the moves as they went. The shaven-headed man behind the counter was already making Alexa's latte.

'And for your friend?' he asked, emphasising the last word.

Alexa hesitated, glanced at Leigh and shrugged.

'Espresso,' said Leigh. 'Please.'

This was not a place where it was easy to be angry and that gave Leigh comfort, even when Alexa sat as far away from her as she could and folded her coat over her knees. Posters by the counter were advertising a gig: *Ash Gray & The Burners*. The image showed a man with a mane of curly hair, mid-song, play-ing the guitar left-handed. There was a double bass propped against the wall, the colour of cherry-red Doc Martens, and exotic drums rested on stacked vinyl. It was as if the café had music poured into it each weekend, the hot, bright water of phrases, and held it, kept it long after it had cooled. It was a place to be known or to be unknown, whatever you wanted. A man in a flat cap and burgundy necktie sat down on the edge of their table and smiled at Alexa. He was tall and slim with a neatly shaped beard and intelligent, kindly eyes. Every movement seemed gentle and precise. Within moments, a couple came to join him, leaving their seats on the other side of the café and knocking the table as they leaned to hug him. Alexa dabbed at her spilt coffee with a napkin.

'Here.' Leigh handed her a handkerchief and Alexa didn't take it.

'Who carries one of those?'

'Grandads, mostly. And hipsters.'

Alexa didn't smile.

Behind the counter, the man was singing along to a band he'd put on the iPad. It was a full, mellow sound, old-fashioned and modern at the same time.

'Can you play?' asked Leigh, nodding to the instruments.

'No.'

'Me neither. I've always been shit at music.' She laughed. 'Shit at most things, really.'

'I don't know who the bass belongs to. Jonny's maybe.'

'Who's Jonny?'

'This is Jonny's place.'

'Right.' The espresso had made Leigh's mouth dry. Dry and bitter. She wished she'd asked for water. 'Do you know everyone in here?'

Alexa didn't smile. 'Everyone apart from you.'

'Yet,' said Leigh. 'You don't know me yet.'

'I don't know if I want to.'

'You asked me to come for coffee.'

In the silence, Leigh busied herself with the Bird&Bee's Firewood Collection poster on the wall.

Oak. The king of trees has a sparse flame.

Sycamore. Will not burn when green. Season well.

Sweet Chestnut. She spits and she sparks but burns well.

Roast the nuts, too!

She tried to imagine what each branch looked like, but she could only think of the taste of chestnut, the rich sweetness of it. Alexa was stirring her latte. The two men and the woman next to them were hunched over the table, talking softly. She caught the names of local streets, varieties of tree. She remembered a newspaper article in the *Star* she'd seen weeks ago in the shop café, how leafy suburban Rustlings Road was being threatened with tree-cutting, how the council maintained it was a way to make the pavements safer, and how the protestors camping in Endcliffe Park disagreed. There'd been rumours of contracts signed, money promised to a road-contracting firm. She wanted to listen, wanted to be part of their intimate circle, their three heads bowed together.

'They're going back to the Vernon Oak tomorrow,' said the woman. 'There's been a tip-off.'

The man in the flat cap sighed. 'And can we stop them?'

'We can slow them down. Make life bloody difficult,' countered the other man. He had John Lennon glasses that suited his face and white stubble. His partner was petite, alert. She had the quick hands of an artist and she wore a red and white spotted dress, hair gelled slightly.

'And there's the money,' she added. 'Last week on St Ronan's Road we delayed them by days, they had to come back three times. They were raging.'

Leigh was nervy and distracted. Why would Alexa ask her here if she didn't want to talk? She didn't seem angry, more indifferent. On the drive from Hathersage, Leigh had murmured to herself as she passed the gated houses on the south-western side of town, the insubstantial, elegant trees at Brincliffe Edge, rehearsing apologies and declarations. *I never meant to meddle in your life. But once I had, I wanted to make it right.* Nothing sounded the way it did in her head. *I did it for Pete. I did it for you. I didn't think ... I wasn't thinking.* Now she was in Alexa's presence, she couldn't bring herself to try.

'Another coffee?' she asked, weakly, picking up her wallet.

'I'll get them.' Alexa stood up abruptly. As she reached for her coat, the slim, gentle man opposite put his hand on her arm.

'Jasvinder?'

'Sit down, love,' he said. He had a slow and deliberate way of talking, it seemed to make the whole room gather around him. 'These are on me. There's something I wanted to ask you.'

* * *

The oak was larger and broader than Leigh had expected, the road quiet, apart from the protestors who stood with hushed reverence around the base. It was draped with yellow banners and bunting. The weeks since her meeting with Alexa in the café had been frantic, her phone buzzing with news about roads where trees were under threat or where action was planned, covert attempts by the developers, red herrings and hoaxes. The police had arrested two elderly women for obstruction. In one demonstration near Ryle Road, a protestor tried to get in front of a chainsaw, and they only switched it off when he started clutching his small terrier to his chest, too. A mother had been cautioned for taking her baby on a protest.

Ever since Jasvinder and his friends had coaxed them into their circle that day in Cafe#9, Leigh had been lit with energy, ready to leave the house whenever she could. She was reminded of a customer in the gear shop who belonged to the Edale Mountain Rescue Team, how he'd spring into life as soon as a call came through. She felt indignant, hopeful and giddy, which, she realised, was better than she'd felt in months.

On their first walk to a watch together, Alexa had softened and started to talk. They discovered they had the same stride length and could match each other's pace. There was no great apology, no need for Leigh to beg for forgiveness. But, with the trees to talk about, their silences became shorter. That night, Alexa had sent her articles on WhatsApp, links to vitriolic pieces by George Monbiot, tweets and endless petitions. *This is how state and corporate power subverts democracy. Trees are the lungs of the planet.* Over texts, they began to joke with each other. They risked emoticons – smiley faces and thumbs-up. Alexa was more forthcoming behind a screen. She told Leigh how she was getting on with her dad, and Leigh pretended Pete had told her nothing at work. Leigh was careful not to push her with questions, but in time she began to mention Caron, too, how they were in occasional contact, civil but not quite friends. Alexa and Leigh met for pints at The Union, a gig at Cafe#9. Leigh always drove to Alexa's neighbourhood. She began to feel at ease in the café. They learned her order and started making it when she walked in. There were regulars she didn't talk to, but was happy to see all the same. The girl with Fifties headscarves. The four men who always made a show of ordering scrambled eggs, but then barely touched them. Halfway through, one would always get an important call on his mobile and slouch outside, then the rest would follow. She sat alongside each of them the way you sit with afternoons.

Dore was grey under a veil of cloud this morning. A few cars passed and pipped their horns at them. A woman who seemed to be in charge gave Leigh coffee from a thermos and checked she had all she needed. A smile was twitching at the corners of her face.

'If this comes off, it'll be the best publicity we've had yet.'

'No pressure!' yelled a burly man in an anorak and everyone laughed.

The green of the trunk matched the green of the pavement underneath. It reminded Leigh of the privacy of the woods above Hathersage, close to North Lees, where the air smelled of bluebells and blackberries, and the leaves made a paste under your feet. She checked her balaclava to make sure it covered her face fully. She plucked at her jumper, dark, fashioned with black wings to make her look like a bird, a crow or a raven. One for sorrow. Wasn't that magpies? She needed good luck. She couldn't afford to fall or fuck up. Then she started to move, slowly and deliberately up the tree, high into the branches, where she sat and looked down and waited for the cameras.

The Trees

At night the trees call to each other across the roofs of the houses. There are so many, but there are never enough for an army. Some of them are splayed and ancient with voices like church doors. The saplings sound like bicycle brakes on a wet day. They shout from every corner of my body, a choir in Ecclesall Woods, a small cough from the corner of the Botanical Gardens, a single, loud voice on Ryle Road, where a tree is an island, intervening, steering the movements of people. Even when the felled trees whisper, they are louder than owls. They talk about their suffering, how they were cut. But mostly the trees yell to each other like men across a building site. In summer they announce who they've seen: the loiterers, the smokers, the ones who try to speak to them, flat palms against their trunks, forgetting that they don't understand the language. They laugh, a ripple that starts in the branches and spreads until it tickles the stars. Some of them have stood for hundreds of years, but they are calm. The saplings speak about magpies and penknives, the sly touch of the sun. Somewhere in the suburbs, you are awake and – though you don't know it – it's them you listen for, alone at your attic window, hugging yourself tight.

Leigh

Leigh passed a hand across her face as if she could wipe the sun from her eyes. Apparent North seemed to shimmer in the heat. It was the best day of the year, the wind still for once. Even the midges weren't out. She watched a clot of cyclists move slowly up the road below, leaning into the gradient, chugging their way to Burbage North and the brief downhill. They were half a rainbow, red and orange and blue and green.

She saw the leader pull away from the others, then they came together again as the incline steepened and the others reeled him in. He would get ahead again and then they would catch him, overlap. That was how it would always be. She felt the burn as if it was in her own thigh muscles, the sweet ache of uphill, of work. Then she turned back to watch the woman on the rock, the short, blunt buttress she was climbing, stubborn as a thought. Her white helmet was too bright in the sunshine. Her quickdraws clinked as she shifted her weight. All the routes here had ungainly finishes, few holds at the top. The woman bellyflopped her way over the edge, laughing.

Alexa stood up and looked down.

'Safe!' she yelled.

Pete took her off belay and grinned up.

'You've got my stylish moves,' he said. 'Like father, like daughter.'

Alexa stuck her middle finger up at him. Leigh stood slightly apart from them. She was part of the day, but something told her not to get too close, give them space. She watched Pete putting on his shoes. Quick, practised movements. But not bored ones, not over-rehearsed. Each climb was a new climb, however soft. However hard.

'Hey, Pete,' she said. He angled his head towards her. Safi sat next to him. She angled her silvery head, too. 'She's got your approach to gear as well.'

He looked over his shoulder. Alexa had placed one large cam in the crack; she'd moved it up with her as she climbed. *Practically a solo*. Leigh heard him chuckle.

From the top, Alexa didn't say anything, but her face was alive. She was wrapping a sling around a rock, content and absorbed in the movement.

'Should I go up and help?' asked Leigh.

'Nah. She's OK. She's a fast learner.'

Leigh nodded. She had hoped he would say that. Going near either of them felt like a kind of trespass.

'Besides, if her belay's crap, it's only my tin skull we've got to worry about.'

Safi had seen a grouse lift out of the heather below, its call startled from it as it rose. Her legs tensed and her ears flattened. She started forwards and stopped, as if something was tethering her to Pete and Alexa, an invisible loop of their rope. Leigh knew how she felt. She was leashed to the rock, walking away from it in smooth arcs, always drawn back again. Perhaps she'd been tied to Stanage all her life. The cyclists had vanished over the top of the hill, but they would be back, too, back next week and back the week after, pitting themselves against the same roads, imagining they'd tire of them, but never tiring, not really.

Alexa took in and the rope pulled taut on Pete's harness.

'Alexa?' he called up.

'What?'

'It was a pleasure. Holding your ropes.'

'Shut up and climb, Dad.'

In the car on the way up, Alexa's speech had been peppered with it. *Dad. Dad.* Trying the word on again, like something she thought they'd both grown out of. Pete had started climbing. Alexa was giving him too much slack, but he didn't seem to mind. There was a route to the right of her that Leigh could solo, an old favourite, steep for the grade. She was content to stand in the shade, hardly moving. Last year she would have been moving. Last year she would have done six routes by now. But it wasn't last year. And she was stiller.

She yawned, a cat-like, wide-mouthed yawn. She was knackered from Tom's engagement party. Her head was clear, though – she'd driven, not stayed long at the hall, clutched an orange juice. Practised saying 'Sophie' when people asked her name. When they toasted the happy couple, she lifted it high and caught Tom's eye and gave him a proper, teeth-out smile. The kind of smile your eyes join in with. And if he felt anything like embarrassment or regret, his face didn't show it. Tom and Rachel walked off through an archway thick with roses. The stray petals on his suit looked comical, like bird shit. She'd thought about sharing that with someone, with the gangly, bearded academic on his own by the drinks table, by text to Tom himself, but there was no good reason, and she'd stopped doing things unless she had a good reason, so instead she took a photo of the couple as they walked away. She placed the card she'd got for them and a single bluebell on the gifts table, and she'd left the drone of pissed gossip and small talk and driven back through Hope, the road straight as a promise all the way home.

Alexa and Pete were on the descent now. She could hear their voices, the clatter of their gear as they got closer. They had the same gait. She didn't know why she'd never noticed it before. They came back under the edge and stood next to her, looking up at the rock. Alexa was breathing hard in the heat.

'What's that route over there?' asked Alexa. 'The one that looks like a battleship.'

'That's Black Car Burning.'

'The route Caron wanted to climb?'

'She'll climb it,' said Leigh. 'She'll be back.'

And she would. She'd be back stronger and leaner, with hard fingertips and feet that knew the route in the dark. She'd be back, this year or next year, and Leigh would hold the rope for her and she'd do it properly this time, do it so that she was almost climbing with her as the sequence came together, as her own heart lifted and stalled and lifted again. Caron would stand on top of Black Car Burning, and something in her would be quenched and Leigh would help to quench it.

'Have you ever thought of going for it?'

Leigh smiled at her.

'I'm not that kind of climber,' she said.

318

'Don't listen to her,' said Pete. 'She could do anything if she put her mind to it.' He hitched the rope further over his shoulder. 'Besides, she's full of shit.'

Leigh watched them walk down along the path together, the path that was really an outline, someone's idea of a path, leaning into each other's sentences and laughing and passing a water bottle between them. Alexa's hair matched the light. She'd untied it and it ran down her back, moving when she moved. Leigh felt something she couldn't place as she watched them get further away from her, something like the feeling on a crux, the second just before you make the move. An elevated kind of feeling. She wiped the sweat from her face with her T-shirt. It was early. There was so much daylight left.

A wide black shadow passed over her. It was as if the lights had gone out on the whole afternoon. Then it shifted and the sun came back again. She looked up and saw two paragliders arcing over Stanage. They were more like bats than birds. But they were giants. Their span was huge and sturdy. Now she was under the shadow of the second one. They moved in perfect silence through the air, describing something beyond words. Safi scampered underneath and barked and barked at them, confused by their size and slowness. Leigh squinted as their darkness left her. They were entirely quiet, utterly contained. She had never thought about flight before. Pete always called them *mad bastards*. Them and the cavers, seeking out the coolness underground; hidden, tight places that gave Leigh the creeps. But now, watching them planing over the rocks, nothing seemed more logical, more necessary, than the way they moved, not rising but gliding, looking across the whole valley, changing it with their passing.

Somewhere far away to her left, she heard Pete shout 'Climbing!'

One day she would do it. One day she would stand somewhere higher than this. She would walk to the edge and trust that all she had could hold her. She would step out into the air.

Hillsborough Inquest, 2016

When the courtroom erupts it's like the roar at a football match. People fling their arms around each other. Some of them have wet cheeks and red eyes. I'm there on shoes and skin, on sweat and held breath. I'm a trace on the clothes of everyone who ever set foot in me, ever touched me, ever said my name aloud. I'm a film on every tongue, the saliva on the roofs of their mouths. For months I've stared out from the faces of the families in ordered rows, the muttering police and their barristers, the photos of the 96. I've settled on their smiles, their flat cheeks, the sheen of their reproduced, familiar images, those faces that hardly seem like people at all any more. I seeped into the clock and looked down on the heads of the nine jurors, the six women and the three men, noticed which were nervous, which were bold. I have heard everything. I have heard the words *gross negligence* and *cover up*, the words *drunk and disorderly*, over and over again. I know each spoken name by heart now, the way I know my own street names and shops, even as they change, even as the signs get painted over and graffitied. And then, this morning, the great pause and the clenched knees.

Unlawful killing. A 7–2 majority vote.

Pete is near the back of the courtroom, alone, his left leg twitching like he's operating a sewing machine. He stands, unsteadily. I get inside his jacket, then. I cling to him. I've known him so long. He walks out on to the courtroom steps. It's a beautiful spring day. He takes his jacket off and he slings it over his shoulder. The shadow of a bicycle overtakes him as he walks. He checks the timetable for trains to Liverpool. Pete stops at the florist to buy a bunch of flowers – extravagant pink lilies and broad carnations. He goes to Bank Quay and he loses himself in the crowd.

Acknowledgements

Thank you to Parisa Ebrahimi, Charlotte Humphery and Clara Farmer at Chatto and to my agent Peter Straus. Thanks also to Alan Buckley, Claire Carter, Ian Cartland, Hannah Copley, Heather Dawe, Jess Edwards, Niall Fink, Andy and Janet Mort, Miranda Pearson, Ben Wilkinson and Jonathan Winter and everyone in the Derbyshire Irregulars Climbing Society. I owe a debt of gratitude to Douglas Caster and the University of Leeds for a Douglas Caster Cultural Fellowship from 2014 to 16. Thanks also to Laynes Espresso, Leeds, and Cafe#9, Sheffield, where much of this novel was finished. Thank you to the production team behind the BBC2 documentary *Police Under Pressure* for making the footage available to me after broadcast.

penguin.co.uk/vintage